Rachel'

Fiction

The Serial Dater — 31 dates in 31 days

The Serial Dieter — 31 dishes in 31 days

Various Henry Houdini long short stories

Morgen's books

Fiction

After Jessica — money and a girl gone missing

Hitman Sam — a trainee hitman and love triangle

Oh, Henry — the first in the Henry Houdini series

One for the Road — a hit-and-not-run novel

Short Story Collections: Shorts & Flashes

Non-fiction

The 365-day Writer's Block Workbooks
1000+ exercises and 50+ tips per book

Editing Fiction ~ A Writer's Guide
Morgen's guide to writing a story then pulling it apart

Oh, Henry

A British dog detective novel – the first in the Henry Houdini series

Rachel Cavanagh
and Morgen Bailey

Oh, Henry

Copyright 2020 © Rachel Cavanagh and Morgen Bailey

ISBN: 978-1-913633-06-6

The rights of Rachel Cavanagh and Morgen Bailey to be identified as the Authors of the Work has been asserted by them in accordance Copyright, Designs and Patents Act 1988.
Published in 2020 by August Publishing UK.

Apart from any use permitted under UK copyright law, this publication may only be reproduced, stored, or transmitted, in any form, or by any means, with prior permission in writing of the publisher or author/s or, in the case of reprographic production, in accordance with the terms of licences issues by the Copyright Licensing Agency.

All characters in this publication are fictitious and any resemblance to real persons, living or dead, is purely coincidental.

www.augustpublishing.co.uk

Cover design by Caroline Vincent

Discover other titles by Rachel Cavanagh and Morgen Bailey at https://morgenbailey.com.

Thank you for purchasing this book. If you enjoy this story, please encourage your friends to purchase their own copies.

Thank you for your support.

For the young in all of us.

There is some swearing in this book
so please bear this in mind
when sharing with younger readers.

Chapter One – Not Your Ordinary Dog

Henry sat glued to the television, giggling, and wagging his tail at the old cartoons.

He'd not seen this one the first time round, he was too young, but was hooked as Danger Mouse hovered over an alligator pit, and Baron Greenback threatened to flick the switch. Of course, Penfold came to the rescue. Henry knew there was no way the hero of the programme would be lost forever.

As the show ended and was replaced by *Tracy Beaker*, Henry pressed the remote's red button and the screen went blank.

He looked at the clock, five past nine, and there was no sign of breakfast. He was about to bark when the door opened and in walked the lab assistant, Gwynne Davies, holding a tray. She put it down in front of him and waited.

He looked at the two bowls: the food, the semi-skimmed milk, nestled next to a copy of *The Times*. Henry looked up at Gwynne. "Is that it?"

"It's your usual."

"Ruff's Complete, I presume."

She nodded.

"Getting a bit bored of it, to be honest."

"Let me guess… smoked salmon? Caviar?"

Henry lifted a paw and scratched behind his ear. "Mmm… sounds quite nice. Fish instead of meat. But no… I'm a carnivore. I should be eating meat." He looked at the blank television screen. "I know." He looked back at Gwynne. "I know exactly what I want."

"Right…"

"Yes. It's perfect."

"Go on, surprise me."

Henry grinned. "I am your prized possession, am I not?"

Gwynne said a hesitant, "Yes."

"I can have anything my heart desires?"

"…Yes."

"Okay then. I shall have alligator."

Gwynne laughed, but stopped at his serious expression.

"See what you can do?"

Henry didn't hear what Gwynne mumbled as she took the tray back to the kitchens but, although his stomach was rumbling, he thought he'd be more than happy to wait to see what would be in the bowl when she returned.

Henry tilted his head and heard his neck click. "Oh dear, that's not good." He whistled but that didn't alleviate the boredom. "Not as patient as I thought." He stared at the TV. He could switch it on again but felt he'd outgrown the children's channel. He knew how to change to another station but there was nothing he really fancied seeing, even though he'd not tried.

So he looked around: water bowl, bed… of sorts. No, the floor was much more comfortable, and plain. The beanbag thing he'd been given had pictures of other dogs on, he assumed to keep him company, but they had the opposite effect. There were a couple of half-eaten rawhides but they took more energy to eat than he felt they gave him. Then there was the other distraction… ah yes, that would do nicely.

Gwynne looked down at the ripped toy, then into Henry's big brown eyes staring up at her.

"It wasn't me."

"Really? Then who was it? There's only you and me here. I know you're hungry, but your breakfast won't be long."

The big brown eyes kept staring. "All right. I confess. It was me but it's your fault for–"

"Henry! You've become so cheeky since we gave you the ability to talk."

Henry wagged his tail.

"I thought that toy was your favourite."

"I was only playing."

"It's got dribble all over it. You were shaking it, weren't you."

Henry nodded. "It's what we do. We're dogs. We chase rabbits, cats and things."

"Anything that moves, I know."

"So you give me a cat toy and I'm going to–"

"Chase, Henry. You didn't need to rip it to shreds."

"It's not shreds. An ear's come off, that's all."

"What did I say about you being cheeky?"

"Just speaking my mind."

"If I'd known…"

"What?"

"Nothing. Never mind. Now, Dr Moss and I have some questions, and we want your honest answers, okay?"

Henry nodded.

On cue, Dr Templeton Moss entered the lab, studying a clipboard. "How is he today?"

"I'm well, thank you."

Moss looked up from his notes. "Henry?"

Henry smiled. "That's me."

"So everything's okay? Voice all right?"

"More than all right," Gwynne answered. "Can't shut him up."

"I did think it was weird to start with," Henry said ignoring Gwynne. "I could hear myself. Of course I could always hear myself but it's like it was clearer, louder and…"

Moss watched Henry's lips move as he waffled on. "Your lips are moving."

Henry stopped mid-stream. "Of course. I'm no ventriloquist."

The doctor laughed, looked at Gwynne's scowl, and laughed again.

Henry turned to Gwynne. "You said you had some questions?"

"Yes. Dr Moss?"

The doctor looked back down at his clipboard. "Number one. How do you feel?"

Henry frowned and repeated, "I'm well, thank you."

"Number two. Has anything else improved since the implementation of the medication?"

"'Implementation of the medication'," Henry mimicked. "Like what?"

"Memory? Vocabulary? Desires? Motivations?"

"Erm…"

"Maybe a bit too much all at once," Gwynne suggested.

"No, it's okay," Henry said. "Memory. The same, I think. Born, eat, poop, chew…" He looked at the toy. "I couldn't help it."

"That's okay, Henry," Dr Moss soothed. "That's what they're there for. Any frustrations?"

"Apart from it not being a real cat?"

Dr Moss laughed and added a 'sense of humour' box.

"You asked about vocabulary," Henry continued.

"Yes," Gwynne butted in. "And desires, motivation."

"Vocabulary. Now I like hearing the sound of my voice–"

"We can tell," Gwynne mumbled, receiving a dirty look from Henry.

"It's not like I've studied a dictionary since you gave me that stuff."

"Interesting," Dr Moss said while chewing on the end of his pen.

Henry didn't find that interesting at all. He'd quite like to spend his time studying not only a dictionary but an encyclopaedia as well, but thought that a step too far at this early stage. "As for desires. I still desire to rip up…" He looked up at Gwynne and paused. "Desire to play with my toys. That was an accident. Motivation, being given a fake cat is a good one. And breakfast."

"Very good." The doctor nodded and jotted more notes. "Question four. If you could be any animal, what would you be?"

Henry cocked his head.

"Would you like me to repeat that?"

Henry straightened his head. "You mean you can change me into something else?"

Dr Moss laughed. "Of course not, Henry. We can only work with what we have."

"That's a silly question then, isn't it."

"It's hypothetical."

Henry wished he'd had that dictionary.

"Pretend," Gwynne explained.

"A giraffe."

The two white-jacketed humans looked at each other.

"A giraffe?" Gwynne asked, looking back at the dog.

"Why a giraffe, Henry?" Dr Moss asked.

"It's obvious, isn't it?"

The doctor shook his head.

"Because all I see all day are ankles. Knees if I'm begging, which I don't plan on doing any time soon, by the way. If I was... were, a giraffe I'd be able to see anything, wouldn't I. Even more than you. Any more questions?"

Dr Moss nodded. "A few, but I think that's enough for today."

Gwynne looked at him, so he beckoned for her to join him in the corridor.

Henry watched them leave then turned his attention to the one-eared cat. "They'll be giving that stuff to you next, although they'd have to sew your ear back on or you wouldn't be able to hear their questions."

He then looked back at the glass pane in the door, saw the ecstatic expressions on their faces and said, "If you're like that now, just wait until I show you what I can really do."

Chapter Two – How It All Started

Gwynne flicked the end of the needle, just like they did in movies. She wasn't sure why but it seemed appropriate at such a vital stage.

"Final dose for today, Gwynne." Dr Moss pulled his glasses down slightly then peered at his clipboard. "35mg?"

Gwynne nodded.

"If this doesn't work we'll have to review," Dr Moss said returning his glasses to their original position.

Gwynne nodded again and eased the needle into the dog's fur. "Sorry, mate."

The dog sighed, padded back into its cage, and lay down, keeping its eyes fixed on Gwynne.

Gwynne turned to her boss. "Should we wait for it to take effect or…?"

Dr Moss smiled. "I know you're impatient – we both are – but it could take hours, an hour at least before–"

"Would you mind if I have a nap while you're waiting?"

The white-coated humans turned to the cage.

"What?" Gwynne looked back at Dr Moss. "Did you say something?"

The doctor shook his head.

"No. It was me."

Gwynne stared at the cage. "Henry?"

Henry stood, looked around the stark laboratory, frowned at the lack of colour, then stretched and yawned before licking his lips. "Yep."

"No." Gwynne shook her head. "You can't…" She returned to face Dr Moss. "He…"

Moss said nothing but his lower jaw could have caught flies, even a bird, it was so far open.

"Oh my…" he said finally.

"God? Buddha? Mohammed?" Henry offered. "Then there's Adonis, Apollo, Hephaestus, Nike – not sure if they named the running shoes after her, maybe you could check for me? And then of course there's the fishy one, Poseidon." Henry took a slurp of water before continuing. "They had an adventure in the movies with him back in the…"

"Seventies," Gwynne finished. "One of my boyfriend's favourites. Don't know why because–"

Dr Moss coughed.

"Sorry."

"He…" Dr Moss said, mouth not closed but less of a fly-catching tool. He looked down at his clipboard, back at Henry then to Gwynne. "He…"

"I know." Facing Henry, Gwynne said, "You can speak."

Henry nodded. "English. Yes… though not quite what I imagined."

"What do you mean?" Dr Moss asked.

"My voice is lower than I expected. It sounds higher in my head but when I hear it out loud... Distinguished, not quite Bertie Wooster but…"

"Bertie Wooster, hey…" Dr Moss said, noting something on the clipboard.

Henry strained to see but was too low, so returned to his general sitting position. "Yes. I'm a Jack Russell."

"Of course," Dr Moss said then screamed, making Henry recoil until he hit the back of his cage.

"Sorry, Henry. It's just that…"

Henry crept forward.

"We never imagined this side effect." Gwynne smiled.

Dr Moss nodded. "We were only hoping for… It's a long story. We'll explain another time. You understand everything we're saying. You really do, don't you."

Henry nodded. "My English is good, although there's always more to learn, isn't there." He didn't wait for a reply. "I also speak… another long story."

"Go on," Dr Moss encouraged.

"Another time. I'm quite tired actually." Henry yawned then repeated, "Would you mind if I have a nap while you're waiting… for whatever else it is you're waiting for?"

"Waiting?" Gwynne asked.

"Yes. Earlier you said it would take an hour or two. A few, I think you said. Another side effect?" He looked down at his side. "Am I supposed to sprout wings like that car in *Chitty Chitty Bang Bang*?"

Gwynne smiled again. "You know your films."

Henry liked Gwynne. She seemed impressed… more so than the doctor but Henry had had more interaction with Gwynne than Dr Moss. "Am I okay for a bit of shut eye?" Henry shut one eye dramatically before opening it again, making Gwynne laugh. "And then maybe later some lunch?"

"Later, certainly," Dr Moss agreed. "We have to wait two hours for the Diaphosfor… for the medication to get around your system before you can have anything to eat. Water's fine, obviously."

As the doctor spoke, a droplet fell from one of the hairs on Henry's chin. He felt it fall so looked down to see it splatter onto the plastic-coated bed. It landed on the face of a cartoon Rottweiler, making Henry giggle.

"Henry?" Gwynne asked.

Henry looked up. "Huh?"

"Okay?"

"Oh, yeah. Everything's fine. Left foot's… paw's a bit tingling – this one…" He moved his front left paw slightly. "But I was lying on it so bound to feel odd."

"Pins and needles?"

Henry looked at the syringe's needle Gwynne had placed inside him then laid on the stainless steel work surface surrounding most of the large laboratory. He wanted to growl but knew it was an inanimate object so had no choice what happened to it… to him.

Gwynne followed his gaze then apologised.

"It's okay," Henry soothed. "I know you have to do it. Looking at all the money you've spent on this place, it must be important."

"Very," Dr Moss said and made another note on the sheet on his clipboard.

"Will you be disappointed if it doesn't work?" Henry asked.

Gwynne and Dr Moss looked at each other then back at Henry. He could tell they were battling whether to say 'the right answer'. Yes and Henry would feel guilty, No and they'd know he'd know they were lying.

"Then I hope it does," Henry said and rested his chin on his paws. He wiggled his front left paw to get rid of the pins or needles – he hoped it was only pins as they were much smaller – then closed his eyes and was soon snoring.

Gwynne smiled then looked at her boss, whispering, "What will we do if it doesn't work? The previous didn't and we're running out of options. Sir Alfred, Sir Walter, what will we tell them?"

Dr Moss didn't need to look at his clipboard to know what to reply. "He talks." Moss grinned. "He talks!" The doctor then looked at Henry, who was still snoring, and lowered his voice. "Henry talks. We've created the world's first talking dog!"

"But what about why he's really here?"

"We can work on that. The Sirs will be so thrilled with this. Of course they won't believe it until they see it for themselves."

Gwynne gulped.

Moss sighed.

Chapter Three – Dr Moss's Report

Hands hold still! It's no use. I just… I can't believe we did it; the world's first talking dog!

I'm meant to write a report to my bosses, the Board, financial backers. I'd rather phone them, blather on about our first conversation, me and Henry's. Of course they'll want to see for themselves, hear for themselves. I'll have to tell him to be on his best behaviour, less of the cheek, but I know it was just excitement, bravado, having someone to talk to.

Can you imagine how frustrating it must have been, all that time, to want to say something and not be able to, to talk but know that all we hear is barking, whining and the likes? Still, he's only young, not even a teenager in human years. You'd think we'd have chosen a puppy but they'd be immature, not have a grasp of the English language.

Good thing we didn't go with a Schnauzer. Not really practised my German since school. Irene and I did go to Berlin for a weekend, a few years after the wall came down, but we were surrounded by other tourists with a common language of English, so we were lazy. Irene had her phrasebook and used it to order food and so on. I hardly said a word, but then that's Irene all over.

Talks the hind legs off a talking dog, she does. Actually, that's not a bad idea. Not that I can tell her yet. You can imagine how frustrating… but then she wouldn't keep it to herself. Made that mistake not long after we were married. She'd make a rubbish spy, but then I don't suppose they'd take anyone under five feet tall.

Henry. Report. I guess I can start with the tick boxes and fill in the text as I go along.

Dr Moss jerked when the phone on his desk rang. "Hello? Yes, Janet, put him through. Thank you… Good morning, Sir Alfred, and how are– of course, yes. Just writing it up now. Typing, yes. Email, certainly. Half an hour, hour tops. Oh, are you? Half an hour it is then. Lower handicap, have you, sir? That's impressive. I don't really play golf, no. Relaxing, yes. I'm sure it is, Sir Alfred. Oh yes, I'd seen Bruce Forsyth play on the television. Once or twice, I'd say. Sir Walter? Of course he'd be very welcome. Of course he wants to see where his money– Tomorrow? That's no prob– Report, yes, right away, Sir Alfred."

Dr Moss stared at the screen. He'd ticked the relevant boxes but there was a gaping section for 'Comprehensive Reportage'. Not just reportage, or even report, but comprehensive. He scrolled down… and down… and down. He reckoned he'd need a couple of thousand words at least to satisfy the Board, to satisfy the notorious Sir Walter no-relation-to-Sir-Bruce Forsyth. Dr Moss had never met Sir Walter but his reputation preceded him. Dr Moss knew it would be tough enough to please Sir Alfred, but… What was he worrying about? The dog talked. The dog actually talked. Henry would open his mouth, chat about something inane, but at least they'd see it. Him.

"Oh no," Dr Moss said to the screen. Henry. It wouldn't just be inane, it would be inane with attitude. Dr Moss had seen enough episodes of Family Guy to know how much trouble a dog with attitude could cause. Barry. No, it wasn't Barry. Bobby? He remembered the other characters' names but always struggled with the dog. Stewie, the baby, was the other reason Dr Moss watched it.

He and Irene had always wanted children, and used to have fun trying for one, but it soon became evident that it wasn't going to happen, not without some help. Dr Moss had offered to go for tests but Irene had declined. "Don't want to be poked and prodded," she'd said, snipping the head off a Princess of Wales rose. Dr Moss had watched the flower fall into the wicker basket. It had had a guillotine feel about it and he'd been glad the rose had been named after British royalty rather than French. He knew that was all there was to be said.

He'd have gone all the way; adoption, IVF, but it wouldn't have been him being stuck with needles. He'd seen the procedures on TV, watched people practise with oranges, like Hugh Laurie and Joely Richardson in *Maybe Baby*, one of Dr Moss's favourite films. He kept little from Irene but he knew she'd never want to watch it. "Too painful," she'd say, had he had the nerve to ask, although the subject of children had never come up again.

So the DVD had sat in his office desk drawer ever since it had been given away with a weekend paper, *The Mail on Sunday*, he thought. He didn't get much time to watch films at work but sometimes he just needed a break; a little humour from the seriousness of reports, budgets and... reports! He looked at the tiny time display on the computer screen.

He had eleven minutes to get the report to Sir Alfred. So he'd start at the beginning, coming up to date, include the question and answer session – he had those stored anyway so could just copy and paste. Of course he'd tone down Henry's cheekiness somewhat but emphasise how advanced his English was, is. That, surely would impress Sir Alfred and if it impressed him, Sir Walter would be a pushover.

Brian. Brian the dog. That was it.

Chapter Four – Steak Unlikely To Ever Be Alligator

"Got a cold, Henry?" Gwynne asked, tapping information into her computer.

"No."

"Okay for water?"

"Yes."

"Then what's with all the coughing?"

"Have you forgotten something?"

Gwynne opened her desk drawer. "Mobile. Purse. Keys. No, I don't think so."

Henry growled.

After taking a sip of coffee, Gwynne turned and glared at him. "Speak, Henry. You can speak now."

"I know."

"I know, you know. Don't growl, it's childish."

"I am a child. I'm nineteen months."

"Which is… ten… eleven and a bit in dog-to-human years?"

"That's a myth."

Gwynne put down her mug. "Is it?"

"Of course. Silly thing to say. Do I look a week older than yesterday?"

Gwynne wasn't sure how to work that out. "Erm…"

"Exactly. As I said, it's silly. Now, are you going to feed me, or what?"

"Oh, God! Sorry, Henry. I took your tray back and completely–"

"I know. Surprised you can't hear my stomach rumbling from there."

"Your stomach rumbles too?"

"Just because I'm canine, it doesn't mean…"

Gwynne was looking back at her screen, typing something.

"What are you doing?" Henry asked.

"Typing."

Henry tutted. "I can see you're typing. I can hear you're typing. What are you typing?"

"Notes."

"About me?"

"Yes, Henry. About you. I have to write everything that happens, however trivial."

"Thought so."

"Why?"

"There's a saying I've heard on TV. 'It's not all about you, you know.' But it is, isn't it? Everything you do is all about me."

"Not exactly everything, Henry."

Henry looked around the lab. "Don't see any other pets here."

Gwynne chuckled then stopped.

"What's so funny?"

"You called yourself a 'pet'. It's quite sad really."

Henry exhaled. "Dogs are pets, aren't they?"

"Usually."

"When they live in houses. It's not the same here, is it."

Gwynne shook her head sadly. "No it's not."

"But you take me for walks, feed me… sometimes, and…"

Gwynne pushed back her chair. "Sorry, Henry. I'll go get it now."

Henry nodded and smiled as Gwynne left the room.

Gwynne passed the other labs, the squawking, squealing, and chirping. Her clearance allowed her into most of the other rooms but she'd never been. There was a code amongst the lab staff; you didn't venture into others' domains uninvited, and given the cool reception she'd received in the canteen since her arrival at Forsyth Medical Research Sciences, she'd not been surprised they'd not been forthcoming.

FMRS certainly had a 'village' feel about it. If you weren't born there, you'd never be accepted. That had made her wonder if any of them had actually been born at FMRS, some of them did look a little odd, but then they were scientists, it was a given.

Apart from nineteen-year-old Eddie Parker, Gwynne was the newest recruit. One lunchtime, Eddie had been more than happy talking about the projects he was working on but when he'd paused, waiting for Gwynne to reciprocate and she hadn't been able to, he'd picked up his tray and joined the other lab assistants a few tables away.

Breakfast a distant memory, Gwynne walked past the rows of empty tables and into the kitchens. She was ignored by most of the staff who were busy washing dishes, wiping down surfaces, and putting away unused foods.

At the back of the kitchen, about to enter a huge stainless steel pantry, a tall lanky man in white jacket and black and white check trousers, spotted Gwynne, took a step back and shut the pantry door. “Hi, Gwynne. Thought you'd forgotten me.”

Gwynne laughed. “Adam, you're the only man I know who has to duck through every doorway. Who'd forget you?”

Adam smiled, turned to the nearest work surface, and picked up a tray.

Of course Gwynne hadn't asked for alligator, but whatever meat Adam could spare.

“Not the finest sirloin, but I've tried to avoid gristle.” He handed the tray to Gwynne who took it and looked at the contents. The bowl of stale milk had been replaced with fresh, *The Times* Gwynne added later, as it was sitting by her computer, but the dog food had been replaced with meat in gravy. It still looked like dog food to her, albeit not dried pretending to be meat and vegetables, but the human food Adam prepared was usually lovely so she had no reason to doubt him this time.

“Bored with the dry stuff?” Adam asked as Gwynne thanked him.

“I thought I'd treat him. Sorry to put you to any bother.”

“Oh, no bother at all,” Adam said in his soft Scottish accent. Gwynne had never asked but guessed it to be Edinburgh. It wasn't as harsh as Glasgow and she couldn't think of where else it could be, her visits to Scotland countable on one hand, minus the thumb, and half of those to weddings at Gretna Green which barely counted.

She thanked him again and carried the tray back to the lab.

"There we go." Gwynne placed the tray onto the platform they'd given Henry so he didn't get neck ache from eating at floor level.

"Mmm."

"Mmm?"

"This isn't alligator, is it?"

Gwynne laughed and shook her head. "No, it won't be alligator."

"Won't be? You mean it could be now?"

"No, Henry. It's not now and it won't become alligator. They're not that easy to find."

"There was one on the television. More than one, I think."

"That was on the television. It's fiction."

"Fiction?"

"Not fact. The opposite of fact, like stories in a story book."

"Fiction like talking dogs."

"Not really, but–"

"If it's not alligator, what is it?"

"I don't know. Adam didn't say."

"Adam?"

"Head chef."

"Head chef. So this could be someone's or something's brain?"

Gwynne laughed again. "You are funny. No, not brains. At least, I don't think so." Gwynne could almost feel *her* brain whirring. "Adam did mention sirloin steak."

"Steak?"

"Not the finest, he said."

"Of course. This is a laboratory, not a Michelin-starred restaurant."

What Henry did and didn't know always amused Gwynne. It made sense that Henry's knowledge bank would come from his surroundings, mostly the television. She thought they should have better control over what he watched; she knew the system had parental controls but it only had the family package so he couldn't get up to much mischief.

She watched Henry tuck into his breakfast, taking stops to lap up the occasional slurp of milk.

"Oh, I've got *The Times* for you as usual." Teaching Henry to read was the next milestone they hoped to achieve, perhaps get him a computer with an application that he could dictate to and that would talk back to him. But that was weeks, perhaps months, away. There was so much to learn by just talking to him and who knew how long that would take?

Henry finished chewing his mouthful of steak-unlikely-to-ever-be-alligator and swallowed.

Gwynne nodded, noting that despite his cheekiness and his bravado, Henry was a gentleman, or rather, gentledog.

"I like *The Times*," Henry said.

Gwynne was going to say something but Henry continued.

"But it's a bit stuffy."

"Stuffy?"

"You know… business, world news… which is interesting but not all relevant, is it? Could you maybe bring in a selection tomorrow? Maybe something less…"

"Less?"

He looked up, almost cross-eyed. "Brow high?"

"Highbrow. Posh."

"Yes, highbrow. Less posh."

"I'll see what I can do."

"Thank you. In the meantime, do read me today's highbrow."

As Gwynne read to him, Henry sat, listening intently. Every now and then, he'd tilt his head, understanding what he was hearing. He mulled over his secret. Should he tell Gwynne that he was able to read? He decided against it, he liked her reading the paper to him.

He knew he could ask if there was something that didn't make sense but during the whole fourteen-page dissection – Gwynne never got past page fourteen – Henry would always lie down and close his eyes as if to signify that the reading session was over. Gwynne would fold the newspaper and tuck it into her bag to take home. Henry wondered if she then read it to her boyfriend, Dan, and Henry imagined him lying down and closing his eyes when he'd had enough; perhaps also around the business pages.

Chapter Five – Turning Fact Into Fiction

Gwynne looked at the stainless steel clock above the lab's double sink. She knew the time was displayed on her computer screen but always remembered after she'd looked up at the wall. She never trusted the computer, despite it always matching, within a minute or two. Computers go wrong, have a mind of their own, she'd think, not realising that the clock on the wall was powered by a satellite, by computers, but assumed that the battery was replaced by the maintenance staff before it ran out.

She stared around the lab. Almost everything was made out of stainless steel, brushed steel or steel-effect material. Clean. Clinical. Cold.

Gwynne liked to think in threes, write in threes, work in threes; Henry, Dr Moss, herself.

Henry was taking a nap, so when the clock's minute hand caught up with its hour hand, due north, midday, Gwynne flicked over to Word, opened up *Henry novel v1.0.doc* then scrolled down to where she'd finished typing the day before, partway through Chapter Four. She read the final paragraph so she could regain her flow. She'd meant to email the document to her private address but she knew she wouldn't have time to add to it, Monday being her and Dan's movie night.

She'd started the book as an autobiographical account but then realised that she'd signed a confidentiality agreement when taken on at FMRS so she'd made it fictional. She'd kept the document as *Henry*, she'd decided, until she found a name she liked, a name that suited the two-dimensional talking dog as much as the three-dimensional. She'd kept its gender as male and would wait to see if it suited its skin.

Final paragraph read, she carried on…

With Henry sleeping, and snoring, ~~Gwynne~~ George…

Gwynne had always fancied having a name that could be male or female, and Georgina felt distinguished, plus It kept her first initial so helped her track who was supposed to be who.

With Henry sleeping, and snoring, George…

Gwynne also thought the names Henry and George suited each other so she'd have to choose a name for Henry that went just as well, assuming she kept George.

With Henry sleeping, and snoring, George settled into writing more of her novel…

Yes, Gwynne was writing a novel about someone writing a novel. She'd read one like it – she couldn't remember what but she'd enjoyed it so thought she'd have a crack at doing it herself. This was her first crack at writing fiction so she could… should experiment.

With Henry sleeping and snoring, George settled into writing more of her novel, taking it back to where it all started; how she and Henry had met. George had recently been made redundant from being a secretary to the famous scientist, ~~Stephen Hawking~~ Shelby LaVine.

Gwynne wasn't sure where the name Shelby LaVine had come from, like much of her inspiration to-date, a few poems and short stories, it came "inexplicably and without method" as Emma Thompson had quoted in Gwynne's favourite movie, *Stranger Than Fiction*.

She'd been searching the local paper's job columns circling anything and everything she thought she was capable of doing, and some that were highly unlikely but if you didn't apply…

"Undertaker's assistant? Really?" ~~Dan~~ ~~Stan~~ Ben, her ~~loyal and gorgeous~~ ~~supportive~~ boyfriend, asked, peering over her shoulder, mug in hand, its contents threatening to spill onto the paper. George uprighted the mug.

"Is uprighted a word?" Gwynne asked as the computer underlined it in red. She shrugged and thought that if you couldn't make up words when you were writing fiction, there'd be no fun at all, so she left it in and continued typing.

"A secretary is an assistant. It shouldn't be very different."

"I know, but undertaker? Do you really want to be wearing black all day?"

George looked at Ben's charcoal-grey suit, his black and grey tie, then looked ~~at his face~~ into his eyes.

"It's grey," Ben defended. "Besides, it's not really what you

wear it's your surroundings. You know, dead people." He shuddered.

George looked back at the paper and scored through the advert for Downes Funeral Care. ~~She didn't look up at Ben but~~ She could feel Ben's eyes boring into the paper. She glanced up at the mug which was again threatening to spill its contents. "Ben, please."

"~~Oops~~ Oh shit, sorry."

Gwynne had gone out with a guy for a while whose favourite phrase was "Oh shit, sorry". Not favourite exactly, but most regularly used because he was always making mistakes, letting her down. 'For a while' had turned out to be a month and a half. He had been one big mistake. But now she had Dan and was happy. Blissfully. Most of the time.

Gwynne looked up at the clock, then down at the computer screen's time display. A minute different, so she had twenty-eight or twenty-nine minutes left of her lunch break. "Eek."

"Huh?"

Gwynne swung round to Henry's cage, thinking he'd spoken to her but he was just repositioning himself. She looked around the room but knew the only other living thing was a plant. One that was in serious need of some watering. She opened her drawer to remind her – something she'd started doing with her bedside table when she had to remember something the following morning but didn't want to switch the light on – to write down whatever it was she was opening the drawer for, for fear of waking Ben. Dan.

Gwynne shook her head. This writing lark wasn't as easy as everyone made it out to be. Just write, or in her case, type a few words and the rest would come out? It worked up to a point but she knew she'd have to start making notes, for consistency… what was it they called it? Continuity. Green eyes at the beginning and still green eyes at the end. She'd read books where details differed and it bugged the hell out of her.

So she created 'Henry notes.doc', typed in the characters names she had so far… not many; George(ina), Henry (to be changed), Ben and Dr… what would she call Dr Moss? She'd stick with that for now and change it later. A simple find and replace. She had no foliage in her novel so there wouldn't be any other kind of moss.

Her stomach rumbled as she clicked on save then close, leaving just *Henry v1.0.doc* on the screen. She'd been working on it for a couple of weeks and had been pleased with her progress but at a few lines every lunch break, it would be months before she finished it. Dan had a demanding job – in finance – a little beyond Gwynne's understanding but then he didn't talk about it much anyway. They were comfortably off, her current job paying much better than the previous, and that was all that mattered. There was enough to worry about in life without adding money to it.

In the drawer Gwynne had opened, lay a couple of ham and pickle sandwiches so she carefully removed one and ate it, washing it down with a lukewarm cup of coffee. It didn't matter too much if she went over the hour. She'd certainly made up for it by coming in early and staying late on several occasions; she'd always felt it gave a good impression when in a new job. She still felt like a rookie so half an hour either side of the day wouldn't hurt. It wasn't as if she had anything really to go home for. Dan worked in London where a seven-to-seven day was the norm. Gwynne sighed and returned to the document.

"~~Oops~~ Oh shit, sorry."

George laughed. "You are funny." Ben leaned down and kissed her forehead.

"No." Gwynne had always found kissing of foreheads patronising and although Ben (Dan) could sometimes be a pain in the bum, he and George (Gwynne) had a good relationship.

Ben leaned down and kissed her cheek.

Gwynne paused again. "Does it matter which cheek? Does it matter whether he's standing on her left or right?" She'd imagined him on her right so it would be her right cheek and while Gwynne had heard writers talk about giving a story detail, she'd also heard that less is more, a term first attributed, in her mind anyway, to decorating a house. So the cheek stayed as a cheek, no right or left.

Ben leaned down and kissed her cheek. ~~George~~ She put her hand up to the moist

Gwynne sighed again. "Too much information. No, just write it. Worry about detail, too much or otherwise, later. No wonder it took most writers a year or two to write a novel. At this rate, Gwynne thought, she'd have probably not finished the chapter. "Come on, George. Hunker down."

Ben leaned down and kissed her cheek. ~~George~~ She ~~put her hand up to the moist~~ smiled and continued looking for jobs while Ben cooked their dinner. She felt guilty that while he'd been working hard all day, she'd been home but it wasn't as if she hadn't been busy. The house was even more immaculate than normal. Ben liked it that way and it was only fair that she made it nice for him to come home to.

Gwynne blew a raspberry. "Schmultz" so she scored through from 'She felt' to 'to come home to'. Why shouldn't Ben cook dinner? It wasn't as if he was doing it every evening. It would have been nice if Dan did once in a while but he burned everything he touched. Gwynne smiled as the image of The Human Torch from *The Fantastic Four* sprang to mind. It was then replaced by Drew Barrymore in *Firestarter*, another of Gwynne's favourite films. Top ten anyway. "Okay, so she'd look for jobs and he'd cook dinner. That's enough methinks for that little scene. Let's skim forward."

Only two of the adverts she'd circled had led to interviews, but one she really pinned her hopes on…

"Pinned her hopes. Isn't that a cliché? Oh, well." Gwynne shrugged and continued typing. Clichés could die in her first edit. It was just about getting it down… out.

Only two of the adverts she'd scored through led to interviews, but one she really pinned her hopes on was the one at Forsyth Medical Research Sciences. She hoped it wasn't one of those places that tortured animals. She could never work somewhere like that. So she'd gone on the internet, before submitting her application, and done her homework – she'd have to do that anyway as interview preparation. They were, their website promised, an ethical company working for ethical clients. Details were fairly hazy but anything that included the word 'ethical' had to be okay. Besides, she could check it out when she was there.

~~Twelve days~~ Two weeks later, she was sitting in a stark meeting room at a long oak table opposite four interviewers; three in suits and one in a lab coat. They were all older than her, in their ~~fifties and sixties~~ forties and fifties, and as serious as she had feared. George felt embarrassed.

"No. No 'tell'. Show, Gwynne, show how the character feels… how George feels."

George could feel the heat rising ~~from her skirt suit jacket~~ up her neck. She scratched it subconsciously.

"Adverbs. Stephen King hates adverbs. The 'ly' words. Oh heck. Never mind." Gwynne looked at the clock, growled then looked over at Henry as he shifted position again. His right leg kicked and Gwynne wondered if it was just a reflex or whether he was dreaming and fending off an attacker. "That's good. I'll use that." Gwynne stretched her neck, pulling out a muscle that had tightened overnight. She growled again.

George could feel the heat rising up her neck. She scratched it subconsciously then smiled ~~at the panel~~. The only woman on the panel asked her why she wanted the job. That was a question she'd always dreaded but knew they'd include, though perhaps not this early. They usually told her about the job first so it threw George but she'd rehearsed her answers to most eventualities so replied, "From the description in your advert~~isement~~, it looks a very interesting and challenging role." She knew better than to call it a 'job'. The panel could call it that but to her it had to be a role, a career, long-term, show them she meant business.

She continued. "I have worked in a number… a small number of different positions ~~since leaving school~~ but have gained a wide variety of experience in a number of fields." She knew she could ramble if she didn't keep her answers concise. Repetition of 'number' was perhaps only noticeable to her, and did it really matter? They weren't writers, editors, publishers, they were scientists, probably mathematicians, they loved numbers.

"I do feel that I have the experience that you are looking for. I work well on my own as well as in a team." Repetition of 'well', George thought but smiled again and sat up straighter in the chair. Not that she'd been slouching, but she needed to feel in control… of herself, anyway.

Twelve forty-five. Another fifteen minutes and then Gwynne would have to do some proper work. Notes. She'd have to make some notes, get some kind of structure. Plot. She knew from her short stories that the characters would take over but if she got stuck…

George felt the redness in her neck fade as the questions continued – answered, she thought, calmly and professionally. She hoped the man in the white jacket would be the one she'd be working with because he was the nicest of the four, treated her like a human being rather than a ~~sheep~~ ~~cog~~ number. They'd still told her nothing about the job, it had been all too one-sided until they'd asked her whether she had any questions. "Do you perhaps have a job description? Tell me something about the position? The advert was rather–"

The lab-coated man apologised and read from a piece of paper. "Assistant to Dr Moss. That's me, by the way." He pointed to his chest then looked down to the absence of a name badge and frowned. "Where did that go?" The other panellists looked at his jacket then back at George. They did so with precision timing, and it felt like a scene out of Doctor Who. They were definitely the baddies.

George kept looking at Dr Moss and took notes as he continued reading the job description. It didn't seem very different to being a secretary; working to deadlines, support to the doctor – George almost laughed at that point but coughed to hide it – but must also be able to use own initiative.

George found herself nodding at everything he was saying. It seemed simple enough. Like any job, it took a while to get to know people and systems. Three months, George reckoned, and if, as it would be working for him, she was sure she'd enjoy it. Not that she fancied him, he was the oldest member of the panel, but he felt like a father figure and having lost her father

Gwynne could feel the tears welling up as she typed the words. She'd lost her father ten years previously and she still missed him, thinking about him every day. Would she be that cruel to George? It would certainly change the way she felt about Ben, as it had for Gwynne with Dan. He was only four years older than her but sometimes he felt like her father, taking control when something went wrong. She realised how much she depended on him and hoped he didn't feel taken for granted, but she often told him how much she loved him, so there was no need to worry.

Not that she fancied him, he was the oldest member of the panel, but he felt like a father figure. He then talked about the salary she would be on, two thousand five hundred pounds a year more than she'd been on at Shayle Components, the other benefits; a small pension, discounts at affiliated establishments – George was going to ask where they were but Dr Moss continued – promotion opportunities. When he'd paused, George asked him how many people there were in the department and was surprised when he'd said, "Just you and me at the moment but we're getting two technicians. It's a brand new project. Very hush, hush." He tapped his nose.

You and me. Did that mean he wanted her, or was it just a figure of speech? There would be plenty of other applicants, with more experience than her, she was sure. She'd never worked in a science lab.

"Yes, she had." Gwynne scrolled back up, remembering a reference to Stephen Hawking replaced by Shelby LaVine.

There would be plenty of other applicants, with more experience than her, she was sure but hoped that personality could play a part, that he felt they'd get on.

"Oh come on, Gwynne. This isn't a dating show. Type, edit later." She knew there would be days when the flow was stilted but she felt time pressured because she had to fit her writing into a lunch break. It would be better to email it to her personal address, go home on time, and get cracking, stopping only to prepare dinner for Dan when he texted to say he was getting on the train.

It was a system that had worked well; she'd time it so it was hot when he got home, serving as he was upstairs getting changed. The only times it went awry was when the train had been delayed, unexpected substances on the line, a cow here, fallen leaves there, the wrong kind of snow.

With the clock showing she's a minute left, Gwynne saved then closed the document and emailed it to gwynne.davies191@hoppellnet.co.uk (the 191 standing for her and Dan's house number). It was usually time for Henry to have his lunch but given how late he'd had his breakfast and how comfortable he looked, she decided to leave him be. She'd get something for him, she wasn't sure what, given his new dislike for the dried food, when he asked for it.

Asked for it. Even though it had been a few days since he'd been able to speak, it still felt like a novelty. "Of course it is," Gwynne said to herself. "The world's first talking dog. It'll always be a novelty. For a while at least." She assumed they'd get other dogs, try the same thing on them, the same drugs, but who could tell whether they were going to work?

They'd been lucky with Henry. What if they tried a meaner dog? A Staffie? A pit bull? She knew she was stereotyping; there were probably nice Staffies out there, she'd just never met any, and as for pit bulls, they were banned in the UK so they'd never source one, get a licence for one, even if they wanted to. No, they were better off sticking with the softies, but then a Jack Russell was still a terrier. Henry could still have a dark side that hadn't surfaced yet.

She looked over at the cage and wondered.

Chapter Six – And Fact Into Fact

Henry was lying on his back, legs akimbo, one kicking out, with the occasional whimper. Gwynne reached across the desk to pick up the departmental camera. Ensuring the flash was off, she took a couple of photographs then switched to movie mode and took a couple of minutes' worth of footage.

She placed the camera carefully back on the desk and opened up a daily log they used for Henry's progress. Dr Moss kept his own version for his reports to the Board but this was more thorough, and a copy in case he'd missed anything.

Skimming back to day one, she read through what she'd entered already.

Day 1 – Monday 1st April

Dr Moss has selected today to begin the trials. I reminded him that it was April Fool's Day to which he laughed and said that it was even better. The world wouldn't find out what they were doing, especially not if the experiment failed, for some weeks, months perhaps but today would be memorable either way.

Patient Name: Barnabus Audicious Roman III

Adopted Name: Henry Forsyth I (HFI)

Species: Canine

Breed: Jack Russell (pure?)

Age: 17 months

Weight: 7.1kg (16 pounds)

Height: 12 inches (30cm)

Length: 18 inches (45cm)

Width (shoulders): 6 inches (15cm)

Doses: 100mg of drug coded 'XTFB12-17', the contents of which are only known to Doctor Moss (DM), Felicity Davenport (FD) and Kelvin Johnson (KJ), technicians of this department. 100mg deemed safe level for initial implant. Subsequent 10mg doses every six hours (6am / 12pm by Gwynne Davies (GD) then 6pm / 6am by A.N. Other) if patient showing no sign of ill effects to a maximum of another 100mg in any seven-day period.

Initial trial: one month from day one with interim reviews every twenty-four hours, weekly reviews and Board-level reviews at the end of month one. The decision will then be taken whether to continue with the treatment.

Following securement of monitoring equipment onto the patient (HFI), for which he showed no signs of distress or discomfort, initial implantation was actioned at 6.01am in the presence of DM, FD, KJ and GD. HFI was conscious and alert. He did not resist implantation, and accepted, and ate, the dry gravy bone treat given subsequently which FD and KJ had confirmed would not conflict with XTFB12-17.

The aforementioned four members of staff remained vigilant to the welfare of the patient until 7am by which time no effects were evident upon HFI other than tiredness, which was agreed by all to be normal. FD and KJ returned to their stations, leaving DM and GD in the room with HFI to monitor his progress ongoing and administer subsequent doses until such time as a reaction was noted.

8.10am: HFI awake and aware of his surroundings. Angling head from side-to-side when spoken to (normal). Scratched left ear for approximately ten seconds (normal). No obvious signs of skin irritation. No objection to physical examination. No abnormal behaviour noted. Standard reaction (excitement including barking) to squeaking of toys. Conclusion: Behaviour as before.

8.59am: HFI consumed usual quantity and substance of breakfast (one half cup of dried *Ruff's Complete*, 200ml semi-skimmed milk) as prepared by kitchen staff member Adam Roberts (AR). Access to bowl of water (untouched within 6.01:8.59 time duration). HFI currently playing with squeaky toy (pink and yellow hippopotamus) – no outwardly aggressive or violent behaviours noted.

9.42am: GD and HFI returned from walk of approximate half-hour duration within FMRS boundaries. HFI personality outwardly normal, no other animals encountered and therefore no interactivity to report. GD talked to HFI to which HFI viewed

GD but no vocal attributions made by HFI.

Gwynne skim-read the rest of the day's report which followed a similar pattern with no effect produced by the subsequent 6pm 10mg dose.

Knowing what happened the following day, Gwynne jumped to that.

Day 2 – Tuesday 2nd April

Patient details: as before.

8pm (1 April) to 5.30am (2 April): notes taken by KJ. Also see DM records. No reporting of unusual behaviour in advance of, during, or subsequent to 12am dose.

5.59am: DM administered a further 10mg. Reaction awaited by DM and GD. HFI drowsy but no outward or unexpected emotions recognised.

6.13am: HFI asleep. Breathing apparent, estimate normal.

7.04am: HFI asleep. Breathing apparent, estimate normal.

7.41am: HFI asleep. Breathing apparent, estimate normal.

8.12am: HFI barked with unusually high level of tail movement. DM absent. GD paged DM and approached cage with caution.

8.14am: DM returned to laboratory suite. HFI still vocally active (barking).

Chapter Seven – More Than This

"Sorry about that, Gwynne," Dr Moss said, somewhat out of breath. "Just checking in with Irene."

"How is she?" Gwynne had only met Mrs Moss twice but both times they'd chatted as if they'd known each other for years. She spoke far more to Gwynne than she had to her husband, and it hadn't gone unnoticed.

"Oh, fine. I just caught her actually. She was off out to collect some clothes for the village's jumble sale."

"Jumble sale? I didn't realise people still did those. I thought it was all money-grabbing car boots."

"Not at all. They have four a year and do really well, although I think a lot of the stuff they get is boot sale leftovers but people seem to buy anything."

"As long as it's a bargain."

"And going to a good cause."

"What's Irene's?"

"Usually the church roof, which has always amused me because we're not churchgoers, but this time it's the flooding in Bangladesh."

"That's terrible. The flooding, I mean. You'd think of that part of the world as having droughts, being such a dry country."

Dr Moss nodded. "It's the Ganges."

"Yes, I heard that on the BBC. It makes us appreciate the odd bit of rain we get."

"Excuse me. If you don't mind."

Gwynne and Dr Moss turned round to Henry's cage. He was looking up at them, toy abandoned. Henry scratched his ear, stretched his neck, and yawned. "I'm here, you know."

Dr Moss grabbed a clipboard from the work-surface next to Gwynne's computer. "He speaks such good English."

Henry coughed.

Gwynne stared at him.

"It's rude to stare, you know."

"Where did he pick up 'you know' from?" Gwynne asked.

"Where does he pick anything up from? Us, the TV, radio.

He's... eighteen months old so–"

"Nineteen."

"Exactly. He's only been here a couple of months so wherever he was before us, it'll have infiltrated his learning systems. He'll be repeating things he's heard."

"But he knows what it means. In context. He's speaking of his own free will. He's not mimicking. Are you, Henry?"

Henry shook his head.

"See?"

Dr Moss grinned then looked at Gwynne who was standing, staring at Henry, her mouth agape. "Gwynne?"

"I can't believe he speaks."

"I know."

"I do," Henry said, sighed and lay down.

All he wanted, all he'd ever wanted, was a decent conversation, where humans could understand what he was saying. He'd been listening for... he wasn't sure how long but it felt like years, forming words in his brain, constructing sentences, repeating them until they felt right. He knew he was clever; he only had to be told something once and it stuck.

He'd enjoyed listening to the study channels. Henry's former mistress, Carmen, had been Spanish, an 'illegal'. Henry had heard Mick, her English boyfriend, call her that often enough. Henry knew what that word meant from all the illegal items in their house; the ones that smelled so nice when Mick smoked them – Henry wouldn't have done even if he'd been given the chance, and the lovely black shiny guns that Mick spent most of the day polishing before he went out, taking them with him, then polishing them again when he got back.

Mick would call Carmen stupid for wanting to learn English. "We get on okay, don't we?" he'd say to her. Henry thought it was because Mick struggled with the language himself and didn't want her, or anyone else, bettering him.

In the end, the police had turned up, arrested them both, not without a lot of resistance and swearing. Henry had been taken away too, to a long pen with lots of other dogs. He was used to being kept in a cage, so that hadn't bothered him – it still didn't

– but he liked peace and quiet, and apart from the arguments between Carmen and Mick, he'd had a pretty good life. Being surrounded by at least a dozen other dogs – a dozen other cages, Sesame Street had taught Henry to count – and Henry could hear more, wasn't peaceful at all.

"So..." Gwynne stepped nearer to Henry's cage. "Are you... okay?"

Henry stayed lying down, head rested on paws, but looked up at Gwynne and mumbled, "I'm fine, thank you. Just a little tired."

"We're not long back from a walk," Gwynne explained to Dr Moss, who nodded.

"A boring one, if you ask me which I know you didn't but..."

Gwynne and Dr Moss looked at each other then back at Henry.

"It's the same trip every time. Couldn't we go outside... you know, properly outside, to a park, let me off the lead, let me run around. I'm a dog, not a prisoner."

"I don't know..." Dr Moss started. "I'm not sure we can take that risk."

Henry lifted his head off his paws. "Risk? What risk?"

"Of you running away."

Henry laughed, making Gwynne laugh. "Why do you think I'm going to run away?"

"Because you know you have to come back here and be put in the cage," the doctor explained.

Henry looked at his cage, the bars wide enough to fit a cat through, the cage measuring at least five feet by four. His bedding was soft... ish, there was constant water, food came fairly regularly – when it wasn't late – and he had all the toys he could possibly want. With the exception of on-the-tap treats, there wasn't anything missing. He even had undivided attention and the occasional cuddle from Gwynne when the doctor wasn't around. "So?"

"Don't you want your freedom?" Gwynne asked, walking over to her desk and sitting down.

"Why?"

"You know," the doctor started, looked at Gwynne, then back at Henry. "To run around any time you like, chase… things."

"Chasing's tiring. Ever tried it?"

Dr Moss shook his head. "No, can't say I have."

"Let me assure you, it is, especially squirrels. They have the same number of legs, ears, head, tail, and so on, but they go like the wind. It loses its appeal after a while. Cats are fun because they make more noise but the ones that are brave… or stupid enough, fight back and that's no fun. My mate, Butch, nearly had an eye out because of a hulk of a ginger tom." Henry had added the last bit for effect. He'd never met another dog called Butch, only seen one on TV, and other than Carmen, had never had any friends, canine or otherwise, but liked the way it sounded.

"What happens now?" Gwynne asked Dr Moss.

"Erm… I'm not sure. I hadn't… we hadn't anticipated it actually working."

"What?" Henry stood. "You mean you gave me that stuff, which stank, by the way. Couldn't you have made it meat-fragranced, or flowery, or something?"

"Sorry," Gwynne said.

"That's okay," Henry replied. "You won't have to give it to me now anyway, will you? I mean, I can talk and everything. You're… it's job done, isn't it?"

"Erm…" Dr Moss repeated. "I don't know." He referred to his clipboard.

Henry lay down again. He was disappointed that these people didn't seem as clever as their white coats implied. They certainly didn't know very much. Carmen knew everything about everything, as long as it was in Spanish. She'd watch *Preguntas Preguntas* every weekday lunchtime and score as much as the runner-up, sometimes even the winner. Henry had tried to tell her that she should take part but she couldn't understand him. She'd just say, "Si," and tap him on the head. Initially it had felt patronising but he knew she loved him, just as he thought Gwynne had, did, does, and he liked the contact.

It was Mick who insisted Henry be kept in a cage. "We've

got some powerful shit here," he'd said. "We don't want him getting any of it." Henry knew what shit smelled like, he'd sniffed plenty in his time; his own, other dogs'. He'd not sniffed humans' but what it smelled like when they burned it, smoked it, certainly wasn't any shit he'd encountered.

Henry watched Dr Moss study his clipboard. The doctor shook his head every now and then. Gwynne was looking at her screen and smiling.

Henry had been expecting more than this. Whenever Carmen had been excited about something, she'd made lots of noise, jumped around, but these two were more than subdued. Maybe it was the Spanish custom to show feelings. Henry had heard, on TV he thought, about the English stiff upper lip, although Gwynne's and Dr Moss's didn't look very stiff. Dr Moss's were narrow, quite pale, like his face, as if it rarely saw the sun, only looking as tanned as it was because of the white coat he always wore. Now that did look stiff, and always very white.

Mick had been grubby, his hands especially. He'd handle the guns, the 'shit', often while eating whatever Carmen had made for him, never saying "Thank you" when she put it in front of him. She'd pause, wait for some act of recognition, even a derogatory comment which was forthcoming often enough about her clothes; they were always too many when they weren't going out, too few on the rare times Carmen and Mick did leave the house together – or her hair; too dark, too pale, too long, too short.

Nothing she ever did was good enough for Mick but Henry was easily pleased. He'd have leftovers as well as his regular food, all so healthy that he never got fat. He didn't get much exercise but when Carmen knew Mick was going out for long enough, she'd open the cage door, let Henry wander around the house then walk him round the block to the local dog park.

He'd never been bothered about other dogs, all that sniffing of backsides, going round in circles. He'd done it to be sociable, but it felt a bit demeaning, although the other dogs seemed to enjoy it. He'd soon wander off, check his surroundings, spend some time alone. Apart from the dog walks, grocery shopping or going out with Mick, Carmen never went anywhere, so Henry was rarely alone.

Of course Henry wasn't Henry back then. He'd been Jack. How original; a Jack Russell called Jack. Then the rescue centre had called him Tim, which he didn't think suited him at all. So when FMRS had renamed him Henry, he was delighted. It sounded smart, regal.

He'd watched enough of the History Channel to know about Henry the Eighth and all his wives. Henry even knew how to spell 'eighth' because it was the only word in the English language to end in 'hth'. Some would say that Henry had had a rough start in life but he had no complaints and when he'd arrived at FMRS he'd thought he'd be okay too. They'd warm to him and vice versa.

Henry sat looking from Dr Moss to Gwynne and back again. He imagined they were playing tennis. Rafael Nadal and… who? Henry couldn't think of a Spanish female tennis player. Then he began to doubt that Rafael was Spanish. Carmen used to cheer him on, watch re-runs until Henry could repeat the commentator's reports word for word.

"Gwynne?"

Gwynne looked up from her screen. "Yes, Henry?"

"Is Rafael Nadal Spanish?"

"Sorry?"

"Rafael Nadal, the tennis player. Is he–?"

"I think so. Let me find out for you." Gwynne flicked from Word to Safari, her Mac's internet programme, and Googled Rafael Nadal. She clicked the second of the forty-nine million offered entries, opening Wikipedia's.

"Yes. He's from Manacor, Spain, wherever that is."

Henry didn't know either. Carmen had mentioned a cousin from Barcelona and an ex-boyfriend from Valencia – when Mick wasn't there, of course – but she'd never mentioned Manacor. Henry would have remembered.

"Oh, okay."

"Why?" Gwynne asked.

"A friend mentioned him once or twice. Just curious."

"Oh," Gwynne said calmly, despite feeling all but calm inside. She wanted to scream, jump up and down, shout from the rooftops, or at least out the window that she was talking to a dog and it... he was talking back. Really talking back, a real conversation... about Rafael Nadal. Henry knew who Rafael Nadal was. Amazing.

Gwynne joined Dr Moss at Henry's cage. Dr Moss crouched down so he was face-to-face with the dog.

"Hello, Henry."

"Hello, Dr M."

Dr Moss looked up at Gwynne, who shrugged, then looked back at Henry. "Henry, I–"

"Yes, Dr M."

"You're okay, are you?"

"Pretty good, thank you."

Dr Moss shook his head.

Henry tilted his. "Am I not okay?"

"Oh yes. Of course you are. I... erm. I need to report to the Board, any news of a progressive nature."

"A progressive nature?" Henry asked, head reverted.

"Progress, yes. If there are developments."

"Like me talking?"

Dr Moss gave a nervous laugh. "Ha, yes. Anything they should be made aware of, would be interested in."

"The Board? People who haven't got enough to do?"

Dr Moss looked up at Gwynne.

"No, Henry," Gwynne stepped forward. "Not that kind of bored. It's a group of people who pay money to make things happen."

"Like me talking."

"Like you talking, Henry," Dr Moss rose, shaking his right leg.

Henry looked around the lab. "Costs a lot of money, doesn't it. To run this place."

Dr Moss and Gwynne looked at each other but said nothing.

"Of course it does." Henry lay down. "If there's nothing else,

I'm going to have a nap. It's been quite a tiring morning." It hadn't actually but he was bored… spelled, however it was spelled. Toys or no toys, he'd rather have reciprocated interaction, of the human kind if it was on offer, but it hadn't been particularly forthcoming so he'd have a nap and see what happened when he woke up, or was woken up. They might decide they'd waited long enough. Ask him some really exciting questions. Have a bit of fun, some thrill-seekment. Henry wasn't sure if that was a word but as long as he knew what he meant, and they did when the time came, that was all that mattered.

A three a.m. police raid was a hard act to follow, but of course Dr Moss and Gwynne didn't know that. As far as they knew, he'd lived a sedentary life in a normal English house until whoever had owned him had tired of him, kicked him out to wander the streets. He didn't actually know what they knew but a life of destitution behind him sounded more realistic than a drugs bust. And everyone loves a sob story. You only had to watch daytime TV to know that.

Chapter Eight – The Resistance

Gwynne's heart sank as she turned off the main road and headed down FMRS's long drive. Placards of varying sizes and colours greeted her as she approached the front gates.

The FMRS security team was keeping the protestors back far enough for Gwynne to drive through but she still heard them bang on her car, clunk against the red Ford Focus's paintwork. Heart pounding, she wanted to shout back, tell them not to hurt her car but enough of them thought she was hurting animals so she felt the triviality of something materialistic a weak argument.

She'd been warned that this could, and likely would, happen, that there were people who didn't understand that they'd never hurt animals knowingly, that no animal had died there of anything other than natural causes, mostly old age. FMRS had open days where the public could come in, see the work they did, but of course there were areas where they couldn't go and those who wanted to cause trouble used that as an excuse.

FMRS's accounts were available to anyone who applied, the members of the Board had no known blemishes against them and yet, every few months, a small group would congregate until they felt they'd made their point heard and left before the police were called. As long as they didn't cause any property damage or injuries to FMRS staff, they were left alone.

It wasn't such a bad experience, Gwynne thought, to spend a morning outside a former stately home where peacocks had once roamed and the gardens still housed a huge fountain and maze so big you could easily get lost.

Her heart was still pounding when she walked to the main reception. "Morning, Lauren."

"Morning, Gwynne."

Lauren Sanderson, FMRS's receptionist, placed a pile of envelopes on the ledge in front of her. "Nothing interesting-looking today, Gwynne. Probably bills mostly. No love letters, that's for sure."

Gwynne laughed. "Just as well. Dan wouldn't be very happy

if there were."

Lauren pointed her chin towards the half-glass half-wood panelled front door. "I got here as they were congregating so I drove straight in, but the security guys have their work cut out today."

"They certainly have. Wouldn't want to be them but then I guess that's what they're paid for; using their brawn."

"Another exciting day planned for you then?"

Lauren was always fishing for gossip. Gwynne couldn't tell her what they were doing but Lauren tried anyway.

"Same old, same old."

Lauren smiled then took a call.

Gwynne mouthed a "thank you", clutched her post, and swiped her ID card to let herself through to the labs.

"Morning, Henry."

"Morning, Gwynneth."

"Gwynne, just Gwynne."

"Are you not a Gwyneth, one 'n', like the actress… erm…"

"Paltrow."

"That's it. Her husband's a singer, isn't he?"

Henry knew exactly who Gwyneth Paltrow and Chris Martin were; Carmen also loved keeping up with all the celebrities, but he knew he could come across as too cocky sometimes and it didn't do any good.

"Two 'n's but yes, Henry. Although he's not been her husband for ages, I'm impressed."

"Too much TV."

Gwynne murmured something out of Henry's earshot and he hoped she didn't take that literally. He loved watching TV and hated the thought of them restricting it so decided to backtrack. "As long as it's educational, of course." Not that he wanted to just watch study programmes. Children's TV was designed as instructional too, wasn't it? Young brains needed stimulating and he knew his had much more learning to do.

"Mrs… do you have a last name?"

"Davies. Miss."

"Oh, not married."

"No."

"But you have a boyfriend. I've seen that look…"

"Look?"

"You know. Far away. Dreamy. You look like Meredith Grey in Grey's Anatomy lusting after McDreamy."

"McDreamy?"

"Yeah. Derek Shepherd, the brain surgeon."

"Oh."

"You must have seen Grey's Anatomy."

"Can't say–"

"Everyone's seen… never mind. Do you have satellite TV or the likes?"

"…Yes."

"There'll be repeats of it, I'm sure. UK Gold. Living. One of those."

When Lauren had asked Gwynne whether she had an exciting day planned, chatting about TV programmes wouldn't have come under that heading. Chatting about them with a talking dog, Gwynne figured, definitely would.

As if reading her mind, Henry said, "Another exciting day then today? Another walk round the grounds or…"

Gwynne looked at the clock. Eight forty-five. Dr Moss should be around but Gwynne had not thought of going to the end of the corridor, past the technicians' lab and knocking on the doctor's door.

As she thought of him, the door opened and in came Dr Moss, clipboard in hand. "Morning, Gwynne."

"Morning, Dr Moss."

The doctor turned to Henry. "Morning, Henry."

"Morning, Dr Moss."

"And how are you today?"

"I'm well, thank you."

"Good… good." Dr Moss took a pen from his jacket's breast pocket and ticked a box.

Henry looked at him, waiting for further comment or

instruction, but the doctor just stared at the piece of paper.

"I was going to make a drink. Would you like one, Dr Moss?" Gwynne asked.

The doctor looked up from the clipboard. "Thank you."

"Coffee? Tea?"

"Coffee, please."

Gwynne nodded. "We were talking about TV programmes and celebrities."

Dr Moss looked back at Henry. "You were?"

Henry nodded. "We were. Can you believe she's never seen Grey's Anatomy?"

Dr Moss turned to Gwynne. "Really?"

Gwynne shook her head.

"One of my favourite programmes. But then I've got lots of favourites."

"Mine too," Henry chirped up. "Ooh... I've got a joke for you."

"You have?" Gwynne asked.

"About a boy and a dog."

"Go on," the doctor urged, sitting on a chair by a spare desk. Gwynne sat on her own chair.

Henry coughed then looked at his captive audience. "A boy takes his dog to the cinema. It's an old-fashioned cinema with a high single-desk ticket office. He buys a ticket for himself but doesn't mention the dog. The salesman doesn't spot the animal so says nothing. The boy and his dog go into the cinema."

Gwynne and the doctor look at each other and smile.

"The usherette... it's an old cinema, remember."

Gwynne nods.

"The usherette goes up to the boy and says, 'We're not supposed to have dogs in here, will he behave?' 'Oh, yes,' the boy says. 'He's very good. You won't hear a peep out of him.' 'But it's *Lord of the Rings*,' the usherette says." Henry turned to Gwynne. "It used to be *Gone with the Wind* but I've updated it."

Gwynne smiled and nodded so Henry continued.

"'It's a really long film,' the usherette says. 'He'll be no trouble. Really,' the boy says. 'Okay,' the usherette says and returns to her station. She watches the pair of them during the film and they're both glued to the screen, the dog occasionally wagging its tail. As we do."

Dr Moss laughed and Henry continued. "During the break, the usherette's too busy selling ice creams to speak to the boy who remains in his seat. The second half of the film is much the same; the boy and his dog are glued to the screen, the dog occasionally wagging its tail. As we do."

Henry paused for the doctor to laugh again but it wasn't forthcoming so Henry continued. "When the film's over, the usherette goes over to the boy and says, 'I can't believe how much your dog liked the film.' 'Me too,' the boy says. 'He hated the book.' Ta da!" Henry put out his front right paw for effect but Gwynne and the doctor were already laughing.

"I'm rubbish at remembering jokes," Gwynne said. "But I must remember that one to tell Dan."

"Very good," Dr Moss said, looking at his clipboard. "Very good." Henry watched the doctor's pen as he ticked off another box.

"What was that one for?"

"Sense of humour. Two ticks now."

"Oh," Henry said.

"Drinks," Gwynne said. "Two coffees coming up. Want anything, Henry?"

"Would you like."

"Sorry?"

"I was taught to say 'would you like' not 'do you want', although you didn't say 'do you', just the 'want'."

Gwynne looked worried. She turned to Dr Moss then back to Henry. "Who taught you to say that?"

"Grover. Sesame Street. And I wouldn't mind a spot of milk, if it's not too much trouble."

Gwynne smiled and relaxed her shoulders. "Not at all."

"Thank you," Henry said as he watched the doctor pull his chair nearer to the cage.

Gwynne left the room and the doctor turned over a sheet and tucked it behind the clipboard. He fiddled the page straight, frowning as he did so, then removed the sheet, leaning back in his chair, and put the sheet down on the desk.

"Couldn't trouble you for another blanket, could I?" Henry asked the doctor.

"Are you cold?"

"Not now, but at night. Was a bit chilly. I think they turn the heating off, whoever 'they' are. I always wondered that. 'They' have a lot to answer for… or is it 'to'?"

Dr Moss made a note on his clipboard. "Anything else?"

Henry thought he sensed a bit of sarcasm in the doctor's voice but decided to let it go. "Thank you, but no. Although…"

"Yes, Henry?"

"Having the milk warmed a bit would be nice. But, no, I wouldn't want to trouble…"

"Maybe we can get you something from the kitchen."

"It's okay. Another time." Having no success with Gwynne earlier, Henry asked again, "Another exciting day then today? Another walk round the grounds or…" He let the questions hang in the air, waiting for the doctor to process them.

"We're having some visitors."

"Oh, yes?"

"Some very important people."

"The Board?"

"You know about…? Oh yes, yesterday. Board vs bored. I remember."

"So they're coming here?"

"Yes."

"To see me?"

"Yes, Henry, to see you."

"And they're the ones that pay for all this, aren't they?"

"They are."

"So… I have to behave?"

"Yes, please, Henry."

"I'm sure I can do that."

"Would be appreciated."

"Would like my warm milk though…"

"Okay."

"And a new toy. These are getting a bit shabby. Wouldn't

want the Board to think you don't look after me."

"We'll try, although…" Dr Moss looked at the clock. The Board would be there in just over an hour. Not a good day to have protestors outside. He looked out through the window. There was only a slight view to the front gates but there were still plenty of people milling around, placards at forty-five degree angles as they waited for someone to show them to.

Dr Moss could instruct Security to get rid of them but he wanted the Board to know what the staff had to face occasionally. They'd instructed complete honesty at all times; transparent procedures, clinical methods logged at every stage, regular reports, so that's what they'd get.

Gwynne returned with three plain white mugs, evenly balanced on a narrow sandwich tray. She pointed one end at Dr Moss who took his mug.

"Thanks, Gwynne."

"No problem." She put the tray on her desk, took the middle mug and placed it on a coaster by her computer monitor. She then walked over to Henry's cage, remaining mug in hand, and put it on the floor by the cage door.

"I may be clever," Henry said, "but my tongue isn't Gene Simmonds long."

Gwynne laughed, recalling how her brother, Neil, had been a 'Kiss' fan as a teenager, with posters of the rock group plastered on his bedroom wall, including one about four feet high with Gene's torso and stuck-out tongue. Their mother rarely ventured into his room because of it… and the fact that she couldn't cross the room without having to step over something.

"It's okay, Henry. I'm not leaving it there. Just need my hands free to open the cage." She pulled a chained bundle of keys from her jacket pocket and removed the padlock.

Henry looked at the padlock. Carmen had never put one of those on her cage. She'd trusted him.

Gwynne followed his eyes. "It's not that we don't trust you, Henry. We don't want anyone to steal you."

That hadn't occurred to him before. It made him valuable. Loved, even.

Chapter Nine – Meeting The Board

Henry drank the milk that Gwynne had poured into his food bowl. “Very nice, thank you. Nice and…” He looked at Dr Moss. “Chilled.”

Dr Moss looked down at his clipboard again.

Henry wanted to growl, to ask him why he kept looking down. There were things he wanted to say, probably ask him. The first time they’d had a question and answer session it went okay. What was stopping him this time? “Uh oh.”

“Uh oh, Henry?” Gwynne took a mouthful of coffee.

“Were you planning a walk before the Board gets here?”

Gwynne turned to Dr Moss. “The Board’s coming?”

“In an hour. Sorry, meant to tell you. I only found out this morning, when Sir Alfred called from an early round of golf. Not all of them, I think. Just him, Sir Walter, and one or two more.”

Henry whistled in Dr Moss’s direction. “Two ‘Sirs’. Very impressive.”

Dr Moss nodded and scuttled out of the lab, mumbling about how much he had to do before his bosses arrived.

Henry looked back at Gwynne. “Anyway, as I said, ‘Uh oh’.”

“Oh, yes. You want to go for a walk?”

“If it’s not too much trouble. May well make a puddle otherwise and that would be embarrassing.”

Gwynne walked to the lab door, unhooking a lead from one of four coat pegs. She looked over at the cage, which was empty, and gasped.

“I’m down here,” a voice by her feet said.

“Oh, phew.”

“Didn’t think I’d escaped, did you?” He looked around the room. “Unless I was actually a giraffe, there’s no way I could get out the windows, especially as they’re shut, and even I have my limits, and you’re by the door. Where else could I go?”

“Sorry, Henry. Just a bit nervous.”

“The Board.”

“Yes. I’ve not met them all before and–”

“It doesn’t sound like you’re going to meet them all now.”

"No, I know but the two Sirs are the top of the tree."

"I guess they'd have to be… what are they doing at the top of a tree?"

Gwynne laughed. "Not literally. It's just a figure of speech."

"Oh," Henry said, posting that one into his brain banks. He'd heard someone say, probably on TV, that humans use a tiny percentage of their brains to store all the information and they could do so much more. Henry didn't know the proportion of his capacity to theirs. Maybe Dr Moss could have told him but he didn't hold out much hope. Still, the Board must have placed their faith in him, and Gwynne, and the two other people in white coats that called in from time-to-time, Felicity and Kelvin. Henry had never had a conversation with either of them, not two-way anyway.

They'd looked over at him, talked about him, Felicity even came over and said some baby speak to him, but that was before he let them in on the fact that he understood every word, and was willing to give as good as he got. Very willing actually. Up to then, he'd been quite restrained, they were nice enough people, and the women were especially nice to him, but if anyone riled him, he'd let them know who was boss. Not anyone in a white coat, that was for sure.

"Can we go for this walk now?"

Gwynne had been staring at him for the past few seconds and Henry didn't know how much longer he could contain the milk he'd drunk.

"We can't be long, Henry, so please curb the stopping and sniffing. Okay?"

"Okay."

"And no talking while we're out."

"I won't if you don't talk to me."

"I'll try."

Henry grinned. "But I know what you're like."

"What am I like?"

"You're like me."

Gwynne laughed. "A talking dog?"

"No. You can... What's the phrase? Talk for England."

"I don't know about that."

"Wales then."

"All right, yes. I can live with that."

They turned left out the lab and to the exit just past Dr Moss's office. They then went through a single door next to double fire doors. Gwynne turned round to make sure it was shut after them, then patted her trouser pocket to check she had her keys. Henry thought that a bit Irish, to do it in that order, which was especially strange because Gwynne was Welsh.

"Okay. Just the short version this time. We can come out again later. Okay?"

Henry said nothing but sniffed at the bottom of a drainpipe.

"Henry?"

Trying not to move his mouth, Henry mumbled, "You told me not to talk."

Gwynne looked around. "There's no one here."

Henry wanted to be sarcastic, say something like "Make your mind up" but instead just said, "Okay."

Gwynne, using an expandable lead, wandered on, picking a pace that implied that Henry should keep up. Every now and then she would gently tug at the lead or tap her thigh to chivvy him up but he was always lagging behind. "Henry!" she called through gritted teeth.

Henry tutted and plodded on. As well as the drainpipe, he watered four rose bushes, the edge of the fountain – much to the Head Gardener, William Wilson's annoyance, and Henry was about to cock his leg against a wheelbarrow but Gwynne yanked the lead.

"You know better than that, Henry. You'll have Old Mr Wilson on my back."

Henry shuddered. He couldn't imagine Gwynne wearing him as an appendage, and Henry knew neither of them would have been able to carry the man's weight. Despite all the walking Mr Wilson got, he was terribly overweight but then Henry figured he probably just went around shouting orders at the other gardeners and never did any work himself.

As Henry and Gwynne went back inside, Dr Moss was locking his office door. "Oh, thank goodness! I wondered where you were."

"Just taking Henry out before–"

"They're here already. Early. I'm not ready. We're not ready. Henry's all damp and…"

"It'll be fine. Do you want to put him back and I'll go through to recep–"

"No, no. I'll go. They wouldn't expect anything less. No offence."

Gwynne shook her head.

"I expected them to be late," Dr Moss continued. "Sir Alfred was playing golf. He always spends hours. He's probably still in his get-up. Expect 'loud' when he comes through. Ooh, Gwynne, could you rustle up some coffees? Use the cups and saucers. Make sure there are no chips. And if you could find some biscuits that would be–"

"You go. I'll get everything ready." Gwynne looked down at Henry. "He'll be on his best behaviour, won't you, Henry?"

Henry sighed. "Yes. Boy scout."

Dr Moss laughed nervously and walked down the corridor before thrusting his hand in the air. "Clipboard. Where's my clipboard?"

Gwynne had already unlocked the lab door and stepped inside but came back out. "It's on the spare desk here. It's all ready for the Board."

Dr Moss puffed. "Thank you, Gwynne. Okay, here goes."

Gwynne walked Henry to his cage, unclipped his lead and ushered him inside. She shut the door after him but didn't lock it. She knew the Board would want him out, walking around, when they were done asking questions. They'd want to see that in any other respect, he was a normal dog; walking, sitting, begging (despite Henry having said he wouldn't… maybe Gwynne would 'forget' that he knew that) and lie like any other Jack Russell, any other dog.

Gwynne went to the kitchenette next door, filled the kettle

and returned to the lab.

Henry was rolling around the cage floor, part on his bed, part off.

"What are you doing?" Gwynne asked.

"Practising."

"For what?"

"The Board."

"Rolling around on the floor?"

"That's the kind of thing they're after, isn't it?"

"I don't think so."

"Don't they want me to be like a normal dog or just one who talks?"

"Let's see, shall we?"

"Were you making a drink?"

"I am."

"Could I have some milk?"

"Not just yet. Later, maybe, after they've gone. Don't want you widdling on the floor."

"Widdling?"

"Yes, you know. Doing a number one."

"Number one?"

"Going to the toilet."

"Oh. Why didn't you–?"

But Gwynne had already left and Henry could hear her clinking cups, and opening and closing the fridge door.

When the door opened next, it wasn't Gwynne but Dr Moss followed by three men and a woman. Two of the men were even older than Dr Moss, both had grey hair and were dressed in business suits. One had a walking stick, the other was more agile. Henry assumed the latter was Sir Alfred as he played golf and Henry was disappointed that he wasn't dressed accordingly.

"As you can see, Sir Walter..." Dr Moss pointed around the room but was talking to the man with the stick. "We have all the appliances in place to ensure an effective and prolonged testing process. We are obviously only at the beginning of that process but are encouraged by the results so far."

The group was ignoring Dr Moss and were all focused on Henry. The woman detached herself and walked to the cage.

"Careful, Olivia!" Sir Alfred called out. "Don't get too close. You don't know what it's capable of yet."

"That's quite all right, Sir Alfred," Dr Moss said. "He is very gentle."

"But even so…"

"It's okay, Papa," the woman said and stepped closer to the cage until she was about a foot away. She crouched down and said, "Hello."

Her voice, Henry thought, was like butter. He'd heard that expression on TV and although he couldn't imagine a voice being yellow and full of fat, he knew it was a compliment. He wanted to tell her but decided against it. He'd wait for instruction from Dr Moss or Gwynne before speaking. The first words, Henry knew, would stay with Sir Alfred and his entourage for the rest of their lives; not long judging by the looks of the two Sirs, but the daughter was still quite young, about the same age as Gwynne, Henry thought.

Unnoticed, Gwynne had come in with a tray of drinks and placed it silently on her desk. When the woman turned to see what Henry was looking at, she stood and smiled. Gwynne smiled back. "I've made some coffees but if you prefer tea, do let me know."

"Coffee will be lovely, thank you." Olivia held out her hand and took the proffered cup, placing her hand flat underneath the saucer. Holding out her right pinkie finger, she took a delicate sip then slowly brought the cup back down onto the saucer. Henry could only see part of what she was doing but was spellbound. Olivia turned to face him. "Isn't he lovely?"

"He's very good," Gwynne lied, then added, "He has his moments of naughtiness, as all dogs do, but on the whole he's no trouble." Gwynne looked at Henry and winked.

He wanted to wink back but didn't. *Best behaviour*, he reminded himself.

Henry sat, head up, shoulders back, as models do on the catwalk… Henry could never understand why it was called a catwalk and not a dogwalk. There was so much to learn about the English language. So many questions he wanted to ask Gwynne, get her to look things up on her computer. He wished he could have a computer of his own so he didn't have to keep bothering her but she never seemed to mind. And of course he didn't have any fingers.

"Henry?"

Henry focused and looked up at Dr Moss.

"Henry. Today is an ordinary day but we have some special visitors here to see you. To see what you can do."

Henry looked at the two Sirs who were facing each other. They didn't look impressed. He stared at them until they looked back at him. *Okay*, Henry thought. *I need to impress them.* "Hello, my name is Henry. Je m'appelle Henri." He thought pronouncing his name without the 'H' would add a flourish. He felt like bowing as Sir Walter Raleigh had when he dropped his cloak onto the muddy ground so Queen Elizabeth I could walk onto it without getting her feet dirty.

Henry thought it a bit pointless because she would have been wearing shoes but she had seemed to be pleased, although that was before she locked him in the Tower of London for marrying one of her ladies-in-waiting without the Queen's permission. She was a fickle woman. It wasn't as if she wanted to marry him herself. Henry didn't understand the royals, although the younger generation these days seemed to have their heads screwed on, which was just as well, Henry thought, because the kings and queens seemed to take such pleasure in chopping them off.

Henry continued. "Ich heisse Henry. Soy… mi nombre es Henry."

Sir Walter hobbled forward, nothing like Sir Walter Raleigh. "Were his lips moving? I didn't see his lips moving." Then he turned to Dr Moss. "Is this a tape you're playing? A CD perhaps?"

"Not at all, Sir Walter. Everything Henry's saying is of his own free will, although we didn't know he could speak any French, German and er..."

"Spanish," Henry added.

"Thank you, Henry."

"You're welcome, Dr Moss. De rien... Willkommen..." He was tempted to add a 'de nada' but thought that would be showing off.

The two Sirs looked at each other again then back at Henry.

"Ask me something, anything," Henry added, "and I'll reply. I'm not shy and I have nothing to hide."

Olivia giggled.

"Go on then, Olivia," her father said. "Ask him something, anything."

Olivia cleared her throat. "How old are you, Henry?"

Henry wanted to cough but thought she'd think he was being rude, copying her, like he was tempted to do with Sir Alfred's posh accent. "I am nineteen months old."

"Ask him something more complicated," Sir Alfred pressed, but Henry continued anyway.

"I shall be two years old in five months. I don't know the day exactly because I'm a rescue dog and Carmen... that's my previous owner, is in jail so they..." He turned to Gwynne and Dr Moss then back to Olivia. "Couldn't ask her when I was born. I think I lived with her all my life, before coming here because I don't remember being anywhere else, other than the rescue centre, but..."

He looked at the third man of the group, who was scribbling notes. Henry wanted to suggest he use a dictaphone because he could just point it at Henry and make notes later, but the man was smiling as he wrote, smiling with his tongue sticking out actually, which Henry had first thought was quite rude but then realised that it must be helping him to concentrate because he wasn't looking at anyone, just at his notepad and writing things down.

"So, yes, nineteen months old, which feels a lot longer. They say that there are seven dog years to every human year so technically I should be..." Henry looked down at the floor. He could add up but multiplication took him longer.

"133 months. Eleven years and a month," Olivia said without appearing to think about it.

Henry nodded. "Yes, thank you."

Gwynne had dispensed the other coffees with their required milks and sugars, and was offering chairs to the two older board members. They took them willingly and were sat a few feet away, with the note taker standing next to them. Olivia was still close to the cage and hanging on Henry's every word. She turned round to the old men. "Would you like to ask him something, Papa, Sir Walter?"

"Ask him if he likes it here," Sir Walter suggested.

"I do, thank you." Henry looked again at Dr Moss then at Gwynne, who smiled.

Sir Alfred shuffled on his seat. "Good. Very good. Now, tell us about the whole process. What happened when the drug first took effect?"

Dr Moss stepped forward and looked down at his clipboard. "On–"

"No. Henry, if you don't mind."

Dr Moss coughed and stepped back. "Certainly, Sir. Henry?"

"I'd been here about a week, I think. Of course I can't tell the days, I don't have a calendar, but it had got dark and then light again six or seven times."

"Okay," Sir Walter said. "Go on."

"They… I mean Dr Moss and Gwynne, Miss Davies, were doing all sorts of tests, nothing bad, just checking I was okay. The heartbeat, glossy coat, eating everything they gave me, and so on."

Sir Walter nodded.

"Then they gave me injections. They said "sorry" and that it shouldn't really hurt. It didn't much, just a little sting but they gave me a gravy bone afterwards, which I love, although those stinky tripe sticks are really my favourite but I know they're really fattening so I mustn't have them very often. I used to have sweets that look like shoes which was fun because I like tugging at the laces, but then I chewed one of Mick's trainers which got Carmen into trouble and she said I couldn't have any more, although by then I was old enough to know the difference, but I don't think she wanted to risk it."

"Carmen? Mick?" Sir Walter asked, tapping his hearing aid.

Henry wanted to tut, to ask why Sir Walter had such a bad memory seeing as Henry had told him earlier who Carmen was but then put it down to his age, that the old man's brain must have so much in it that everything would be fighting for space and maybe the fact that Carmen was Henry's previous owner had been knocked out by Sir Walter trying to work out Henry's age… or the difference in months between the two. That or what he was going to have to eat when he left FMRS.

"Henry's previous owners, Sir Walter," Dr Moss explained. "He's mentioned them to us a few times but we know nothing about them because we got him from a rescue centre, as you know, Sir Walter." Sir Walter nodded. "Apparently they are in prison, or are awaiting trial. Very unsavoury characters so I understand, but then they would be going to prison."

"Carmen's lovely," Henry blurted. "She was just caught up with a bad man. He's the one to blame, if you're going to blame–"

"It's okay, Henry," Dr Moss soothed. "There's no blame." He then faced Sir Walter. "I'm surprised Henry turned out as balanced as he did."

Henry pictured himself sitting in one of Lady Justice's scale bowls and would normally find it funny but instead gritted his teeth. He didn't like anything bad being said about Carmen, especially from someone who had never met her, but he liked Dr Moss too and he was right, people going to prison are usually bad, or at least they've done something wrong to warrant them being there. Henry wanted to ask them to find out how Carmen was but suspected it was 'no' to his history and how it would stay. He had to accept that this was his present life and he had to leave his past behind.

"Sir Alfred. I have some questions for Henry if you'd like to–"

"I think we've seen enough, thank you, Moss. You have clearly done a marvellous job here. We never doubted you.

That's why we hired you, and gave you two of the most expensive technicians available. And all this equipment." Sir Alfred made a circular motion with his right hand. "Gwynne was obviously your choice," he added, still looking at Dr Moss. "But I'm sure she's getting on just fine."

Henry could tell Gwynne was battling whether to say something or not but decided that because Sir Alfred wasn't looking in her direction, there was no cue for her to speak.

"Right," Sir Alfred said, causing Dr Moss to shudder. "Are Felicity and Kevin in? May we go and see what they're up to?"

"Felicity and Kelvin? Certainly, Sir Alfred. Right this way."

Sir Alfred stood, prompting Sir Walter to do the same, although he winced as he relied on his walking stick. Gwynne pulled back their chairs and watched the men leave the room, led by Dr Moss, and closely followed by the note taker.

"Sorry about that, Gwynne," Olivia said. "He's excited really. I'm sure they both are. They just don't show it."

"It's fine. It must be a lot to take in."

"Papa is a realist. He'll go away, thinking that it's all clever effects then come back armed with a series of questions of his own. This was rather impromptu, I'm afraid. Something someone said on the golf course, not about here – they don't know anything about Henry – but something made him think. He came here mid-game. Wants to get back to the old duffers he hangs around with."

Gwynne smiled.

"That's what he calls them but they're younger than him, late sixties, retired for years, in banking and suchlike. Papa is mid-seventies but has always been active. Doesn't want old age to catch up with him. A form of denial if you ask me, but he has, we have, all the luxuries you could possibly want and when you live like that, it's easy to feel younger than you actually are."

"Are you in banking… and suchlike too?" Henry asked.

Olivia laughed and turned to Henry. "Goodness me, no. Papa's money was from his father's successful clothing company. He's no longer involved… not to the extent he was. My brother runs it now but it didn't interest me. Menswear, gents' suits, all top of the range, of course. No, I'm more of a hands on, don't mind getting my fingers dirty, kind of person. I trained to be a vet. I have my own practice in town. Only small, but it ticks over."

"Really?" Gwynne asked. "I don't remember one called Crawley."

"No. It's Yandersip Veterinary Surgery. Named after my late mother. A distinctive name, you'll agree. Although easier to remember, I didn't want the Crawley name to influence our clientele. Not that I think it would have been a bad thing because they trust the name but they may not think I've been through the right training. Have got the job through being… you know."

"That's understandable. Is that why your father wanted to have animals here?" Gwynne asked.

"Not really. Of course the kind of things they want to trial here certainly needs animals but it was more my mother dying. He was always working too much to take notice of how thin she was getting, I was at school with lots of homework, and we had a housekeeper. Mother had always kept herself busy, too busy to eat sometimes, so we all thought she was burning energy. My father regretted not making her life easier. There are so many things he could have done, he said. We had the money, but in the end, money couldn't save her so…" Olivia stared at the ground, then cleared her throat. "I had better catch them up, in case they want me to ask Felicity and Kelvin questions too." She gave an unconvincing laugh. "Thank you, Gwynne." She turned to Henry. "Lovely to meet you, Henry. I hope to see much more of you."

"And you," Henry replied.

Olivia smiled and turned back to face Gwynne. "Thanks again."

Gwynne smiled, they shook hands, then Gwynne and Henry watched Olivia leave, closing the door very gently behind her.

Chapter Ten – Meeting Dullard Mullard

Henry thought he was dreaming when he spotted the light flashing around him. The lab was in darkness apart from that, but he was awake, his eyes open, and yes, there was definitely a light, not flashing exactly, but moving nonetheless.

He wanted to call out, say something but that would have freaked whoever was at the end of the light. *Actually*, Henry thought then spoke in the deepest voice he could muster. "Come out with your hands up! You're surrounded."

The flashlight swung round to the window then disappeared, as the man or woman – from the squeak that had emitted after Henry had spoken, he suspected a woman – switched off the torch. It could only be a torch, Henry decided. He'd seen enough cop shows, hence the "Come out with your hands up" routine.

"Who's there?"

Drat, Henry thought. He wasn't a ventriloquist, he couldn't project his voice across the room let alone outside.

"Come out with your hands up. You're surrounded," he repeated, hoping that whoever it was would think he was a recording.

The flashlight came on again and pointed in his direction then went off.

"What are you doing, Vic?" a voice asked. "Talking to nothing. There's no one here, just a deaf old dog that can't hear for toffee."

Henry wondered what sort of noise toffee had to make for him to be able to hear it. He'd tried toffee once; Mick had thought it funny to give him a piece and watch it gunk up his teeth. He'd planned to get him back but the police raid had intercepted that.

Henry listened to the person with the torch – Vic, Henry assumed – wander around the room, torch back on but never shining above waist height so it couldn't be spotted from outside.

Henry wanted to try the "Come out" sequence again but didn't think it would work any better than the first two occasions. *Try something else*, his brain told him, so he did. "We know you're in there. Surrender now or… put down your weapon." Did the man have a weapon? Henry had by now worked out that it was a man, on his own, who liked talking to himself, the voice deeper than the scream. Again, Henry's words had no effect, the torchlight still scanning the room. Henry wondered what the man was looking for and felt he had nothing to lose by asking, so he lifted his head off his paws. "What are you looking for?"

"Huh?"

He calls me deaf but seems to be himself. "What are you looking for?"

"Who said that?"

"I did."

The torch swung in Henry's direction but didn't reach him until his chin was touching his paws again, his eyes half open.

"Vic, you're hearing voices now," Vic told himself but loud enough for Henry to hear. Vic swung the torch away, towards the computer, and opened the desk drawer.

"Are you going to tell me what you're looking for, or not?" Henry asked in a Spanish accent this time then winced as Vic screamed again. Henry was surprised the security team hadn't burst in but guessed they were more active in the daytime than at night. Maybe they were doing their patrols, with dogs that couldn't talk.

"Hello?" Vic asked, swinging the torch around the room again, this time weaving it up and down as it went. Finally it landed on the cage and an awake sitting up Henry. Vic edged towards the cage and shone the torch in Henry's eyes. He winced and looked away. "Who's having me on, big fella?"

Henry didn't know whether to take that as a compliment; big meaning brave rather than large, or that he'd put on a pound or two since leaving Carmen's. He liked to think the best of people, even ones shining a torch around a deserted lab. Correction: deserted other than a talking dog.

"Me, big fella," Henry replied, referring to his new nickname. Vic said nothing but Henry had a feeling his face was a picture, as the saying went, although that had always baffled him. Of course people appeared in pictures but how was their face one? Vic was in darkness, the torch dropped to Henry's feet, so all Henry could do was wait. He'd been told not to speak to anyone other than Dr Moss, Gwynne and anyone who was in their presence, but Vic didn't seem too bright so even when presented with a talking dog, Henry suspected he wouldn't know what to do. Even Henry made mistakes.

"Holy eff!" Vic growled. "You effin' talk."

"Er, yes..."

"Holy–"

"Yes, we get the idea."

"Is you real?"

Are you, not is you. "What do you mean?"

"Is you a real dog that really talks through its mouth?"

Time to backtrack, Henry thought. "Of course not. How stupid would that be?"

"Eh?"

Not as stupid as you, clearly. "Of course I'm not a talking dog. That's not possible."

"Then how you doing it?"

"CGIs."

"CG whats?"

"CGIs. Computer-generated imagery is the application of computer graphics to create or contribute to images in art, printed media, video games, films, television programs, commercials, and simulators. The visual scenes may be dynamic or static, and two-dimensional (2D), though the term 'CGI' is most commonly used to refer to 3D computer graphics used for creating scenes or special effects in films and television. They can also be used by a home user and edited..." Carmen had looked it up on Wikipedia once, when someone on the TV had been talking about it and she didn't know what it meant. Because her English wasn't brilliant, she'd found it easier to understand when she read something out loud, which meant that Henry heard pretty much everything that went into Carmen's brain, not all of it wanted, in Henry's opinion.

"Oh."

"Oh? Is that it?"

"So you's a computer?"

Henry frowned at Vic's lack of proper English. "No, I'm a dog."

"But the computer talks for you."

"Of course."

"Then how comes your lips move."

"Because I'm not a ventriloquist." Henry was getting seriously fed up with this guy but then figured that if he kept him talking long enough, security would come checking and catch him red handed. "What colour are your hands?"

"Eh?"

"What colour are your hands?"

"I dunno. Pink, human-coloured? What a stupid question."

"So they're not red, then?"

Vic pointed the torch at his left hand, which was gloved in black leather, or pretend leather, Henry didn't hold out any hope that he had much taste in clothes, or money to buy decent ones. From the little Henry could see, it looked like he'd gone out for a jog. Weren't burglars supposed to wear black? Vic's jogging bottoms were a dark grey but definitely not black. "That reminds me."

"What?"

"Have you ever seen Grey's Anatomy?"

"Eh?"

Henry tutted to himself. This guy's vocabulary was far more limited than Henry's, than Carmen's, and the man seemed to be English. "Grey's Anatomy. It's an American TV programme."

"Nope. Don't watch no TV."

Any. That figures.

Vic shone the torch in Henry's direction, fortunately lower than his eyes but still bright enough to start giving Henry a headache. Vic peered in, tilting his head, dog-fashion.

"What are you doing?"

"I'm trying to see the wires."

"Wires?"

"Yeah, computers have wires, don't they."

"I'm... er... wireless."

"Oh, clever. Technology's bit beyond me."

"Mmm."

"Is that what they do here then?"

"What's that?"

"Play with computers and dogs and stuff."

"Something like that."

"Oh. So you are a real dog."

"I am."

"And they treat you okay, do they?"

"Very well, yes."

"You would say that wouldn't you though."

"Why?"

"Because you're their computer. The talking bit anyway." Vic leaned in even closer, until his face touched the bars. Henry was tempted to snap at him, just for fun, but didn't want to get deafened by another scream. "You say," Vic continued, "what they want you to say."

"Not at all."

"But you can't think for yourself."

Henry wanted to snap at him *not* for fun, but took a deep breath and told himself to calm down. It wasn't worth it. "No, I suppose I can't."

"That's really clever. Are you expensive?"

"Sorry?"

"Are you like a new toy that everyone's going to be able to buy at Christmas?"

"A dog is for life, not just for Christmas," Henry quoted, recalling it from a dog charity's slogan.

"No, course not. I ain't got a dog meself. Allergic. Not me, the wife."

So there was a woman behind this man. Henry peered behind him, not really expecting there to be anyone else in the room, but this was another term he'd heard which had never been explained to him. "Oh dear," was all Henry could think of saying.

"Yeah. I'd like one, or a cat, but she can't stand either.

Brings her out in a rash, sneezes, the works."

"Oh dear," Henry repeated.

"So when do they think we can buy one like you?"

"I don't know."

"They'd make it before Christmas, wouldn't they? Maybe not this one. I know things take time, get a schedule on the production line, and that."

"I don't know." Henry felt they needed a change of subject. "So you're married but you don't watch any television?"

"Who said I don't watch no TV?"

"You did."

"When?"

"Earlier. When I asked you about Grey's Anatomy."

"What's that?"

"An American TV programme about interns at a hospital. Seattle Grace. In America."

"Oh, right."

"So…"

"So?"

Henry sighed. "So you do watch TV."

"Only what my Mrs has on. Doesn't interest me."

"You don't watch anything of your own?"

"We only have one set."

"One set?"

"A TV set."

"Set of what?"

"TV."

"I don't follow." *Now who's being stupid?*

"That's what it's called, used to be called. TVs used to be called a set."

"Like badgers?"

"What?"

"That's what a badger's home is called."

"You're too clever for your own good."

"Why? How's it going to harm me?"

"Of course you are, you're a computer."

Henry shook his head. It was hurting the more they talked.

"I'm going to sleep now. You keep looking for whatever it was you were looking for."

Before Henry had a chance to lie down, Vic shone his torch in Henry's eyes. "Ow! Do you mind?"

"Sorry." He lowered the torch again. Henry saw him reach into his trouser pocket and pull out a mobile. "Can I take a picture of you?"

"I don't think that's a very good idea."

"Just to show the wife."

"Not really, no."

"Go on. She won't believe me otherwise."

"You can't tell her about this."

"Why not? It's not a secret, is it? You'll be in the shops eventually anyway."

Henry grunted.

"You got a name?" Vic asked as he put the mobile back in his pocket.

Henry grunted again.

"What is it?"

Henry lifted his nose from his paws just high enough to grunt, "Henry."

"What's yours?"

"Erm… Roger Moore."

"Isn't he James Bond?"

"Okay. It's… Englebert Humperdink."

"That's definitely a made-up name. What is it really?"

"I can't tell you that or…"

"Or what?"

"You'll tell someone."

"I'm a computer programme. I won't tell anyone."

"All right then. It's Victor Mullard."

"Oh."

"See. The others were much more… I don't know. Not boring. The press calls me Dullard Mullard."

Henry sat up. "Press? As in the television?"

"No, the papers."

"You're famous?"

"Infamous really."

"A celebrity?"

"Not exactly."

"Either way. Pleased to meet you, Victor Mullard."

"Pleased to meet you too, Henry."

Henry looked at Vic's extended arm, wrist level with the bars. Henry was pretty sure he could have bitten it off, or at least done some serious damage, had he been so inclined, and he wasn't far off, but stayed still. He knew Vic wanted him to lift a paw, shake a greeting, but he really couldn't be bothered.

He'd been lifting his head off his paws all day and it was as much as he could do to listen. He didn't mind when it was Gwynne or Dr Moss talking but Vic was another matter. Henry was surprised how Mrs Vic put up with him.

Vic then patted his pockets. "Thought I might have a treat in here for you but only keys and mobile. Sorry."

"That's okay. Shouldn't take anything from strangers anyway."

Vic laughed, making Henry wince again, the laugh not dissimilar to the scream, just a few decibels lower.

"You're funny. I'm definitely going to buy one like you for my sister. She'd love you."

"Thanks."

"Do they do them in different sorts?"

"Sorts?"

"Makes. Breeds. She likes Jack Russells and that, but really she's a big dog fan. Would they do a Rottweiler then it can scare her next door's brats?"

"I can ask, but they won't be cheap."

"Money's okay, Henry. Not a problem." Vic laughed again, more resembling a howl this time, and that's exactly what Henry felt like doing. If he could lift the phone, or even get to it, he'd call security, dial 999 if they didn't reply and get this nightmare of a man taken away. Henry had thought if he kept Vic talking long enough someone would come round. Gwynne in… Henry looked at the wall clock but it was too dark to see.

"What you looking at?" Vic asked, swinging the torch round

in the wall's direction revealing it was nearly two a.m.

"Six hours. Five if I'm lucky."

"Eh?"

"Bee."

"What?"

"Nothing. Just practising my alphabet." Henry grinned.

"Oh, clever."

"Thanks. I can do it all, you know."

"Yeah, bet you can."

"If you're a computer, you can do whatever you want."

"I er… guess so. Don't get computers, me."

"No, I don't suppose you do."

"Sister's kids got one. One each, spoilt brats, and they try to show me stuff but it's all Greek."

Henry had always fancied going to Greece. True, they didn't treat their animals very well and they had money troubles too often, but it got a lot more sun than England. "Your sister lives in Greece?"

"No. Why do you think they live in Greece?"

"Because their computers are in Greek."

Vic laughed, fortunately this time more of a chuckle than an out-and-out belly laugh so Henry was spared trying to put his paws over his ears. He'd never been very good at that.

"Why did they choose a Jack Russell and not a beagle? Don't testing places usually have beagles?"

"I don't know."

"Test animals are usually beagles, aren't they?"

"I don't know," Henry repeated.

"Maybe they couldn't get one."

"That could be it."

"You'd think it would be easier."

"Why?"

"With the hunting ban, and all."

"Hunting ban?"

"You know, the government said the la-dee-dah folks on horses couldn't go out chasing foxes, the vermin."

"Foxes do carry diseases."

"I meant the government, the la dee dahs. Poor old foxes."

"Oh."

"So now they can be left in peace, although of course they still go, they just don't get caught."

"Oh." Henry felt stupid with his one-word comments but he didn't feel he could contribute, or certainly didn't have an inclination to do so. "I don't know why they didn't pick a beagle."

"They must have had their reasons. I don't suppose my sister would mind one of those if they only come in you and that."

"I'll ask for you."

"Would you?"

"Sure."

"And tell me?"

"Sure."

"Let me write me mobile number down then."

Henry smiled. No, he definitely wasn't the stupid one. "Don't suppose you've got a business card?"

"Been meaning to get some done but I don't really have a profession."

"No, I don't suppose you do. Mobile number will be fine."

"Ain't got nothing to write down on, mind."

Henry sighed. "There's a pen and paper in the desk drawer."

Vic looked from Gwynne's desk to the spare. "Which one?"

"Either, both probably. That one for sure." Henry looked at Gwynne's workstation.

"Cheers."

Henry watched Vic rifle through the desk then pull out a pen and tear the top sheet off a notepad. He leaned over, torch sat on the desk, highlighting the paper, and with his mobile retrieved, he tapped a few keys. "Don't know me own number, do I. Who rings their own number?"

"Who indeed?" Henry said then watched Vic write down his number, return the mobile to his pocket then put the pen back in the drawer and shut it with a thud. He was certainly one of the world's noisiest burglars.

Vic pointed to the paper. "What do you want me to do with

this?"

"You can leave it there, by the phone. Then I can phone you, can't I."

"Oh yeah. That's a good idea."

"Did you write your name on it?"

"No. Why–"

"I might forget whose number it is."

"Oh yeah. All right then." He opened the drawer, took out the pen and added his name. "Victor Mullard. All right?"

"Absolutely."

"See you again?"

"You never know. Maybe I'll be for sale at Christmas."

"Someone would buy you."

"Thanks," Henry said, hoping it was a compliment.

"Welcome." Vic stuffed his mobile back in his pocket and walked towards the door. "Night then."

"Night, Victor Mullard."

Henry watched Vic crack open the door, peer out, step through, then close it behind him. As the torchlight disappeared through the glass, Henry rested his chin on his paws and went to sleep.

Chapter Eleven – Post-Vic

"Henry, what's this?"

Henry yawned and looked at the scrap of paper Gwynne had slapped against the bars, a little too close for comfort. He pulled back, yawned again, and focused his eyes.

"Who's Vic Mullard?"

Henry pondered. Although Vic had been as thick as Axminster carpet, and clearly trespassing, Henry didn't want to get him into trouble. Besides, Henry blamed the lax security team for not knowing he was there. Didn't they have CCTV? "One of the cleaners?"

"I know the cleaners who cover this building: (a) they're both women and (b)–"

"Maybe a boyfriend?" Henry grinned a little too wide. "Would love some breakfast if it's not too much trouble."

"No, Henry."

No? No, it's no trouble or no, you're not getting any breakfast. Care to elaborate, Gwynne?

But she didn't. She sat in front of her computer, the piece of paper with Vic's mobile number on the desk beside the screen, and logged in. She opened the internet and typed the number into Google. There were no exact matches but plenty for the first five digits and a couple for the remaining six numbers; members of staff at the Welsh Schools Football Association, Indian STD codes. Gwynne opened the drawer and put the piece of paper inside before slamming the drawer shut.

Henry wanted to ask her if she'd got out of the wrong side of the bed, although he knew she had a boyfriend, a live-in one, so she would have had to climb over him to get out which would have been rather unlikely when she could have just got out of her own side. *English is such a silly language,* Henry thought. *No wonder people find it so hard to learn.*

It occurred to him that, other than the bits he'd said to the Board, he'd not told Gwynne or the doctor that he could speak Spanish, and German, with a bit of French. He owed a lot to Carmen and her wanting to better herself. Henry suspected that had a lot to do with the way Mick treated her, but thought she probably would have wanted to anyway, she was that kind of person.

He thought about her in jail, her looking out through her bars as he looked through his. He'd watched enough true crime programmes to know that. They were let out for a few minutes at a time to walk around the outside perimeter then told to go back in. It had been different at Carmen's; at least the times when Mick was away and Henry could have the run of the house, the back yard, being called in when Carmen couldn't risk it anymore.

"Buenos dias, buenos tardes, buenos noches. Good afternoon, good evening and goodnight." Not a literal translation, Henry knew, but buenos tardes, buenos tardes, buenos noches wouldn't have sounded right. "*The Truman Show*. Did you know that, Gwynne?"

"Huh?" Gwynne was still staring at the screen, scrolling down the page of results for Vic and Victor Mullard. There were plenty of those. 'Thief Victor Mullard jailed for twenty-eight months', 'Dullard Mullard caught again', 'Thick Vic never learns'. "Looks like this Vic is a shady character. If this..." Gwynne pointed to the drawer, "is connected to someone working here then we could have some serious security issues."

You're telling me, Henry wanted to say but decided it was best not to. "Maybe it's not the same one? He's probably–"

"He lives three streets from me. There are only two others: one on a 1901 census and another from Australia."

"Maybe he emigrated?"

"In 1885."

"Oh."

"Yes, 'oh', Henry."

Henry giggled. He'd spotted an *O Henry* book on Carmen's shelves – Sesame Street had taught him to read – but now it didn't seem so funny.

"We're going to have words with the cleaners and–"

"No!" Henry blurted. "It's probably nothing to do with them."

Gwynne swung her chair round. "Why? You said–"

"Because..."

"Henry. No one else comes in here. Felicity and Kelvin had left before I did and–"

"Maybe it was Dr Moss? Perhaps Vic's a friend and they were supposed to go out last night, or something?"

"This isn't Dr Moss's writing."

"It's probably Vic's." Henry felt a little better at telling at least one truth.

"Henry?"

Henry looked up at Gwynne, eyes widened and wagging his tail.

"You know something, don't you?"

Henry looked down at the floor. "No."

"Henry."

Still looking at the floor, he blurted, "Okay. All right. It was me. No, not me exactly. It was Vic. He was here and we got chatting and–"

"Henry!"

Henry looked up and tried his puppy dog eyes on her but they clearly weren't working.

Still seated, Gwynne walked her chair over to the cage. "Tell me what happened."

Henry sighed. "Okay but don't get angry."

"Leave that for me to decide."

Henry's stomach grumbled. "Can I have breakfast after this?"

"We'll see whether you deserve it."

"That's cruel."

"Henry," Gwynne growled.

"Okay, okay. Man."

Gwynne tapped her foot on the grey tiled floor.

"He woke me up. Late. Gone midnight. Shining that torch of his. Thought I was dreaming to start with but then realised I wasn't because my eyes were open." Henry fluttered his eyelashes but Gwynne's face still resembled stone. Very much like the floor, Henry thought.

"I didn't want to say anything at first, because you'd told me not to, but then I thought I'd have some fun. I'm sorry but… it seemed like a good idea. He thought he was hearing voices, not like he was schizophrenic or anything, but a recording. "I said, 'Come out with your hands up. You're surrounded.'" Henry laughed.

"Said it twice because he heard it the first time but couldn't get his bearings. Then he finally worked out it was me, after I said, 'We know you're in there. Surrender now or… put your weapon down.'" Henry mimicked the voice he'd used the previous night. "That really spooked him but by then he worked out which direction it came from and shone the torch right in my face. Almost hurt, it did." Henry could see by the lack of emotion on Gwynne's face that he was getting no sympathy, so it wasn't a good time to remind her that he'd not had any breakfast yet. As for a walk…

"Go on," Gwynne urged, shuffling her bottom back in her seat.

"So we had a little tête-à-tête and then it occurred to me that you wouldn't really approve and I could get into trouble and… yes. So then I came up with the brilliant idea of CGI."

"Right…"

"I told him that yes, because he'd asked, I was a real dog but of course I couldn't actually talk but that it was all CGI special effects. He didn't know what CGIs were… as you can tell from giving me his number, he's not the sharpest playing card in the pack."

"Tool in the shed."

"Exactly. So I had to explain what CGI stood for. As Wikipedia says, 'Computer-generated imagery is the application of computer graphics to create'–"

"I know what CGIs are, Henry."

"Oh, okay. So I explained all that and he peered at me really close and would you believe, he believed it! Believe, believe. To be sure. Mrs Doyle. Father Ted. It's rather f–"

"Get to the point, Henry."

"Okay. He believed me and said that he wanted to buy one of me for his sister for Christmas. He asked when I'd be available. No, not me, because she's not a fan of Jack Russells, which pissed me off a bit, if I'm honest. It's like saying–"

Gwynne growled. "Henry."

"She's more of a beagle fan apparently, although he also said she likes big dogs and if I'm not mistaken, there's not really a lot of difference between..."

Gwynne slid her chair back to the desk, pulled open the drawer and picked out the piece of paper with Vic's name and number. "So why did he leave this?"

"He asked me to let him know when he could buy one."

Gwynne laughed, and Henry expected her stone-face to crack. "He really is that stupid." She then went serious again. "What worries me though is why I had to find out about it from you."

"Oh, thanks."

"No, I mean, that no one phoned me, no one, presumably, phoned Dr Moss. Security mentioned nothing when I came in. There are no emails on the subject. Nothing. So the guy–"

"Vic."

"Yes, Vic. He came in undetected and left again, presumably, undetected."

"I guess so."

"And he's going to tell anyone who'll listen what we're doing here."

"That's all right, isn't it?"

"No, Henry, it's not all right."

"But he thinks it's CGIs and..."

"Special effects, I know. But people love things like that. Dogs. Christmas. Gadgets. We're going to be inundated with nutcases even more than before."

Henry wasn't sure what nuts or their cases had to do with the predicament that Vic had caused, so Henry chose his words carefully. "Sorry."

"It's okay. You weren't to know. Actually, yes, you were to know. We swore you to secrecy. You promised not to tell anyone."

"I know but you've given me the ability to be understood and do you know how long I've wanted to be… oh never mind, you wouldn't understand. You've always been able to talk, always been understood."

"Not always."

Henry sat up. "Really?"

"Not when I was a baby."

Henry slouched again. "That doesn't count. No one understands babies. They talk goo and they get goo back." He wasn't sure goo was the right word but it was the one that sprang to mind. That and chorradas, quatsch. He couldn't remember what it was in French but remembered that merde was shit, but didn't share that either with Gwynne. She'd not been interested in his earlier offerings. "So what are you going to do?"

"Tell Dr Moss. We have a serious lapse in security so he needs to know. It'll all be on the CCTV. The Sirs are very hot on CCTV. Protective of this place. If not, I have an old camcorder at home. I'll bring it in tomorrow. It's digital so not actually that old but I only tend to use the camera and video settings on my phone now."

"Oh, okay. And Vic?"

"He was trespassing. Bet he broke in, a window or something. Someone will find out. He's got form–"

"Form?"

"Previous. He's been to jail, and not just once. This'll be his third time at least, so he'll have the book thrown at him."

Henry wanted to ask her which book, whether it could be an *O Henry* so he could have it when they'd finished with it, but decided she probably wouldn't know, or care. It would be a heavy one at least because otherwise it wouldn't hurt. And it didn't seem that much of a punishment.

"Leave it with me, Henry," Gwynne concluded and turned back to her computer.

Henry knew there was no point in fighting Vic's corner, had Vic got any. He looked quite round to Henry. There also seemed no point in asking for breakfast or a walk, so Henry lay back down and went to sleep. He knew it was what dogs did best… those that didn’t talk.

Chapter Twelve – The Real Thing

Henry lashed out, kicking his paws as he was yanked by his collar.

"Come here, you!" a man growled.

Even asleep, Henry was determined to put up a fight, kicking and wriggling around in his cage. This dream seemed so real. He didn't often have bad ones but at least knowing this was one, made it easier to deal with.

"Mind he don't bite," a voice behind the man said. Henry couldn't tell if it was male or female. Male, he thought, but he'd got Vic wrong so he'd keep an open mind for now. Not that Henry knew what an open mind looked like – not very nice, he thought, all the squishy bits leaking out, so probably better to keep it closed. He knew it wouldn't be Vic because Vic knew Henry's name.

"I don't bite," he wanted to say, but knew he wasn't supposed to talk to anyone who didn't already know he could, and he certainly didn't know these people. So even though it was a dream, he remained silent, and waited to see what happened.

The other person, an older man, handed the first man Henry's lead, the one hung by the door. *Bloomin' cheek*, Henry thought, *using my own lead to steal me. But then they're not really stealing me. How did they open…?* He looked round and saw the padlock lying on the floor in two pieces. The older man was holding a tool large enough to have easily broken the padlock. Henry wanted to ask what the tool was but again he couldn't speak, knew he shouldn't.

Henry also knew this was a dream because the lights were on in the lab. If these were real burglars, they'd be using torches. There were windows all along one side of the lab. They wouldn't risk being spotted by the… rubbish security team, which wouldn't now be rubbish though because Gwynne or Dr Moss, or both, would have torn strips off them. Henry had never seen anyone having strips torn off them before and although he wasn't as blood-thirsty as Mick, Henry was curious enough to witness it at least once.

These two men were certainly more organised than Vic because whatever he'd been after he'd not been able to find. Henry remembered him leaving with nothing on him but his keys and his mobile. Vic had said as much and he'd seemed like the honest sort.

These guys though knew what they wanted – Henry – and they were already out the lab door. Henry knew the exit routes; Gwynne would take him one way one day, the other the next. Depending on where these guys were parked, Henry assumed, would determine the route they took to get out.

As he thought they would, they took the nearest exit, Henry trotting between them. The first man, the one who had pulled Henry out, who he thought looked a similar age to Mick, so thirty-something, slammed the silver horizontal bar keeping the fire exit doors shut. During the day, the only time Henry had ever been out that way, there was no problem but at night, opening the doors activated the alarm and Henry's ears fell flat as the siren wailed.

"Well done, Billy," man number two snapped as they bundled Henry into the back of a small white nameless van.

"Not my fault, Norm. You're the plan man."

Plan man. Love it, Henry thought, as Billy hooked Henry's lead to a ring on one of the van's inside walls. Beneath it was a thick beanbag-type bed, waiting for him to curl up and snooze while they took him to their destination of choice. Henry hoped there would be plenty of food wherever they were going. It didn't matter what sort, some humans gave their animals leftovers of their own creations. Sure, Henry was fussy at the lab but who'd want something that tasted as if it had gone stale, or freeze-dried like astronauts' packet stuff?

So Henry padded round in a couple of circles, until the bed was just how he liked it, and went to sleep.

Chapter Thirteen –  Living With Norman And Co.

"All right, you. Up you get."

Huh? What? Henry opened his eyes and looked around him. This wasn't the lab. And it wasn't a dream. *Uh oh.* Henry pursed his lips together, just in case whatever he'd been thinking spilled out.

"Come on, you." 'Norm' unhooked Henry's lead from the van and tapped his right leg, encouraging Henry to come of his own free will. Henry wasn't sure he had any at the moment, free or otherwise. The lab or who knew where? Gwynne or...? Gwynne. He missed her already, despite her being mean to him the last time they'd spoken. She was getting slacker at bringing his breakfast on time. Henry couldn't understand why she had to keep going to the kitchen. They had cupboards, clean tap water. She could have just kept the supplies there.

Henry plodded out of the van and dropped onto concrete. They were in a garage, a residential one, with two bicycles hanging on the wall, an array of tools – a gap where the one that Norman had been holding looked like it belonged – and a washer dryer that was part-way through a spin. Henry couldn't see much through the door because it was going so quickly but there was a lot of pink. That had to be a good sign; a woman. Either that or these men weren't as macho as they tried to make out.

Billy put the tool on a space on a shelf and unlocked a door to his right. "Come on, Norm. Bring him inside."

Norman, beanbag in one hand, lead in the other, led Henry through a door into the inside of the house, into a long narrow hall with the front door, utility room, lounge, kitchen diner, toilet and stairs leading off. All the doors were open and Norman led Henry into a small utility room. At one end was a cage next to two bowls: one of water, the other empty. Henry's stomach rumbled.

"Put him in there until we've worked out what we're gonna do with him."

So, Henry thought, *they're not as organised as they made out, unless Norman the plan man had all the plans but hadn't shared them with Billy.*

Norman placed the beanbag onto the cage floor then nudged Henry inside. With no choice open to him other than making a run for it but only the house to explore, he settled on the bed and watched Norman lock the cage.

"Sorry, mate. It'll be all right, really it will."

Henry sighed, lowered his chin onto his paws and closed his eyes. With any luck he'd wake up and be back in the lab, although he knew that wouldn't be the case, and there was certainly no sign of any food forthcoming. His stomach rumbled again in agreement. Henry lowered his ears, and went to sleep.

What seemed like seconds later, he heard a clanking noise. Without lifting his head, he put up his ears and opened his eyes. A woman, younger than Carmen, maybe Gwynne's age – Henry had no clue how old she was, but like Gwynne, this woman had no small wrinkles around her eyes – crow's feet. He thought that would have been painful and wondered why anyone would want a bird to do that to them.

The woman was filling the empty bowl with dried food and Henry's heart sank. Not more dried food. Did these people have no imagination? She then opened a cupboard and brought out a yellow sachet. Henry watched intently as she peeled off the top and squeezed some of the contents on top of the dried food. *That's better*, Henry thought. The woman then spun the bowl to mix the contents and put it on the floor. Henry then expected her to unlock the cage but she turned and walked out.

Thanks very much. How am I supposed to get that now? You people are so cruel. Don't feed me for hours and then when you do, I can't–

Henry's thoughts were interrupted by Norman coming back in the room. He leaned over, unlocked the cage, and pushed the food bowl into a corner. He then fetched the water bowl, the contents of which looked quite fresh, and placed it next to the food.

Henry wanted to say "thank you" but didn't. He'd remain as impassive as he could, as silent as he could, until he knew whether they were a threat or not.

Norman left the room but didn't shut the door so Henry could hear everything they were saying in the lounge next door. He listened, eating as quietly as he could until the food was gone.

"It was your idea."

"No, it was Vic's idea." That was a younger voice. Billy's most likely.

Oh, Henry thought. *So he is involved. Then why didn't he come and get me? He'd already been there and–*

"She's not to blame for this."

She?

Vic's not a she. Okay, so Henry's conversation with Victor Mullard was by torchlight but he definitely wasn't a she.

"You would say that, she's your daughter."

Henry's brain hurt. The Vic he knew was not only male but he was also only a few years younger than Norman. Henry didn't know a whole lot about human biology but he was pretty sure that Victor Mullard couldn't be Norman's daughter.

"Victoria's never let us down before."

That settled it; two Vics. One male, one female. Not related. Henry felt relieved that his Vic had nothing to do with this, but then he felt sad because his Vic would have been kind to him. They had a bond, despite only knowing each other for a few minutes. Maybe Henry could use his big brown eyes on the woman he'd seen. Too young to be Norman's daughter, a granddaughter perhaps?

"When's she back, Norm?"

"Finishes work at five. Coming straight home, so half-five."

"Why did she go to work? She knew we was–"

"So she wasn't implicated. Everyone knows her involvement with the Animal Freedom Foundation. She'd be the first one they suspected."

"And you'd be next in line, Norm."

"Maybe, but we ain't at mine, are we. No one knows about you and me. They'd never come here."

"And she ain't what the plan is."

"Not exactly."

"What does that mean?"

"She knows I can't keep secrets."

"That doesn't help me though does it, Norm?"

Norman shook his head. "Sorry, Billy."

Henry wanted to cough, remind them that it was rude to talk about people behind their backs, although he was actually facing them so it would be in front of his front but he didn't suppose it made much difference. He looked around the room. Apart from a bookcase in the corner, filled with large factual types, there wasn't a lot there; a couple of cupboards above a sink with no room for the washer dryer that had finished its cycle in the garage a few minutes before.

There was a clock but the second hand wasn't moving so Henry suspected it wasn't the right time. He always seemed to be hungry so could only tell whether it was daytime or night-time from whether it was daylight or not. He could hear a radio, he thought coming from the kitchen and the woman singing to a pop song.

Henry didn't recognise it; Carmen, Mick nor Gwynne listened to anything like that, but the radio DJ announced it as One Direction. That didn't mean much to Henry but he wondered if they kept going in one direction or whether they'd ever stop. Some groups went on for years; Carmen had liked the Beatles and they'd watch a TV programme where they'd been playing on television when programmes were only in black and white.

When Henry had first seen it, he'd looked from the television to Carmen's lounge and back. He couldn't understand why they had taken the colour out of the studio that they were filming from when somewhere as ordinary as Carmen's house was still very colourful. That was something else he'd ask Gwynne if he ever had the chance again.

Henry heard footsteps padding through the hallway and heading in his direction, so he lay down, chin on paws, and closed his eyes.

"Oh, good dog," the young woman said. "You must have been hungry."

Henry was finding it hard to keep quiet, to keep his eyes

shut but he stayed as still as he could, waiting for her to leave or say something else. She did the latter. "Hello, dog."

Henry hated being called 'dog'. Of course he was one but it was so impersonal. He had a name and wished people used it. He didn't call them 'man' or 'woman', did he. That would be rude.

He heard a clink on the bars and a hand tug at his collar. The hand twisted the collar round until it found the nametag. "Let me see, now. Oh, Henry."

Henry wanted to laugh. O Henry. *Just one laugh, please*, but he stayed still. He was getting good at this acting lark.

"Henry," the woman called softly.

"Becks!" Billy shouted from the other room. "You done our lunch yet?"

Rebecca let go of Henry's nametag, sighed and padded out of the room. "Couple of minutes. You want beer or–"

"Course we want beer."

Mick all over again, Henry thought as he heard Rebecca opening the fridge and pouring the beer into, presumably, two glasses. *At least they're using glasses.*

He heard her wander through into the lounge and Billy swear. "What you go do that for? It never tastes the same unless it's in the can."

"Sorry, Billy." Then Henry heard a thud followed by Rebecca crying and running out of the room.

"That was harsh, Billy," Norman said.

"Does her good to put her in her place once in a while. Trying to impress you, I know she was."

"I prefer a gla… never mind."

Henry listened to Rebecca make up the men's lunch and take it through. There was a clatter of plates, Billy swore again and Rebecca ran from the room. She closed the kitchen door, turned the radio up louder, but Henry could still hear her sobbing.

"Pathetic woman," Billy said during mouthfuls of lunch. "She never used to be like that. Was fun when we first got together but you know what it's like when you get married."

"Not really," Norman replied.

"You married though, aren't you, Norm?"

"Forty-two years."

Billy whistled. "Longer than I've been alive. Don't look that old, mate."

"Thanks."

"So what's your secret? Don't look henpecked." Billy laughed showing a mouthful of beef and ketchup sandwich. He added a couple of chips and carried on chewing, mouth open.

"I look after her."

"What?"

"I'm nice to her."

"Nice, shmice. Keep 'em keen, Norman."

"It doesn't work with many of them."

"You don't know women, Norm. Bet you've only ever been with…"

"Ursula."

"Ursula? Is that foreign? Like Ursula Andress in that bikini?"

Norman smiled weakly. "They're both Swiss, yes."

"Nice."

"So what language does she speak?"

"German, Swiss German, French, and English, obviously."

Henry's ears pricked up and he wagged his tail.

Rebecca padded back through to the lounge to remove the empty plates and glasses. "Can I get you anything else?"

"That was lovely. Thank you, Rebecca," Norman said in a warm soft voice.

"Another beer," Billy grunted with no hint of an endearment or gratitude.

Henry heard Rebecca go to the kitchen, place the plates and glasses on the draining board, get more beer from the fridge, and return to the lounge.

"Give Norman a glass, Becks."

"It's okay, Billy," Norman said before Rebecca could reply.

"No, it's all right. She'll get you a fresh one, won't you, pet."

Rebecca just smiled then returned to the kitchen. She opened a cupboard, removed a glass and walked it back through to the lounge.

"Thank you, Rebecca," Norman said, taking the glass. "There really was no need, I–"

"Nonsense, Norm. Becks is only too happy to, aren't you, Rach."

Rebecca squeaked a "yes" and returned to the kitchen. She shut the door and yanked up the radio.

Henry growled as he listened to Rebecca cry. She and Norman were the good guys, albeit in on a dognapping, but it was Billy that Henry really had it in for. He wasn't sure what he'd do, what he could do, stuck behind bars, but if there were an opportunity, a slight chance, then Billy would get his comeuppance.

Henry looked at the clock. Three p.m. Victoria would be back in a couple of hours. What would happen then? Would he be ransomed? Henry knew enough about that from watching Mick's American cop dramas. They usually ended up as dead bodies by the roadside… but then they were humans. People didn't kill dogs, did they? If the ransom wasn't paid, they'd just keep him wouldn't they? He'd use his big brown eyes, be as adorable as he could. Everyone liked dogs… except Mrs Mullard, and that was only because she couldn't.

Man's best friend. Gwynne would pay the ransom. FMRS anyway. They needed him. He knew they could just go to the rescue centre and get another dog and inject that one but they'd formed a bond. They loved him. Okay, so he'd caused a bit of trouble with Vic mark I but he wasn't going to say anything.

And Henry wasn't going to speak to Vic mark II or the price would go up. He knew Sir Alfred and the Board had lots of money, he'd heard Dr Moss talk about their deep pockets, although that made Henry laugh because it must get quite tiring carrying all that money around. Wouldn't the pockets rip eventually?

Yes, they'd ask for a ransom, wouldn't be much, he was only a dog… *Oh no.* Henry remembered what Norman had said about Vic mark II. That she belongs to the Animal Freedom Foundation. There's no way she would let him go back in there. He needed to tell her he wanted to be there, that he'd made friends with Gwynne and they were going to have fun. He looked around the room. Rebecca was nice, maybe Victoria was nice too. She cared about animals so she'd care about him. Wouldn't she?

Henry sat listening to Billy and Norman talk about football then fishing – the latter which Henry battled with as it thought it cruel yet he loved eating the creatures, when they weren't wriggling of course. The men moved on to their spouses (with Norman trying to persuade Billy of their virtues) then the weather. Henry was about to lie down, go to sleep, when he heard the front door open. He stared at the door into the lounge but only caught sight of a tall slim woman as she went into the kitchen.

"Hey, Becca."

"Hi, Vic."

"Oh, shit. What's the matter? Didn't it go well? They're here, aren't they?"

"It's fine. Billy and your dad are here. They got the dog, a very cute Jack Russell called Henry. He's been fed, ate everything so was obviously hungry."

"That's good, isn't it? What's the matter?"

"Nothing. It's fine."

"Becca … what's that mark? Was that Billy?"

"It's fine."

"Bec! You must stand up for yourself. What was it this time?"

"I poured his beer into a glass instead of taking the can through. I thought your dad would like–"

"The pathetic little–"

"Vic, please. Don't stir. It's fine."

"So you keep saying."

"They're chatting away. I'm in here. You're here now. Billy likes you. Everything went to plan. You tell them what's next, they'll be happier. Billy'll be happier and everything will be okay. Please, don't get angry. That only makes him worse when you've gone. Says I tell you too much, that it's none of your business."

"It is my business, Becca. I'm your best friend, matron of honour, although why you ever married–"

"He has a good side, a soft side, really. He's just under pressure with losing his job and…"

"Not in a hurry to get another one though, is he."

"He's trying."

"Yes, very."

"Vic, be fair. He goes down to the job centre every morning."

"Does he?"

"Sure he does."

"You see him there?"

"No, but…"

"Then how do you know he goes?"

"Because he tells me. He wouldn't lie. Besides, he tells me about the jobs he applies for."

"Like what?"

"Cashier at Cost Savers, dishwasher at Barnard's Bakery, road sweeper with the council, Customer Service Agent at Mac's–"

"So why hasn't he got one of these?"

"Lots of people go for them."

"Is he even invited for an interview?"

"Not yet."

"Why not?"

"He doesn't have any qualifications. They're bound to pick someone with qualifications. It's his dyslexia too. No confidence."

"Do you help him complete the forms?"

"No, they do that at the job centre."

"Mmm."

"I know you don't like him but…"

"He has a soft side. Yes, we know."

Henry dipped his head when he heard the lounge door open

and Billy stomping through to the kitchen, slamming the lounge door behind him. "That you, Vic?"

Rebecca gasped but it was Victoria who spoke. "Yes, Billy. Just chatting with Rebecca."

"Not about me, I hope." Billy laughed a hollow laugh.

"Don't flatter yourself." Victoria joined Billy in the hall and shut the kitchen door, leaving Rebecca to prepare the evening meal.

"So," Billy muttered. "We've gone and got the damned dog. What are we supposed to do with it now?"

"Nothing."

"What do you mean 'nothing'?"

"I'm keeping it."

"What the f–?"

"Billy Maitland. Language. Not in front of the…" She patted her stomach.

Billy put his hand on hers. "How long now?"

"Three months. You know that."

"Becks doesn't suspect, does she?"

"Not a thing. Still thinks you go down the job centre."

Billy laughed, and looked at the kitchen door. "Poor sap. Who goes to the job centre every day?"

"We're going to have to tell her eventually."

"Why?"

"Because we're going to live together." Victoria pulled back her shoulders. "You're going to leave."

"I ain't leaving. What makes you think I'm leaving?"

"But…"

"She's my wife."

"But the baby."

"Ain't my fault."

"But you told me you loved me."

"Course I did. Got you into the sack, didn't it."

"I'll tell her. I'll say it's yours."

"You've already told her what we agreed you'd say. That you was attacked. She helped you through that. You want to lose her too? I'm her husband. Who do you think she'll believe. She can't have kids, you know that. She'll hate you for it. Think you've been doing it to be cruel. Never forgive you."

Vic whined, "But..."

"So what was the story with the dog? You weren't just rescuing it then. I thought we was going to ransom it. Supposed to be simple, weren't it. We go in there, get it. Pay to switch the cameras off for an hour, then we'd ransom the dog, get our money back and loads more. Why you want to keep it now?"

"I've always wanted to keep it. We'll be a family. You, me, the baby, and a dog. We're doing a good thing here. Helping an animal who's being mistreated."

"How do you know it's being mistreated? Looks all right to me."

"You wouldn't know something was being mistreated if it leapt up and bit you, slapped you in the face, told you it was being mistreated. The way you speak to Becca."

"What's wrong with the way I talk to my wife? She just needs respect."

"Treating her like shit doesn't earn respect, Billy."

"Worked with you."

Victoria snivelled.

"Tell her we're hungry in here." Billy pointed to the lounge door. "And say 'hi' to your dad, it's rude."

Victoria wiped her face, sniffed and went into the lounge. "Hello Dad. You okay?"

"Sure. You?"

"I'm fine. Just been helping Bec chop some onions. You know what it's like."

"Would you like some help?"

Billy scoffed. "Leave the women to it, Norm. Too many cooks and all that." He turned to Victoria. "What we having anyway?"

"Chilli Con Carne."

Billy patted his stomach and looked at Victoria's. "Lovely."

Victoria swung round, left the lounge and closed the door behind her, crying loudly enough for Henry to hear.

Oh great, Henry thought. *Not only are they stuck with me, and me them, but I'm going to get a baby as company too?* He'd not had any experience with babies but knew they were famous for pulling dogs ears, fur, paws and other appendages. The thought of that filled him with dread, and he lay down, chin on paws.

He needed a plan, to get back to FMRS without being spotted. He'd been away a few hours so he'd be missed. He thought it unlikely that there would be an announcement on the television, an appeal for his return. No one would make it public knowledge that he could speak otherwise the dognappers would up the ransom, FMRS's work would unravel and he'd be blamed. Okay, so he went willingly, thought he was dreaming it, but they would have taken him whether he wanted to go or not.

Maybe Sir Alfred has contacts, Henry thought, *people in the underworld – beneath the roads – who could make enquiries. Track him down to Billy and Rebecca's house, get him back without a fuss. Just cover their expenses. They don't want him so they'd have to pay to feed him, which could be expensive for someone with no job and a baby on the way, despite Henry only being a small dog.*

Trevor. There was a mutual contact. He worked in security. No wonder it was such a poor department. They'd need more than one person to keep an eye on the whole building, surely. Head Gardener Wilson was a big enough deterrent outside so perhaps they only needed Trevor inside.

Henry had only ever seen one guard come in to the lab, shine his torch around the room and leave again, locking the door back after him. Henry had often wondered what would happen if someone was hiding under one of the desks. The guard, presumably Trevor, would never see him or her, but then they would've had to have had a key to get in. But then Vic mark one got in. Billy and Norman marks one got in.

So, a plan, Henry. He knew they wouldn't just take him back. It wouldn't have been worth their while financially because they'd have to pay again to switch off the cameras for another hour, they'd have to pay petrol there and back, although they weren't in the van long so Henry didn't think they were far away.

One of them could keep him. Norman perhaps? An early Christmas present for his wife? Henry thought he'd probably live longer than Norman so that wasn't such a good idea because his wife would be about the same age and they'd both die, then no one would look after him and he'd die. He shuddered, not liking the sound of that at all.

Billy was definitely a no-no. Rebecca and Billy were a package so he'd have a reasonable life when Rebecca was around but when she was out at work and Billy was home all day – Henry hadn't believed the job centre story either – he didn't know what the brute would do with him. Henry would certainly never be able to talk again. Billy would be a nightmare if he knew the truth and the type of conversations Billy had would be like Chinese water torture, although if their water was anything like their food, Henry would have preferred that.

The only other person left was Victoria and although it had been her idea to kidnap him, and if her belonging to the Animal Freedom Foundation was true, then part of that had been done for the right reasons, she was having a baby. Billy's. The thought of the four… five – Billy, Rebecca, Victoria, Henry and the baby – of them spending time together made Henry feel nauseous.

There was only one thing for it; he'd have to escape. Rebecca liked him and was the one making all the food so he'd wait until she brought him some more but there was a padlock on the cage. What was it with people? Did no one trust him?

He'd wait. He was used to being patient.

Chapter Fourteen – Breaking The Bad News

"What do you mean 'he's missing'?"

"Sorry, Sir Alfred."

"Sorry's no good. What are you doing to find him?"

"Everything we can, sir."

"How did he escape?"

"He didn't, sir."

"Then how…"

"Dognapped, sir."

Sir Alfred guffawed.

"Sorry, sir."

"When did this happen?"

"This morning."

"When this morning?"

"Before we got in."

"Times, Moss, times."

"Sorry, sir. Somewhere between midnight and seven a.m."

"Didn't you lock the lab?"

"Of course, sir. Locked tight."

"And security?"

"They're looking for Henry now, Sir Alfred."

"How did they get to him?"

"They got in somehow to the lab then used bolt cutters or suchlike to snap the padlock on Henry's cage."

"And Gwynne?"

"She's out with security."

"What do we know about who took them?"

"Nothing, sir."

"Nothing!" Sir Alfred boomed.

"Security is looking at the CCTV footage but the camera covering this building wasn't working."

"What?"

Dr Moss held the phone away from his ear. He knew Sir Alfred could be tetchy at the best of times and this certainly wasn't one of those.

"I've spoken with Trevor and he–"

"Trevor? Who's Trevor?"

"Head of Security."

"Trevor who?"

"Thompson, sir."

"Trevor Thompson. Do I know him?"

"I don't know, sir."

"Who took him on?"

"I don't know that either, sir. He's been here longer than I have so–"

"Mmm. Never mind. What do we know about him?"

"Trevor?"

"Yes, Moss, Trevor! Don't test my patience."

Dr Moss didn't think that Sir Alfred had any patience to test but remained calm. Getting agitated wouldn't do the situation any good.

"Do you realise how much we've spent on that dog?"

"Yes, sir."

"Two million.

"Yes, sir."

"Two million pounds. You've just lost us two million pounds. Can you afford to pay us back?"

Dr Moss wanted to point out that it wasn't him who had 'lost' Henry. Moss had checked the cage's padlock, the lab door, when he left the previous evening. Both he and Gwynne had been as secure as they possibly could. Irene used to say that he had OCD because he checked locks so many times but they'd never been burgled so he'd thought it worth the irritation. Having been married so long, there were things Irene did that irritated him but he never mentioned them. "No, sir."

"Then you go out there and find him. Your job's on the line here, Moss."

"Yes, sir."

"I want you to speak to everyone who could have had access to that lab, to the building."

"Yes, sir but that's quite a lot of–"

"I don't care. Speak to everyone."

"Yes, Sir Alfred."

"What are your technicians doing? Felicity and Kevin?"

"Kelvin, sir."

"Kelvin, that's right. Nice lad."

Dr Moss didn't think he was particularly nice. Not dodgy enough to be involved in anything like this… or intelligent for that matter, but not someone Dr Moss would invite home for tea. Not that he ever did.

"So? What are they doing?"

"Processing some tests."

"What? Why?"

"Because they had some outstanding. From the last time–"

"I don't care about last time. I care about the future. We've only just got that dog talking, and you go and lose him."

"Yes, sir."

"Two million, Moss."

"Yes, Sir Alfred." As if he'd needed reminding.

"Get Felicity and Kevin, Kelvin, on the case too. Whatever they're working on can wait. If you can't find that dog, they'll have more time than they'll know what to do with."

"Yes, Sir Alfred."

"And find him today."

"I don't know that–"

"Just do it. Phone me later with the good news."

There was no good news to tell Sir Alfred when Dr Moss had to call him back later that evening. Gwynne had spent the whole day searching the grounds and finally gone home, red-faced from crying so much. Dr Moss had offered to take her home but she said she was fine.

Felicity and Kelvin had had as much luck. Without any CCTV footage, they had nowhere to start. There were no footprints in mud, no squeal of tyre tracks. It was as if a ghost had come in and taken him.

Why didn't he put up a fight? Dr Moss wondered. Did he hate being at FMRS that much? He and Gwynne got on so well, surely he would have wanted to stay for her.

The police were called. They dusted for fingerprints, took the padlock away for forensic examination but without any evidence, didn't hold out much hope. The way the policeman had spoken, they weren't going to take it seriously; it was only a dog.

Dr Moss couldn't tell him that he wasn't only a dog, he was a talking dog, he was a two-million-pound dog. More than two million.

Gwynne had come back the following morning with dark circles under her eyes, and no make-up. Dr Moss didn't know much about women but having seen Gwynne's black-smudged eyes the previous day, he'd assumed she hadn't wanted a repeat of that. Neither had he.

He told her she should take some time off, go away with Dan, but she explained that Dan was on a course and the house was too empty. She didn't want to sit around and mope. She'd rather do that here.

"Thanks," Dr Moss felt like saying but thought that would sound rude so said, "Of course" and patted her on her arm, hoping it didn't come across as patronising.

Felicity and Kelvin were back on the results testing. It was what they did best. If only Dr Moss had confidence in the police. But the police weren't FMRS's best friend. Sir Walter knew the Police Commissioner, others with a multitude of stripes on their shoulders, but they never gave Dr Moss the impression that they'd go out of their way to help, even if Sir Walter called in favours.

Despite there being no evidence of animal cruelty, because there wasn't any, they weren't popular with the locals and it was the locals who paid the police's wages so they had an image to maintain. Help the enemy and you'd be the most unpopular kid in town. That's why Dr Moss never told anyone where he worked. If he was ever asked what he did for a living, he said he worked for NASA but only small fry, not on the actual spacecraft, and people soon lost interest, not thinking that NASA was based in America not central England.

Dr Moss returned to his list of suspects.

Trevor hadn't turned up for work but his colleagues said he'd already arranged a trip abroad with his family and had had it booked for weeks. He had his mobile with him if anyone needed to ask any questions but as far as Dr Moss was concerned, there was nothing he could do or say to solve the situation. The lack of security didn't sit easily with Dr Moss. It was too neat. No signs of a break-in.

It had to be someone on the inside. *You've been watching too much CSI*, Dr Moss said to himself as he put brackets round Trevor's name. Just because he had an alibi, it didn't mean he was off the hook.

Bottom of the list was Gwynne. She could be ruled out: (a) she had no reason and (b) she'd been in pieces ever since. Guilty conscience? Dr Moss shook his head and crossed her out.

Felicity, Kelvin. What reason did they have?

Obviously the Board couldn't be considered. They were funding the whole thing and they had said it had been going well.

Dr Moss opened the top drawer of his desk, put his list inside and slammed the drawer closed again. *Ridiculous*. If the police weren't taking it seriously, why should he? *Because your job's on the line*. He didn't know where to start. On TV the hero would talk to a dodgy contact, find out who's been seen where they shouldn't be, selling what they shouldn't be selling, but Dr Moss knew no one like that.

The only obvious person was Trevor. If only Dr Moss could ask him what he thought. He didn't know him very well but Dr Moss knew the sort of reputation they had. Security were usually former policemen, or women, so knew their way around a case like this. Trevor wouldn't go out of his way for a dog but Dr Moss could say he was asking for a hypothetical human. Security guards were also bouncers and bouncers hear people talk… but about a kidnapped dog? That was the bottom line.

As the day went on, Dr Moss kept expecting the call from Sir Alfred, telling him he was no longer welcome at FMRS. Every time there was a knock at the door – his office or home – he expected one of Trevor's colleagues to tell him to pack his stuff, he had half an hour to clear his desk. But the call never came.

After a week of nervous conversations with Gwynne, who he'd kept busy with plans for when Henry returned (they had to think 'when'); some tests but lots of games, new toys, treats, anything he wanted, Dr Moss had resigned himself to never seeing Henry again, to returning to the Xanadu Rescue Centre for another dog, although his heart wasn't in it. There couldn't be a Henry the Second.

Dr Moss jumped as the door cracked open. "Sorry to disturb you," Gwynne whispered. "I'm off home now if that's okay."

Dr Moss looked at the clock. Five-thirty. "Of course."

Gwynne entered the office, shutting the door behind her. "Do you think they'll ever find him?"

"Who?"

"Henry."

"No, I mean who they?"

"The security team, the police. I don't know. Who's been looking for him?"

"I don't think either of them."

"Then who?"

"We've put posters up and I've been…"

"Yes?"

"I've been driving around most evenings…"

"Me too."

Dr Moss stood. "Really?"

Gwynne nodded. "Especially while Dan was away. Home seemed too empty. I know I wouldn't have been allowed to but I wish I'd been able to take Henry home sometimes. It never occurred to me how lonely he must have been on his own at night."

"Me too."

"Really?"

"Irene would have gone mad but she would have grown to love him."

"As we have."

Dr Moss nodded.

"If he isn't found, will we have to get another dog?"

Dr Moss nodded again.

"From the rescue centre."

"I was thinking about that. Probably not from the same one. They'd remember and start asking questions."

"Can't we go to the press? The local paper. As we've put up posters."

"Sir Alfred doesn't want it too public. I've put my mobile on the poster so there's no connection with here, and Irene doesn't know."

"She doesn't?"

Dr Moss shook his head.

"She doesn't know about him at all, does she."

"No."

"I know we're not allowed to talk about what we do but Dan knows there's a dog. Of course he first thought that we were experimenting, which we are… were, of course, but I told him he… Henry was yours."

"Right. It's not like he and Irene are ever going to meet."

Gwynne didn't reply.

"Okay. You get off home and…"

"Don't stay too late."

"Going in a minute. I have to run an errand for Irene. She's keeping me busy around the house. I think while I'm driving around looking for Henry she thinks I'm at some other woman's house up to no good."

Gwynne laughed, a little too heartily. "Sorry."

Dr Moss smiled. "No, it's fine. It's a ridiculous thought, I know, but once she gets an idea in her head..."

Chapter Fifteen – The Great Escape

It was dark by the time Rebecca came through to collect Henry's bowls. Victoria and Norman had gone home, leaving Billy swearing at the television in the lounge.

"Hello, Henry," Rebecca said, bending down and unlocking the padlock. Henry wagged his tail. "There's a good boy. Are you a good boy?"

Henry wanted to say, "Yes, now let me go!" He wanted to bark but knew that would rile Billy, so just wagged his tail again.

"How funny. You can understand what I'm saying."

More than you know. Henry looked at the padlock on the ground outside the cage then looked up at Rebecca. He stopped his tail wagging.

Rebecca pointed to the padlock. "You don't like being locked up much, do you."

Henry was going to wag his tail again but thought she might have got the wrong idea.

"There's a bolt too. Don't suppose it would do any harm…"

Henry held his head low, his eyes looking up.

Rebecca laughed softly. "Okay. No padlock, just the bolt. You can't get out, can you?"

His eyes seemed to be doing their trick, although he wasn't sure which trick exactly, but Henry kept using them.

"Okay. Just don't tell Billy."

As if I would, Henry thought.

Rebecca took the bowls to the kitchen, shut the door to get to a cupboard behind it and sang along to the radio. Billy was too busy shouting at the TV to hear.

Henry pushed his paw through the bars, lifted the bolt, just as Rebecca had done after unlocking the padlock, then he pulled it back. The door to the cage swung open and Henry was going to step out when he saw the kitchen door open so he pulled back the cage door, holding it in place with his paw.

"Forgot to get the washing, didn't you, Becks," Rebecca mimicked Billy who was still swearing at his programme. "Silly girl, Becks. Here, have another slap."

Henry waited for Rebecca to bring the washing from the garage and disappear into the kitchen.

Releasing the cage door, he edged it open and padded to the garage, thanking whoever was looking down on him – he still wasn't sure if he believed in that afterlife stuff – that Rebecca had had her hands too full with the basket to shut the door properly.

He knew he only had a matter of seconds before Rebecca would return to shut the garage door or Billy would come out complaining about how hungry he was and how long his supper was taking. So Henry made a dash for it, pulling the door to the garage as shut as he could without trapping his paw, and looked around. There were two exits: the one he'd come through and a grey steel panelled door with a lever halfway down it, impossible for even Henry to open.

Henry's heart sank. He was trapped. It was back to a certain beating if Billy ever found out or at worst a telling off from Rebecca, plus a beating – for one or both of them – from Billy. Either way, Henry would never be trusted to have the padlock left off again.

He ducked under a bicycle cover when he heard voices in the hall.

"When's dinner?" Henry recognised Billy's growl.

"Half an hour at the most. I've just been dealing with–"

"Good. Will give me time to get some ciggies."

"Okay, love. We could do with some–"

"I'm not your slave. Get it when you go to work tomorrow."

Henry sensed the garage's door to the hall open and saw Billy walk to the exterior panelled door and open it. Henry was tempted to run but Billy had said he was going out, so Henry had to be patient. Billy would either leave the door open if he wasn't going to be long or have to get out of the van to shut it. He got in the van, started it up and drove off, leaving the garage door open.

Henry pondered for a moment or two then told himself not to be so stupid and ran out of the garage. He waited at the end of the short driveway, looked right and watched Billy's van until it turned again, out of sight. Henry had no clue where he was but turned left. At least if it was a different direction to Billy's van, Billy couldn't see him if he hadn't got far enough away before he came back with his 'ciggies'.

What Henry didn't know was that Billy and Rebecca lived in a cul-de-sac so there was no way for him to get out when he turned left. He ran past a few houses, then the road starting curving right and Henry knew he was now running in the same direction as Billy's van.

It was dark, Billy wouldn't see him. But then Henry was a Jack Russell, and other than a tan heart-shaped mark on one side and tan thigh on the other, almost completely white. Two white objects coming together, which would spot the other first? The van was bigger, an easier target and Henry knew to look out for it. It wouldn't have occurred to Billy to be looking for him.

Chapter Sixteen – DIY Sally

Henry had almost reached the top of the road when he saw Billy's white van turning. Henry dashed into a front garden and hid under some bushes. They were cold and damp but at least they were camouflage.

He watched Billy's van go past then waited a few seconds before appearing. Henry looked up the road to where he thought the house was but couldn't see anything, the garage door being set far enough back not to be visible.

So he made a dash for it. He still wasn't sure where to, but he'd head down the end of the road then decide whether to go left or right. Left hadn't worked out too well for him so far and he knew Billy had turned right going to get the ciggies so whatever that meant, it had to be a good thing, had to mean people. Henry was wearing a collar with FMRS's phone number on it so he'd stop someone who looked kind and they'd call them. Easy. Henry scratched his neck, expecting his nametag to clink but it didn't. He rubbed around his neck. No collar. He didn't remember anyone taking it off and he'd been conscious most of the time. Most. Not all.

Henry sighed. There was no number for anyone to call. How would they get him back now? He remembered having something injected inside him when he was brought into the rescue centre. They'd talked about being able to find him if he ever went missing. So if someone could find out where that something was. *But it's inside you, Henry.* How could he be so stupid? But then how could they be so stupid? Why did they put it inside him? He rubbed where he remembered it hurting, his front left leg. He then moved his paw along it until he felt something long and hard. That had to be it. But what was it? A piece of paper rolled up so small that it could fit into a little tube? But how to get it out? They must have another machine to suck it out. He needed to find somewhere that might have a machine like that.

He got to a small row of shops and looked up at the names: Cost Savers supermarket, Barnard's Bakery, Flora's Chemist,

MacDonnell's DIY. DIY. He remembered Mick saying something about going to the DIY shop. Henry studied the window: pots of paint, a pane of glass with a fake boot and football through it. They'd been cut in half and glued back together again with the piece of glass in the middle. *Clever*, Henry thought.

Then he noticed dog food. Ah, so that's where people buy dog food from. It made sense; human food was from a supermarket so dog food came from DIY shops. *Dogs In Yellow? No. Dogs Involving Y…* Henry couldn't think of another y-word other than yankie – from Sesame Street's episode of the phonetic alphabet – and that wouldn't fit. Besides, they didn't just sell dog food. There was cat food, hamster bedding, allsorts.

Seeing the packets lined up made Henry feel hungry. He'd escaped before Rebecca had fed him again which, on reflection, was pretty stupid but he hadn't wanted to hang around to see what Plan B was going to be. *Put me out with the rubbish*, Henry thought as he saw rolls of bin bags stacked up like a pyramid.

It was then he spotted the tool that Norman had been carrying when he'd first seen it. Bolt cutters. Bolt. Like the talking dog in the animated movie that Carmen had watched once. So this hadn't been a wasted journey. He now had the answer to the tool question. Not as easy as asking Gwynne to Google it but at least he was getting fresh air.

Henry looked at the rest of the shops: a hairdresser's, and two restaurants, Chinese and Indian. No, the DIY shop, whatever it stood for, had to be the best choice. All he had to do was wait until… *Oh no.* The lights went off. That wasn't good.

Henry had needed someone to go in the shop so he could get in while the door was open, find someone in a uniform and look lost. He was lost, looking lost wouldn't be hard, but he'd have to wait until the morning, until the first customer came in. He'd never slept outside before. He was about to walk on, find some shelter when the DIY shop door opened, alarm sounding behind it.

Henry bounced up to the shop owner and barked. The

woman wobbled but managed to shut the door before the alarm stopped wailing. “Hey! You...”

Henry barked again, in case the woman hadn’t heard him the first time. He was pleased to see it was a woman. He’d had more luck with them. He looked up and spotted a name on her blue MacDonnell’s sweatshirt. Sally.

“Okay, let’s see. What’s your name?” She reached down for his collar and Henry was waiting for her to say “Henry” but remembered his collar was missing. “Oh, no. What’s happened to your collar?”

Henry wagged his tail.

“Don’t suppose you’re chipped.”

Henry lifted up the paw that had the implant embedded into it.

“Shake paw.”

Henry dropped his head and lifted his paw higher.

“The chip? It’s in there?”

Henry barked.

“Clever dog. Okay, come in. Let’s see what we can find out.” As she opened the door, the alarm wailed again and she rushed over to a panel on the wall and tapped in five digits. She then went to a computer connected to an advertising display. She tapped the icon to the internet and waited for it to open. Henry recognised Google’s home page and watched her type in something.

“Pet chipping… Pages from the UK only. No… I don’t want it doing. I’ve got… ah, here we go. What to do if you find a lost dog. ‘By law’,” she read, “‘you are required to turn found dogs over to local authorities (animal shelter, pound) where their owner / guardian will be able to claim them. One of the primary reasons why lost dogs are not reunited with their families is that the animal shelter is the first (and primary) location where dog owners search for their lost dogs but it is typically the last location where found dogs are taken (due to the fear that the dog will be euthanised).

“Very few municipal shelters have the resources available to house lost and stray animals more than three days. If you are not willing to take the dog to the shelter, most shelters will allow you to foster (house) the dog while also filing a found report by providing the description, the location where you found it, and your contact information. We suggest you also create a found dog flyer to mail or take down to the shelter so they can post it on a bulletin board. Then if the owner / guardian shows up at the shelter searching for his or her dog, the shelter can put the family directly in touch with you.' Oh, no. We don't want you to be euthanised, do we."

Henry didn't know what that meant, but he was pretty sure that if she didn't want it to happen to him, then he didn't either. He looked up at her, eyes at the ready.

"No, exactly. Besides, they won't be open now. So, looks like you're coming home with me, unless your mummy or daddy are around here somewhere. We'll go outside and have a look, shall we."

Henry barked. What he really wanted to say was that his mummy and daddy, for the sake of giving them labels, were at their different houses and he should be back at the lab, tucked up on the thick bed with all the dogs on it to keep him company. He'd be happy to settle for those.

He liked Sally but he didn't know her. At least he knew *them*. And he missed Gwynne and Dr Moss. He so wanted to speak, to tell Sally exactly where he belonged but he'd promised Gwynne he wouldn't tell anyone who didn't know. It hadn't landed him in trouble exactly, just being a dog had done that, but Sally seemed nice so once she contacted the shelter, they'd ring Gwynne and everything would be all right.

"Let me lock up again and we'll go home, okay?"

Henry barked and watched her put the computer to sleep, leaving the advertising display to tell anyone who walked by about the local double-glazing company's twenty-five percent off special offer, the handyman who didn't charge a call-out fee and for whom no job was too small or too large, and the electrician with seventeen years' experience. Henry wasn't sure what his experience was in but seventeen years sounded like a long time, especially in human years, so he was suitably impressed.

Sally picked up a packet of dog food, a long bit of thin rope which she looped around Henry's neck, then set the alarm and ushered Henry back out the shop. While she locked up, he huddled in the doorway, hoping that a small white van didn't pass while he was waiting.

"Okay, let's go." She led him to a green Mini parked nearby and opened the passenger door. Henry went to jump in but she pulled him back, the rope nearly choking him. "Hold your horses, wait a sec."

Henry didn't realise he had any horses and wasn't sure how he was supposed to hold them, even if his paws would allow him to. He'd tried barking at a horse once when he and Carmen had come back from the park but it hadn't gone well. Carmen had told him off, then apologised to the rider who was struggling to contain the grey mare. Henry had not seen another horse since but had no intention of barking at it if he did.

Sally pulled the front passenger seat forward and led Henry to the back seat which had a cover over it. He wanted to ask her whether she already had a pet but again, had to restrain himself.

Henry watched the scenery speed by as he and Sally headed out into the countryside. Although he'd spent many happy years at Carmen's in the heart of an estate, he loved the green and the open spaces of the countryside. He hoped Sally lived in a big ramshackle place where he could roam around. Now he was her responsibility though, she'd probably leave him tied up somewhere where he'd only be able to look at the horses in the fields – maybe he could ask them if they had any suggestions for how he could hold them – sheep, and anything else that ate grass. It had been a long day, and his brain was getting tired so he could only manage to think of two animals.

He stared out the window and as best he could, made a mental note of the route they were going. If he ever had to return to town, he'd try to backtrack. He was just adding another bend to the memory bank when he spotted a familiar sight. The old converted stately home with the big white board outside.

FMRS. He barked and squeaked.

"You alright back there, boy?" Sally asked as she navigated a particularly nasty corner. "Careful now."

Henry leaned into the window as he saw the white board disappear. He looked out the back window so if they drove, or he walked, this road again, he'd know how to follow it.

The car then turned left, Henry's right, and slowed down. Henry looked out the side window and saw where Sally was going; indeed, an old house, one with a funny-looking straw roof and flowers growing everywhere. It looked like one of the houses from the television programme *Midsummer Murders* and he shivered. He hoped no one was going to get murdered here.

He wanted to ask Sally the name of the village, praying that it wasn't the same one as on the TV, but he just sighed and jumped out of the car when she pushed the seat forward. He'd planned to run, as fast as he could, down the road, turning right, then running until he saw the white board but Sally already had hold of the rope which she'd wrapped round her hand so many times that all Henry could do was pull. "Easy, now. Can't go losing you when I've only just found you."

Henry strained his neck to see down the road for as long as he could until Sally gave one last tug and he was inside.

The house was warm and bright, and as Sally removed the rope, Henry followed her into the kitchen. She put the dog food down onto the work surface and cut open the top. She poured some of the contents into a shallow bowl, filled another with water, and put them both on the floor.

Henry looked at the bowls then up at Sally. "Okay," she said and he took a step nearer, starting with the food and occasionally switching to the water when he felt his mouth go dry. He'd rather have had a tin of meat but knew he shouldn't be so fussy. Food was food and it had been hours since he'd eaten and that had only been a token, Rebecca obviously unaware of how hungry he'd been back then.

He hoped she was okay and wondered if he'd ever see her

again. He hoped not if it meant seeing Billy but somehow Henry knew that given the situation with Victoria, things would change soon anyway. Him leaving did them a favour, he knew that, but he worried about how Billy would react once he saw the empty cage and asked Rebecca to explain.

Maybe he'd care as little about Henry as he did about Victoria and Rebecca, especially knowing there was no money involved. Perhaps he was like that with everyone. He'd been friendly to Norman but even then Henry had sensed a coolness towards the old man, like he was just someone to pass the time with, not really interested in what he had to say, not making any effort with his end of the conversation.

By the time Henry finished the food, he had drunk so much that Sally had to refill the bowl. He didn't think there was anything wrong with what she'd tipped away but he didn't like to complain – couldn't, even he if wanted to.

He sat and looked up at her as she cooked her own dinner. As she moved from sink to fridge and back, he looked around the room. There were photographs on the wall, of her, a man and a young girl. Sally followed Henry's gaze and started crying. Henry wondered whether it was onions – the reason had Victoria given for crying – but couldn't see Sally chopping any onions – or whether it had something to do with the picture, so he went over to Sally and nudged her left hand hanging limply by her side.

"It's okay," she sobbed, then wiped the tears away with her right hand. "It was a long time ago."

Henry sat in the middle of the kitchen floor watching Sally eat. Her make-up was still smudged from her earlier crying session and Henry hoped that there wouldn't be another one. He knew that dogs brought joy to people's lives and wondered whether him being there was destiny. He knew he could bring joy to her life.

If MacDonnell's was her business, then she could take a dog to work with her, couldn't she? The trouble was that FMRS would want him back. They'd paid a lot of money to make him talk. It all depended on what the thing inside his leg said. If it still had his owner as the rescue centre then Sally could adopt him, keep him, be the company that she obviously craved. If it came up as FMRS though, she'd have no option but to take him there.

For now, it didn't matter. They'd deal with that when it happened, if it happened. In the meantime he would keep her company, from a distance, while she ate so she didn't think he was scrounging, then he'd follow her into the lounge to watch TV or upstairs if she was tired enough to go to bed. That's if he was allowed upstairs. Mick had forbidden Carmen from letting Henry upstairs but she said what he didn't know wouldn't hurt him, and Henry was never going to tell, couldn't back then.

It then occurred to Henry that without the 'medication', would he still be able to talk? If so, for how long? When he was alone, he'd speak to make sure he still could. He'd not needed to when he'd escaped because he could hear what he was thinking.

Sally scraped her uneaten food into a small brown bin and put the plate and cutlery into the sink. She squirted a dash of orange-scented washing up liquid on top of them, running the water until it went warm. She let it run for a few seconds then switched it off and scrubbed the dinner things clean.

One by one, she put them on a wire rack and Henry watched transfixed as the soapy water dripped onto the draining board. He was too low to see what happened to it thereafter and imagined a little pool of cold soapy water welcoming the warmer addition. Sally moved to the back door and unlocked it. She picked up the washing up bowl but then looked at Henry and put it back down.

As she walked into the lounge, he followed her then turned round as she did. "Stay here. Good boy," she said and he watched her shut the door. Although it was a small room, the sofa and table weren't near to the windows so when he heard the back door slam, he thought she'd left him but then it slammed again a few seconds later and she let him back into the kitchen. "Sorry, boy, but couldn't risk you running away now, could we?"

Henry wished she had, but barked and wagged his tail because he knew it would make her feel better.

"Poured the water on the plants, in case you were wondering."

He had been.

"Don't think the washing up liquid does them any good but we've not had much rain recently and they say not to waste it. Considering how wet everyone thinks this country is, we never seem to have enough rain. Don't suppose it'll lead to a hosepipe ban but you never know."

Henry couldn't understand why they'd want to ban hosepipes. He'd watched Mick clean his beloved black Ford Escort using a hosepipe and it looked really useful. Of course he couldn't ask him, or Sally, but why something else to speak to Gwynne about, should they ever be reunited. *Think positively, Henry*, Henry thought. *You know how close it is. You'll get there, you just need to outwit Sally and run…*

The thought of that actually made him sad. Here was someone who really cared about him. Wanted him to stay safe, not shut him away in a cage and yet he wanted to leave, return to being injected with Dr-Moss-knows-what, and only get to go outside once or twice a day. Gwynne was always apologising that she'd run out of time to take him for a second walk but he wouldn't have minded if it was only ten minutes – she could have stayed that long, surely.

"We'll go for a nice walk in the morning, okay?" Sally said as she settled on the sofa.

Henry wagged his tail. He wanted to jump up on the sofa, get as close to her as he could, but she'd already looked at him then looked at the sofa and said that although she really wanted to spoil him, she didn't want him to get into bad habits. He didn't mind being spoiled but she was the boss and it was her house so it was only fair.

So he lay on the rug between her coffee table and the sofa,

put his chin on his paws and went to sleep.

Chapter Seventeen – Not For Keeps?

The sound of machine gun fire woke Henry and he instinctively leapt up and barked.

"It's okay, boy. It's the television."

Henry lay back down, chin on paws, but kept his eyes open. Wanting to guard Sally unnerved him. He'd only just met her yet he was willing to give his life for her. Wasn't that what any dog would do to someone they cared about? *Care? You have feelings for her?* Henry let his ears relax.

He looked up at her. It was good to see her smile. He'd been worried that he'd made her unhappy by reminding her of the family she'd lost. He thought he'd probably never find out why. He certainly wouldn't… couldn't ask. Maybe she'd pour her heart out to him.

Don't be silly, he thought. *She's taking you to the shelter in the morning and that will be that. You'll never see her again. And besides, how would she live if she poured out her heart? He didn't want her to die because of him, even if he would for her.*

He heard her laugh so closed his eyes and tried to sleep but his ears were on full alert, listening out for signs of her crying, regardless of whether it was because of the television or anything else. Henry thought about Gwynne, Dr Moss, Olivia. Henry had liked Olivia too. She'd been kind to him and anyone who worked with animals, or sold food for them, had to be okay.

"Okay, boy. Let's go to bed."

Henry opened his eyes and looked up. Sally had switched off the TV and was heading into the kitchen. He followed her and watched her boil the kettle, make a drink – he wasn't sure what but it smelled like chocolate – and fill a hot water bottle. That had been Carmen's routine every night. She'd even made a bottle for him in the winter when the house got so cold he could see her breath as she spoke.

Sally's house was lovely and warm so he couldn't quite work out why she needed the hot water bottle but he knew that sometimes people got into a routine and couldn't get out of it, like the security guards checking at certain times. Or at least they were supposed to.

Henry waited at the bottom of the stairs as Sally walked up to her bedroom, hugging the hot water bottle under her left arm, and holding the mug in her right hand. When she appeared to realise he wasn't following, she turned round. "It's okay, you can come up." He barked and bounded the stairs two by two.

Her bedroom was very feminine, not pink as he would have expected but two shades of purple; a deep rich almost-black purple and a softer lilac. The accessories were mostly cream, and complimented the room, Henry thought, perfectly. Henry stayed studying the décor while Sally went to the bathroom. When he heard her using an electric toothbrush, a sound not dissimilar to one of Gwynne's lab machines, he explored the rest of the upstairs.

Next to the master bedroom was a guest room. Henry assumed this by the lack of personal touches and a pile of what looked like unused royal blue towels. Although this room was heated as well as the others, it felt cold by comparison to Sally's, the walls a stark pale blue. Not as friendly, unwelcoming. Henry wondered how often it was used.

Next was a little girl's room, with everything pink. There were posters of horses and fairies adorning all four walls, a pink television with a built-in DVD player sat on a pink chest of drawers at the end of the bed alongside a pink radio and a miniature silver tree with a vast array of pink jewellery. Henry imagined the two girls, Sally and her daughter, laughing while trying on different accessories. This had been a happy home once, not long ago, Henry suspected, despite Sally earlier saying otherwise.

He wanted to give her a hug, tell her everything was going to be all right. He knew, if they really had gone, that she'd never get her original family back, but things did get better. He knew that. It had happened to him. Here he was, albeit probably only for the next few hours, being looked after by someone who cared about him. She'd find that again, maybe find a new man who already had a family, who had lost its mother, his wife, and they would all be happy again.

"Hi, Kerry. I'm going to be a bit late this morning. No, everything's fine. Just an errand to run. I'll be in when I can. Thanks. Only delivery from Everson's but probably not until this afternoon. Thanks, Kerry."

So, Sally was going to take Henry to the rescue centre, and by 'this afternoon', he'd be behind bars again; at the rescue centre or at FMRS. It would be great to see Gwynne and he was sure they'd have lots of fun but he'd never be free. Even here, Sally didn't trust him enough to be let off the lead outside of the house or car. But at least he could move around, go upstairs, sleep upstairs, on a bed, alongside someone else. He'd never been allowed to do that before. Here he'd felt like a real member of a family, and that's what Sally needed.

Henry watched Sally pour herself a glass of orange juice, tip some cereal into a bowl, soak it with milk, then tuck in. She'd just finished the first mouthful when she looked over at Henry. "Sorry, boy. I can't keep calling you 'boy'. Be glad when I find out your name. You'll get your breakfast soon. Humans first though. It's the rules."

That was something Henry had never considered before; that there were those kinds of rules. He knew humans were more important than dogs; he knew that from their freedom and his captivity. They kept you in check all the time, reminded you that you always came second. He'd been fooling himself that he mattered, that he was family to Sally, that he could be. He wasn't, wouldn't be. He was only a dog.

Although he was hungry, rather than stay and watch her eat, he plodded through to the lounge, and lay on the rug. He'd wait there until she called for him, feed him, then put the rope around his neck – which reminded him of too many hanging scenes in old films – and take him out to the car, to await his fate.

"Ready?"

Henry looked up and saw Sally swinging the rope. He stood, closed his eyes, and waited for her to put the noose over his head.

"Oh, no. I knew there was something." Sally let the rope drop to the floor.

Henry opened one eye then the other and watched her go back into the kitchen – for his breakfast, he hoped. She wouldn't put the lead on *before* feeding him, surely. As he walked through, she was typing something into a laptop.

She looked up at the clock, said to the screen, "We're too early. Could have gone into work after all." Then to Henry, "The rescue centre's not open for over an hour. Do you fancy a walk?"

Henry barked and wagged his tail. A walk in the country was the best thing he could possibly think of doing, with the exception of going to the beach. He loved the water and although he'd never been to the seaside, he loved the thought of biting at the waves as they rushed towards him.

Sally returned to the lounge, looped the rope over his head, and gently pulled him towards the front door. "Sorry about this, boy. If you don't pull, it won't hurt, but it's all I've got. The rescue centre will get you a proper collar, I'm sure."

Henry put down his ears.

"You don't like the thought of that, do you."

Henry hung his tail low.

"But we'll be going in the car. You like going in the car, don't you."

Henry barked but not as enthusiastically as he had done at the mention of a walk. His brain hurt as he tried to work out what would be the best thing. Perhaps he should just go along with whatever happened to him. Now he'd got the rope on there was no way he could escape. They'd go for a walk, restricted by the rope, then he'd be put back in the car and driven to the rescue centre. He'd be shoved into a cage to await his fate.

The walk was better than he'd expected. She'd let him off the rope but they'd gone to a park instead of the woods and into a fenced area with white markings. They looked familiar but he couldn't work out what. They were the same markings as another area next door and it wasn't until two people arrived, both holding rackets, pockets stuffed with balls, that he remembered. Tennis. He and Sally were on an old tennis court, but a grass version instead of tarmacked like the game going on beside them. The grass had been kept short so the lines were still visible but no one had repainted them and Henry figured they'd eventually disappear.

"Go on, boy. Have a run."

That was exactly what Henry wanted to do but he didn't want to go around in circles, be fenced in on all sides, he wanted to break out, run and never stop. He wanted to run past FMRS, run until he found the beach, spend the day biting the surf… and then what? *You need food, Henry*. Yes, he had to be realistic. Whatever destiny had in store for him, he'd always be owned by someone. He knew he wasn't like a wolf, couldn't be self-sufficient. Unless he was someone's pet, someone's experiment, he'd last no time at all.

Sally looked at her watch then beckoned him over. He plodded up to her and lifted his head. She looped the rope over it and he lowered his head again. They walked in silence to the car and he got in the back seat, repeating the action of the previous night without prompting.

The drive to the rescue centre was accompanied by the radio. Sally whistled to one of the tunes occasionally but said nothing. Henry wondered whether she was as sad as he. Did she really want to let him go? Could she, once they'd got there? He knew it was the rules. She had to give him up because he wasn't hers. He belonged to someone else. He belonged to FMRS.

In his head, he sung the words to the Beatles' *Day Tripper*. He wished they were going on a day trip, not one that would only take a few minutes. He wanted them to drive until they couldn't drive any more. She'd let him out of the car, they'd both run free, without a care, then return to the car when they were exhausted. They'd be laughing, joking… talking.

Instead of being scared when she found out he could talk, she'd scoop him up into her arms, tell him what a clever dog he was, say what wonderful conversations they could have. He wondered if she spoke any foreign languages. He didn't think Gwynne or Dr Moss could because they'd been surprised when he'd said what he'd said to the two Sirs. Dr Moss certainly didn't know any Spanish. He'd not even recognised 'mi nombre es'. Surely everyone knew how to say their name. Wasn't that what people learned before they went on holiday?

Henry was still humming inside his head when the car stopped and Sally got out. Henry looked up and saw the sign for 'PetCare Animal Shelter'. Care. He liked the sound of that. Then he realised it wasn't the one he'd been to before. So there was no one to recognise him. Was that a good thing or not? Did he want someone to know him or could he start his life over? *Don't be so silly*, he told himself and he shook his paw, the one with the chip inside.

"Come on then," Sally said opening the passenger door and pulling the seat forward. She didn't have hold of the rope so he could escape but what was the point? He didn't know where he was. He hadn't paid attention when they'd been driving along. Why hadn't he? Was he really that stupid?

After he jumped out, he looked around him, past the car park, the rows of solid grey metal kennels housing dogs whining, barking, in one case howling. No, he didn't like this at all.

"Let's get it over with," Sally said, shutting the door behind him and walked him to the reception.

A kind-looking woman smiled at Sally then looked down at Henry. "Hello, handsome."

He wanted to say "hello" but just wagged his tail.

She then looked back at Sally. "Hello. How can I help you?"

Sally sighed. "I found this dog last night. Actually, he found me. He was outside my shop and I nearly tripped over him. I looked on the internet to find out what I should do and it said I should report him to you."

The woman looked back at Henry, pulling a sad face. "Oh dear. Are you lost?"

Silly question, Henry thought but just stared back at her, tail stationary.

"He's chipped," Sally added. "Left paw. You can feel it."

"Great!" The woman smiled again and unhooked a machine off the wall behind her. "Let's have a look, shall we?"

Henry watched her come from behind the counter and approach him, machine, and arm, outstretched. She crouched down and hovered the machine along the front of his paw, then down the back. Henry felt it tickle so stepped away. "It's okay," the woman soothed. "It won't hurt." She hovered the machine, front and back again. "That's odd."

"Anything wrong?" Sally asked.

"I'm not getting a reading."

"Oh."

Good, Henry thought.

"Let's try again." She hovered the machine, slower this time. "It's supposed to beep. Where's the…" She took Henry's paw in her hand and felt along his fur until she found the chip. She moved the machine up and down, round in circles. "Maybe it's the batteries." She let go of Henry's paw and went behind the counter, to a poster on the wall. She held the machine up to a patterned square and the machine beeped. "No, sounds okay. I can't understand then why… Let me get a colleague. Are you okay to wait?"

"Sure," Sally said.

"Do take a seat." The woman pointed to a row of three blue padded chairs. Sally sat on the third and Henry lay by her feet.

Less than five minutes later, the woman returned, followed by a man so tall his hair brushed the doorway.

"Hello," he said, holding out his hand to Sally.

She stood and shook his hand. "Hello."

"I'm Rob, Centre Manager. I understand you're having a bit of trouble finding… Hello. And who do we have here?"

"I don't know," Sally said. "I found him last night and was hoping your colleague could reunite him but..."

"No, the reader's not coming up with anything." The woman handed Rob the scanner and took up her position back behind the counter. As if it had been waiting for her to return, the phone rang. "Hello PetCare Animal Shelter, Zadie speaking. How can I help you?"

Sally watched Rob try the scanner then frown as it remained silent. "I don't understand. We've never had this before. It, the chip... not this handsome fella..." Rob grinned at Henry who wanted to grin back but just wagged his tail, jumping slightly as it bashed one of the nearby chairs. Rob continued. "The chip must be registered to someone, or somewhere at least. You don't know anything about him?"

Sally shook her head. "He doesn't even have a collar. How irresponsible... unless it came off."

"Unlikely. Maybe someone doesn't want him back and let him loose in the hope someone else would take responsibility for him."

"Or they didn't but didn't care."

"Most likely, although they took the trouble to get him chipped. But then why deregister it? Him. I'm not sure I even know how they'd do that."

"No."

"We only put in the chips here. We have no control over anything after that, other than calling up the details."

"But you can't this time."

"With no beep, the computer won't... or shouldn't. No, it comes up on the scanner here, see?" He held out the scanner.

"Oh, yes. Clever."

Sally was more of a hands-on person than a technophile. It was a little beyond her once it got past emails, photographs and internet searches. Her husband had been good...

Sally sniffed and reached into her bag. "Sorry, got a cold coming, I think."

"No problem," Rob said as he pulled a tissue from a box on

the desk, and handed it to her.

Sally smiled. “Thanks. So, what do we do now?”

“Not a lot we can do,” Rob explained. “Without a collar and working chip, there’s no real way of knowing who he is. We could take him in, although we’re struggling for space at the moment. Does he get on with other dogs?”

Sally looked down at Henry. “I don’t know. It’s only been the two of us. I took him out for a walk this morning but we didn’t meet any.”

“Not to worry. I’m sure he wouldn’t have to share for long.”

“Is there an alternative?” Sally asked, looking back up at Rob.

“The only other option is that you take him home.”

Sally smiled. “Can I?”

Henry barked and wagged his tail.

“Is that an option?” Sally asked.

Rob nodded. “Absolutely. I’ll need your phone number. I mean…” Rob flushed. “I mean, you’ll have to leave your details here so if anyone comes looking for him, we’ll know where to find him.”

“Do you think that might happen?”

“I don’t know. Some people come looking, others see the loss of their dog as an opportunity to go on holiday.”

Sally looked at Zadie who was still on the phone and nodding a lot so she turned back to Rob. “That’s awful.”

Rob nodded and pulled up Henry’s top lip. “He’s not all that old. Eighteen months–”

Nineteen, Henry thought.

“Two years at most.”

“How can you tell?”

“By their teeth. He has a good set, and he’s been looked after well. Overall he seems a happy dog.”

Henry barked, wagged his tail and looked up at Sally.

Rob and Sally laughed.

“See,” Rob said. “He’s certainly happy with you.”

“So it’s okay if I register and take him home?”

"Sure. It would help us out. But if someone claims him..."

"Of course. Is there a time limit?"

"Technically a week but then we wait another week. It's fairer on the animals and their owner. Sometimes they're on holiday and they've trusted their dog with a neighbour or friend. There are all sorts of reasons why they come in to us."

"So if I don't hear from you within a fortnight..."

"I'll... someone will call you in a fortnight unless we've had an enquiry by then. Of course they'll have to prove that he's theirs. See how you get on. You may find it doesn't work out."

"I'm sure it will. He seemed happy enough last night." Sally leaned in to Rob. "He slept on my bed."

"Lucky dog." Rob grinned and it was Sally's turn to flush.

Rob leaned over the reception counter and pulled out a camera. Henry read the name. 'Polaroid'. Mick had had one of those, the type where the picture appears instantly and then takes only a few seconds to reveal.

Henry had never figured out how that worked and he wanted to ask Rob but didn't. That was something else to ask Gwynne... or Sally if he got to stay with her. When they were really close, he'd reveal that he could talk, when he knew it wouldn't freak her out, when he knew she wanted to keep him no matter what.

Rob took the photograph and waved it in the air until it dried and Henry appeared in his white and tan glory. Rob laughed and showed the photograph to Sally. "It looks as if he's smiling."

"Oh yes." She looked down at Henry. "So he does."

Rob looked at his colleague who had put down the phone. "Zadie. Could you please help...?" He paused and looked back at Sally.

"Sally MacDonnell," Sally said.

"Could you help Sally complete an R11, please?"

Zadie nodded, smiled, put the photograph to one side of the counter, then picked a blue clipboard off the wall to her right and handed it to Sally who sat back on the chair and filled in the form.

Henry sat patiently watching her, pleased that at least

something was going his way.

"I'll leave you to it," Rob said, and made for the exit.

Sally looked up. "Thank you. I look forward to your call, but hopefully not for a fortnight."

Rob laughed. "Let's keep everything crossed."

Sally smiled, watched Rob leave, walking towards the kennels, then she completed the form and handed the clipboard back to Zadie. Sally's shop sold pet food but she'd still need accessories. "Can I buy a lead and some toys and things?" She pointed to a display rack between the reception and the exit. Although there were some new items, others looked like they had been donated and Henry hoped it wasn't because the dogs had died.

"Certainly. The profits go to the centre."

"That's great."

"I forgot to ask. If no one claims him, do I come back and pay for…? I don't even know his name."

"I guess if we don't find out what it is, you can pick your own."

"Yes, I could, couldn't I."

"We would ask for a donation but because he's not actually stayed here, there's no obligation."

"Of course. I'd be happy to."

Sally picked a blue lead, matching collar with blank disc, the plastic kind where you remove it from the metal ring, pull out a piece of card, write on it then put it back. "I'd get a proper one done," Sally said, but Zadie was on the phone again.

Henry wagged his tail and Sally nodded at him. She lay the lead and collar on the reception counter and pointed to the toys. "What do you think of these?"

Henry approached her and sniffed at two she held out to him. He nudged the one in her left hand: a green squeaky plastic alligator.

She added that to the lead and collar then picked two more toys and held them out to him. He nudged the one in her right hand: a furry bear, which she added to the pile.

"Okay. Any more?" she asked, adding a squeaky ball and

tug rope then picked two more animals and offered them to Henry. He'd have loved them both – the more the merrier, especially when he was left alone, but thought that would be greedy so didn't nudge either of them, although he liked the look of the racoon glove puppet.

"Okay then. How about some treats."

Henry hadn't realised how hungry he was, so he barked although he did wonder why she was buying some from here when she sold them in her shop. He supposed she was just being generous and they did look nice.

Sally laughed. "Okay. Treats it is." She took three assorted packs from the display and put them on the counter. She then looked at some harnesses and tried to work out the best size. "Medium, I suppose. Got to be safe in the car."

When Zadie came off the phone, she rang the prices into the till. Henry was used to technical gadgets so was surprised that she was pressing buttons instead of zapping at the items. Most people on TV zapped things that their customers wanted to buy but then they were proper shops and not somewhere where they were trying to help others… especially just animals.

"That's twenty-nine fifty, please," she said putting everything into a paper carrier bag with the 'PetCare Animal Shelter' emblem emblazoned on the side.

Sally pulled a credit card from her purse and handed it over.

Zadie thanked her and hovered it above the card reader. It beeped and a piece of paper chuntered up. "At least that one works."

"Sorry?"

"Oh, not your card. The machine. I meant this worked whereas the chip scanner…"

"Ah, yes."

Zadie grimaced. "Sorry, I didn't mean your card."

Sally shrugged. "No, it's fine. My misunderstanding."

Henry was even more grateful than the two women that the first machine didn't work and the second did, because it meant he could go home with Sally, play with the toys, and be taken out for walks without getting strangled. He'd wait the two weeks and see what happened. If Gwynne claimed him then he'd return to the lab. If she didn't, he'd keep Sally company, her and Rob, if he was right about what had just happened between them.

Sally held up the harness. "Do you know how these things work?" she asked Zadie.

"Sure." Zadie came back round from behind the counter.

As she approached Henry, he stood. She picked up one of his legs, looped one of the straps under his chest then the other strap under the other leg. She clicked two sets of black plastic clips together then stepped back.

"As long as the red strip there…" She pointed. "Is vertical down his chest, the rest of it should follow. Make sure the straps aren't twisted and he'll be fine. My dog is a Houdini with these. He gets out regardless of how tightly I do it up. He's thirteen and I've never been able to work out why. So I loop his lead round the seatbelt and clip that onto his collar, as a back-up."

"Thanks, I'll do that. What sort of dog have you got?"

"A cross breed. Jack Russell Cairn. He's usually here, he was a rescue, but my husband has the day off so he's taken him and our sons to the beach. Bertie's about the same size as your chap here but more grey, even more in the past few months, especially round the muzzle. But your chap here has plenty of years in him. How old did Rob say?"

"Eighteen months. Two years at the most."

Nineteen.

"Oh, forgot to say," Zadie added. "There's a metal ring on the top of the harness so it can stay on, and you can clip his lead to it when you're taking him for a walk. Some dogs don't like it but it's better for their necks, especially if you're not going to let him off for a while. Some dogs get too excited for their own good and run as far as the lead will go… when they're on the expandable type, they think it's endless and end up strangling themselves. The trick is to give a little at a time. Or use the harness."

Sally looked back at the display. "I didn't think about an expandable lead."

"Not to worry," Zadie said. "Perhaps for later."

If you get to keep him in two weeks' time, you mean, Henry thought.

"Thank you," Sally said, picked up the bag of purchases and led Henry back to the car.

Henry fidgeted as the harness slipped from side to side as he walked along. He'd be even less impressed if he was going to be shackled to this thing every time they went anywhere. He could tolerate it in the car because he did get buffeted about on the journeys he'd been on so far but it would be no better than being in a cage. It was still a restriction. He sighed but made sure it wasn't loud enough for Sally to hear.

"There we go," she said as she strapped him into the back seat, not easy to do when leaning through the gap between the front and back seats. "Maybe I should put you in the front, although I'd rather you hit the back of a chair than the dashboard."

That didn't fill Henry with confidence about her driving. Okay, so she took the corners a little faster than Henry felt comfortable with but they'd only been on relatively short journeys. Maybe going to the end of the country in search of the beach wasn't such a good idea.

Sally started the car and headed off. She looked at the clock. "Ten-thirty. Not too bad. Wonder what Kerry's going to think of you. She'll love you, I'm sure."

Henry watched out the window as they drove away from the rescue centre, through a small village Henry didn't spot the name of, through an industrial estate, ingeniously called 'New Industrial Estate', then into the road they'd driven away from the previous day.

Sally let Henry out, minus the harness but with the lead, and walked him to her shop. It looked different to him, in daylight, bigger and very green, somewhere rural in the middle of somewhere urban.

Kerry was serving a customer when they came in but spotted Henry and looked from him to Sally.

"Long story," Sally said and went to their staffroom, tying Henry to one of the desk's legs before putting on the kettle. She pulled the bear from the bag and put it on the floor next to Henry. She opened one of the packets of treats with her teeth, which Henry thought looked painful, and put a small bone on her flat palm which she held out to Henry. He looked up at her then down at the treat. "It's okay. You can have it." Henry gently picked it up, then chewed it, swallowed, and barked his gratitude.

"So who's this then?" Kerry asked, making two mugs of coffee.

Sally sat at the desk and looked through a pile of envelopes. "This is... oh, I don't know. He'd got no collar so he's nameless at the moment."

"Oh dear," Kerry said, putting a mug of black coffee onto a coaster by Sally's phone. "We can't have that." She looked down at Henry and frowned. "So he's a boy, then."

"Yes."

"How about Jack?"

"Jack the Jack Russell? That's a terrible idea."

"Okay then. He's a..." Kerry studied Henry's face to the point of embarrassing him. He wanted to look down but was glued to her blue eyes, a sharp contrast to her black bob. "George. Something regal."

"George isn't bad."

"But it's not very easy to call out."

"Why would you want to call it out? Oh, to get him to come to you. All right then, sticking with the regal theme, how about Richard."

Kerry scowled. "Richard? That's worse than Jack."

"What other kings have there been then? Albert?"

A vision of Sir Alfred flashed into Henry's brain. He expected to feel sad, but surprised himself when he realised he wasn't. Being tied to a desk all day was much better than being kept in a cage, and at least he'd have company when he... they went home.

Kerry laughed. A nice laugh, not a condescending one.

"Albert was a Prince. Married to Victoria."

"William. There have been plenty of King Williams."

Kerry shook her head.

"Harry then."

"Harry's a prince too."

Henry looked up at Kerry. *Close.*

"He likes Harry." Kerry twirled a lock of hair in her fingers. "Easy to call out, two syllables. Very up-to-date."

"Harry… Houdini." Sally laughed. "All right then. Harry it is for now, until I think of something better."

"You won't!" Kerry called as she carried her mug of coffee into the shop.

"Are you a Harry?" Sally asked Henry.

He put his head on one side to indicate that while it wasn't spot on, it was close enough. Henry Houdini. Yes, he liked that too. Sounded Italian – not a language he'd picked up much of but there was time. Sally seemed like someone who might watch a variety of programmes. She'd educate him without knowing it.

"Okay then, Harry. You going to be okay here for a while? Sorry the floor's not very comfortable but when we get home I'll look out something that I can make into a bed. Sure I have an old duvet that will do the job."

Home. He liked the sound of that. He'd not considered being at home since he'd been at Carmen's, and Mick had never made it feel welcoming. Sally's was. It was warm, cosy, and once his toys were there, he thought he'd be happy. Very happy indeed.

Chapter Eighteen – Henry Settles In

Sally drew up to her house and switched off the car's engine. She sighed, stared at the lounge's bay window then looked at Henry via the rear view mirror. "I still can't get used to it."

Without explanation, Henry wanted to ask what it was she couldn't get used to then one of the pictures of the family – of Sally, her husband and daughter – flashed into his head. "I know," he wanted to say. He still couldn't get used to not being with Carmen, not being with Gwynne. Mick he could certainly live without.

Henry liked Dr Moss but it wasn't the same. He was a woman's dog – most male dogs were, he knew that – and wanted to settle somewhere. He'd felt settled at Carmen's but not at the lab despite all the home comforts he'd been given. A dog only needed four walls but ones that came in a house not a laboratory or shop. He wanted a house, a 'home' as Sally called it. Sally was looking at the house again so Henry followed her gaze.

Sally turned to Henry and laughed. "Home is what you make it, isn't it, Harry, and if it's only yours for a couple of weeks… a couple of days perhaps… then we'll make it the best one we can. We'll have lots of fun. What do you think about that?"

He wanted to tell her that he couldn't think of anything better. Spend all his time with her – awake at the shop and in the house, asleep on her bed, he didn't care where. It would be better than with Carmen, no Mick to order them about. Sure, there were rules, there would always be rules, but just him and Sally… or him, Sally and Rob. Maybe they'd have another daughter so they could have new photos to add to the original ones. But in the latest photos there would be four of them: wife / mother, husband / father, child…. and dog. A whole unit – one that included Henry. His family. Not Billy's family. A proper family.

"Okay. Enough maudlin dawdling. Let's go get some food."

Henry liked that phrase 'maudlin dawdling'. He didn't know what it meant but he liked the sound, so barked and sprang towards the house as Sally unclipped the lead, locked the car then unlocked the front door to twelve Landside Close.

Sally burped as she patted her stomach. Henry looked at her plate. There was still some pasta and bolognaise sauce uneaten and Henry guessed by the burp – he knew ladies didn't belch, only men did that… men like Mick especially – that she'd finished. Henry looked from the plate to Sally, and widened his brown eyes.

Sally laughed. "I don't know if it's good for you. I know they put pasta and vegetables in tins of dog food these days and the bolognaise sauce is meat but…"

For extra measure, Henry tilted his head, something that had always worked in the past.

"Oh, okay." Sally took the plate into the kitchen and with the fork, scraped it into Henry's left-hand bowl – one of a set of two stainless steel ones Sally had brought down from a cupboard, as if they were always something she had to hand. She retrieved the squeaky ball and tug rope from the 'PetCare' carrier bag and put them on the floor. The toys implied games they'd play; someone would have to throw the ball – which Henry, although not really into servitude, would bring back – he knew how that game was supposed to work – and he couldn't tug the rope by himself. He'd watched some old episodes of *It's a Knockout* on the Challenge channel and always sniggered when one of the teams cascaded onto the muddy field like dominoes.

He hadn't thought they'd put much effort into it and although he'd never really been the competitive type – it rarely made for an easier life – he'd give Sally a run for her money (although why would he need to, he couldn't spend it?) to make her feel that it had been worth buying the toy. Henry had his favourite already – the alligator – but would make sure he'd use everything to show his appreciation. He hoped that whatever happened, that would go with him.

He looked up at the stainless steel clock – the kitchen reminded him of the lab and he wanted to cry but knew that would only confuse Sally – so coughed instead.

"Oh no," Sally said, crouching beside Henry. "Are you okay? Is it too spicy? It shouldn't be. I never have things too spicy. Andy used to like a bit of a kick but I preferred…." Sally sniffed and stood, walking over to a box of tissues.

What she'd said surprised Henry and he squinted, trying to work out why Andy used to like Sally kicking him. Mick had kicked Henry numerous times and there was nothing pleasant about it. Henry wanted to rub his side where Mick had aimed most for, but Henry finished the pasta instead.

He looked up at Sally as she dabbed at her eyes then blew her nose. Henry screwed his up. Even if he could blow his nose, he wouldn't want to with a damp bit of paper. Like Dr Moss – and despite their age differences – Henry was old school and preferred a proper handkerchief. You couldn't beat linen… like the air-force-blue overalls Kerry wore with 'MacDonnell DIY' on them in silver lettering. Henry had thought it classy when he'd first seen it. Most places went for gold but Henry thought that cheap. White gold was okay. A ring Carmen wore on the middle finger of her right hand, something Mick had bought her for Christmas, was supposed to be white gold but Henry had his doubts.

Henry then thought he did a lot of thinking. A lot of head tilting too, but then it helped keep his neck in shape, although he wondered whether tilting it too much one side would make it a weird shape. He didn't get as much exercise as he would have liked – although the running he'd done when he'd escaped from Billy's had been more than plenty at the time. Perhaps when Sally trusted him, Henry, they'd go exploring, off lead. Henry looked Sally up and down. She looked fit, not in the Mick meaning of fit – he'd been only too glad to tell Carmen which female celebrities he thought 'fit' – but Sally didn't look overweight in the least.

Unlike Carmen who sat in front of the TV and ate biscuits most of the day then ate very little when Mick was around, much smaller portions of the food she cooked for them both. Henry hoped Carmen was getting plenty of good food in prison.

He didn't suppose she'd be able to watch as much television or eat as many biscuits but she'd done nothing wrong so she wouldn't be there long. Would she come looking for him or just move back into the house and start again? A new boyfriend, a new dog. A new life without Henry while Henry had a new life with Sally.

Henry followed Sally upstairs, the tissue tossed into the bin on the way out of the kitchen. *At least she won't need that again*, Henry thought as he bounded up the stairs after her.

Sally opened an airing cupboard, lifting up a few different sheets, duvet covers, and pillowcases. She shook her head then dropped a pile of linens on the floor between her and Henry. "Ah ha!" Sally exclaimed then tugged out a big shiny white bullet-shaped package and dropped that on the floor the other side of her. Henry peered behind her legs but couldn't really see what it was. Sally bent down, picked up the linens and placed them neatly back on the shelf. She then pulled out a colourful piece of material from a higher shelf before closing the airing cupboard door and taking the package and material downstairs.

Sally spread everything out on the sofa, leaving no room for Henry. He'd not jumped up there anyway without being invited and this time, the invitation didn't come. He wondered what he'd done wrong but then realised when Sally pulled the white fluffy object out from the package what she had planned.

Henry bolted as the duvet exploded from its packaging.

Sally laughed. "Sorry, boy, I should have warned you."

Henry looked from the duvet to the empty packaging and back again. He looked from one to the other a couple more times until he felt like he was watching a tennis match. Andy Murray playing Federer or Djokovic, except this time Andy would win. Henry wasn't Scottish – he was as English as Sally – but he believed in the United Kingdom and Scotland was England as far as Henry was concerned – and vice versa of course.

He'd never been outside England, probably not outside the

county but he'd seen plenty of the world on TV and Scotland looked beautiful, just like Wales or Ireland – the emerald isle – as Carmen's Irish next door neighbour, Paddy, had described it. That had made Henry want to visit it all the more, thinking of an island full of jewels, like a treasure trove in a pirate movie, but he couldn't see that happening.

Henry watched Sally as she reshaped the duvet into a fairly flat oval, covered it with the patterned material – which he could see had balloons on it, each one with a grinning face. He smiled, then realised what he was doing so looked up at Sally to see if she'd spotted him but she was pulling a weird face, her lips over to one side, tongue stuck out of the opposite side of her mouth, deep in concentration as she folded and sewed, folded and sewed.

Twenty minutes later – according to the purple clock on the white ornate mantelpiece – and Sally was finished. She smiled as she looked at her handiwork. "Mmm, not bad. A bit lopsided but..."

Like your face was earlier, Henry wanted to say, but didn't. It was too early to talk to her – he'd leave it until the two weeks were up and if she got to keep him, he'd share his secret with her then, when it was too late for her to change her mind.

He looked over at the balloon bed. It was obvious, now that it was on the floor, next to a neat box containing all his toys – and some rawhide chews she'd added, including, to his delight, some shoes with laces (he'd ravage those when she wasn't looking) – that it was meant for him. He was pleased there were no dogs to keep him company – he only wanted it to be him and Sally... until she married Rob anyway. Balloons scared him – they popped too easily – but he knew these weren't real ones and couldn't do him any harm. Unless they chased him in his sleep. He knew he was rubbish at distinguishing between being awake and asleep – him being dognapped had proven that.

"Do you want to try it?" Sally asked.

Henry looked at her, the bed, then at her again. He crept towards the bed then stopped.

"It's okay," Sally assured him. "It won't bite."

Henry looked at the alligator in the box beside the bed with all those two-dimensional balloons and imagined them getting together. There wouldn't be any balloons left if the alligator had its way.

Brave, Henry thought, *be brave. You're the man of the house now. Sally needs you.* He wasn't sure if that was strictly true because she'd certainly managed the business on her own... with Kerry, he corrected himself... but at home it seemed a different matter. Henry couldn't understand why she kept the photographs around the house if all they did was upset her but then he'd never understand how humans thought. It took enough of his time thinking his own thoughts without thinking for them too. He wished he had a picture of Gwynne, of Carmen, even of Dr Moss.

Usually, Henry felt grown up, far beyond the human years he was supposed to be, but there were times when he felt like a 'toddler' as Carmen had described him when she'd learned what the word had meant and had explained it to him. Separately, the balloons didn't frighten him but put them next to a vicious reptile, as Sally had done...

Henry looked back at Sally. She smiled and nodded. Henry returned to face the bed, straightened his legs, lifted his chin and leapt at the bed, landing in a rather awkward and painful heap. He could hear Sally laughing behind him, but then stop as he didn't move. She rushed over to him, and knelt down beside him, her eyes looking at his. "You okay?"

Henry felt like the child he was. Foolish. Young. Silly. Foolish. He wriggled round until he was comfortable and nestled into the bed. It certainly did feel comfortable. "Comfy" as Gwynne had asked him as she did the same to Henry's dog bed. Lots of dogs. Dogs bed. Lots of dogs bed.

Henry looked down at the balloons. He'd not counted them before he'd done his long jump lunge but none of them looked burst. He'd not heard any popping sounds. He turned over to face the box. The alligator was still in the same position.

Henry hadn't nudged the box so everything was as it had

been, only the bed had altered its shape, had altered without any choice. That was right. Henry had changed its shape, he was the boss. *And don't you forget it*, he told the bed, or tried to via telepathy but he knew balloons weren't telepathic, nor were squeaky alligators or humans... not the ones Henry had met so far anyway.

Chapter Nineteen – Time Goes So Quickly

Henry loved listening to the conversations that took place in the shop. Over the next few days he'd learned about all the things you could do to a house without actually doing them. Sometimes the names of the tools meant nothing to him unless they were used in context but really, he just loved hearing people talk.

Carmen had the television on whether Mick was there or not, although the programmes were usually different when he was, and at the lab, Gwynne used to talk to Henry – before and after he could talk back – or she'd be on the phone chatting with someone but it revolved around work, and him, so wasn't actually all that interesting.

Here he'd hear different voices, imagine what the people who owned them looked like. Sometimes the door to the staffroom would be open enough to see through to the shop but more often than not he'd only see ankles and could only really tell from those, and the voices, whether the people were male or female, young or old.

The evenings had been a mixture of watching TV, with a variety of food, not just Italian, and being left alone. Sally didn't go out much but the phone had rung a couple of times leading to a date with girlfriends and one with Rob. Sally had almost been a different person when she'd come off the phone with him. Henry wasn't sure who she had turned into but she'd been a happier version of herself once the initial excitement had worn off.

The excitement had peaked again up to the date, and she'd still been on a high when she'd come back on the Tuesday night, a week and a day after Henry had caught Sally closing her shop. In a way it had seemed longer, so much had happened, but it also felt like it had gone by really quickly. They'd had such fun, and Sally was trusting Henry more each day – from not needing the lead going from the house to the car to letting him off from the car to the cordoned-off dog area at their local park – which had brought back sad memories of

Carmen. Another week and they wouldn't need the lead at all.

Unlike dogs on the TV, Henry didn't chase cats. He only chased inanimate objects: sticks, the ball, anything that would be thrown for him and no human would throw him a cat. Henry lay on the bed – which, like him, was also transferred from the house to the shop and back again at night – and thought of the toy cat with the missing ear. If it were possible for Henry to cry, he would have done.

Then the thought struck him that he'd never tried. He'd been sad plenty of times but tears had never come. Would it be possible? He didn't try now – he wasn't really that sad – staying at Sally's, or the shop, beat the cold lonely lab every time – so he'd hope he'd never feel sad again but it would be interesting to know if he could cry… considering he could do much more than talk.

Chapter Twenty – Spotted

It had been a quiet Wednesday and Kerry had grabbed the keys to shut the shop when the doorbell went. Sally was busy filling up a shelf of light bulbs so Kerry served the customer. Henry knew the voice as soon as it spoke. He sat up and listened.

"Hello. Oh, sorry. Are you closing? I'll be very quick."

Kerry smiled. "No problem at all. Take your time."

Henry stared at the door separating the staffroom and shop, seeing only a shadow through the frosted glass. The man looked the right height.

"I'm only after a light pull. My wife would like something pretty but practical, if you have it. It's for our bathroom so nothing too heavy because it's all tiled and Irene does hate it when it clonks against the ceramic."

Irene. Yes. There was no doubt about it.

"I suppose a plastic pull but they can look ugly."

"We don't have much of a choice, I'm afraid. Mostly plastic so I'm not sure we can stretch to pretty."

Dr Moss laughed and followed Kerry to the electrical section.

They returned a few seconds later and Dr Moss paid the £1.79 for the plain white, quite unattractive light pull.

"Sorry we don't have a better range. It's the room really, although they're only small, but we don't get asked for them very often."

"It's fine. It's better than the one we've got already. It's porcelain – nice looking – but it makes a terrible racket and I'm so careless in the middle of the night. Fortunately she's a sound sleeper most of the time but I do wake her up sometimes."

Kerry smiled and went to give Dr Moss his twenty-one pence change.

"Put it in the box," he said, pointing to a children's charity collection tin.

"Thank you," Kerry replied and deposited the coins as Dr Moss went to leave.

Sally finished stacking the light bulbs and took the empty cardboard box into the staff area which led off to the storeroom, pushing the staffroom door open as she went.

"Oh, there was something else," Dr Moss said, turning to the counter. It was then he spotted the dog sitting on a homemade bed. He hesitated and looked back at Kerry.

"Yes?" she asked.

"My wife also said we needed…" He trailed off as he returned to look at Henry. Henry was staring back at him. "My wife also asked me to get a light for the utility room. It's one of those strip things. A two-foot one. It's flickering. Sorry. I should have said when we were getting the light pull."

Kerry smiled. "No problem. I'll–"

"That dog."

Dr Moss pointed to Henry who was in a quandary. *Should I recognise him or not? Bark? Wag my tail? Pretend I've never seen him before?*

Kerry turned to Henry. "Harry?"

"Harry? Is that his name?"

"I don't know but it's what we've been calling him."

"You don't know? You've, er… you've not had him long?"

"A week. Sally found him… sort of found him; he was waiting for her on the doorstep." Kerry pointed to the front door. "Last Tuesday… no, Monday night."

"Waiting for her?"

"I don't think waiting for her exactly, but he was there when she shut up the shop. I'd already gone so I met him when she brought him in the next morning. Why? You know him?"

"I think so. Can I come through?"

"I'll get Sally."

Dr Moss waited at the counter, still in a staring competition with Henry while Kerry went to the storeroom to get Sally.

"You okay?" Dr Moss mouthed to Henry.

Henry nodded.

"Harry?"

Henry shrugged.

Sally came through with Kerry. "Hello."

"Hello. Sorry to trouble you but I think I know your dog."

"Oh."

Dr Moss thought he spotted tears in Sally's eyes. "I might be wrong," he said, knowing he wasn't but still debating whether this was the best thing for Henry. To go back to FMRS, back into a cage, when he clearly looked happy and well cared for.

"He had no collar and his chip didn't work."

"You had it tested, the chip?"

"Of course," Sally said defensively but then softened. "I'm sorry. Yes. I took him to one of the local rescue centres – PetCare – do you know it?"

"Heard of it but don't know it, no."

"They tested the chip but it didn't work. They said he could stay with me until, unless… How do you know him?"

"He, er, belongs to a colleague."

"A colleague? Where do you work?"

"Erm…" Dr Moss looked at Henry then back at Sally. "A pharmaceutical company at the back of the industrial estate. He's our office mascot. Everyone loves him."

"I'd need proof. Does she have photographs?"

Dr Moss nodded. "We do. She does. He has a distinctive mark on his right side, like a heart, and… He's been here just a week? Since Tuesday?"

"Monday night." Sally wasn't sure she was ready to let him go. As the days had gone on, with no phone call from Rob other than socially, she'd become more convinced that the two weeks were going to pass and she'd get to keep Harry, officially, for ever. She'd come to need him as much as he needed her. She looked round at the dog. "What's his name? His real name?"

"Henry."

Sally laughed. "So we weren't far off."

"No." Dr Moss mouthed Henry a 'sorry'. He wished he didn't have to do this, that he could just walk out the shop and never come back, go to the out-of-town DIY supermarket in future, but it was done. He knew Sir Alfred would make his life hell until they'd retrieved Henry. He was too precious, dangerous, a commodity to have on the loose.

The good thing, or so it appeared, was that Sally didn't know he could talk. Could he still talk? The reactions were there so Dr Moss hoped he could or all their hard work would be undone. "I can bring in some photographs tomorrow. I quite understand that you don't want to let him go until you're sure I'm telling the truth. Could I see him now, just so I know one hundred percent?"

Sally stepped back so Dr Moss could come behind the counter.

As he approached Henry, Dr Moss crouched down. "Hello, Henry."

Henry wagged his tail.

"He's pleased to see him," Kerry whispered to Sally.

"He does that with everyone. He's been tied up since lunchtime."

"Are you okay?" Dr Moss asked Henry.

Henry looked at Sally then barked.

Sally sniffed and pulled a tissue from her jeans pocket. "Getting a cold," she said to Kerry who nodded sympathetically.

"I'd feel the same," she said.

Dr Moss looked at Henry's right side and nodded. "I'm afraid it's definitely him."

"And this colleague of yours," Sally said, shoving the tissue back into her pocket. "She treats Henry well?"

Dr Moss turned. "Yes, she does."

"He seems to love being around people."

"She brings him to work and gets lots of fuss, from us and the customers."

Dr Moss neglected to mention that Henry was in a cage all day and abandoned at night. It was no life for a dog and the doctor still contemplated lying, saying it wasn't him after all, but he didn't want to lose his job. He knew at his age it was unlikely that he'd get another, and he was respected.

They did good work, and Henry had allowed that to happen. They needed him. But, he thought, from now on they'd treat him better. No cage, or at least more breaks out of it, no solitude at night. He'd come home with him or go to Gwynne's, if she didn't mind. They did get on well. They did seem happy together.

"That's good," Sally said. "So you'll bring photographs in tomorrow."

"I could get them tonight and–"

"Tomorrow is fine. He'll be here. We're open nine to half five. Come anytime between then." Sally wanted to tell him to wait a week, so the two weeks was up but she knew it didn't work like that. The man had seen him after a week. Too early.

"Thank you." Dr Moss stood and looked at Sally. "I know how hard this must be for you. If it's any consolation, we've all been so worried about him."

"All? Your colleague has family?"

"Just a boyfriend. They live together. I meant me, our other colleagues. Henry's become part of the furniture, in a nice way. It's really not been the same without him."

Sally looked at Henry who was looking at her, ears down. "And it won't be here. I'll have to phone the rescue centre. They may want proof."

"Of course," Dr Moss said. "I'm sorry… I really am."

She nodded. "Thank you." She knew it would be hard without Harry… Henry, but it had made her appreciate how lonely she'd been. She'd go back to PetCare, have a look at their other dogs. They must have plenty, judging by the noise they'd made when she'd driven into the gravelled car park.

She wondered whether they'd done that on purpose, gone for gravel instead of tarmac so the animals would hear and anyone visiting would feel obliged to take something home with them. She'd get another small dog, no bigger than Harry… Henry. She couldn't get 'Harry' out of her head.

She could call the next one Harry but then she'd have a constant reminder of the companion who'd got away. Of course the man could be lying but he'd mentioned the heart-shaped mark on Henry's side before he'd seen it.

"Until tomorrow then."

Sally nodded and gave him a weak smile.

After selling Dr Moss a two-foot replacement light, Kerry showed him out, and locked the front door.

"Shit," she said as she walked through to the back.

"I know," Sally said, removing the money from the till, and counting it.

"It won't be the same around here."

"It'll be fine," Sally lied. "We were without him a week ago so it'll just go back to that."

"But… no, you're right. It'll be fine. He's been getting in the way anyway."

"Kerry!" Sally snapped as Henry put his ears down.

Kerry leant over to Henry and stroked his head. "Sorry, mate. Didn't mean it. Just said it so we'd feel better but we won't. It's been great. Really going to miss you."

Henry whined, making Sally burst into tears and dash to the toilet.

Henry wished that Sally hadn't come in when she had, hadn't pushed the door so hard, that he'd not recognised Dr Moss's voice, that it had all happened in another few days, when it was too late, when Henry was officially hers, but 'que sera sera' as the song went.

He was trying to remember who had sung it. Edith Piaf? No, that was *Je ne regrette rien*. Not even the same language. It was from a film. What was it? He couldn't remember but pictured the actress sitting at the piano singing it. Who her? Blonde. In a western as… *Annie Get Your Gun*. Doris Day. Ooh yes. With the man who imagined the rabbit? Henry knew it wasn't but giggled then quickly turned it into a sneeze. It wouldn't do any good now for Sally to find out the real him.

No, he just had to wait another few hours, twenty-four at most, then he could natter to his heart's content. He'd been worried he'd talk in his sleep but Gwynne had said all she'd witnessed was kicking of legs and whimpering. Sally certainly would have said something if he'd had.

He'd grown to like Kerry, despite her weird singing and funny laugh. She and Sally were like daughter and mother. No, more like younger sister, older sister. They looked out for each other. They spent little time together outside of work; Kerry had only come over one evening during Henry's time there and they'd talked mostly about work, both passionate about the business that Sally had bought with her husband, almost abandoned when he and her daughter, Joanna, had died.

Henry still hadn't found out how that had happened but he knew what effect it had had on Sally ever since. He'd seen hope in her eyes when she'd met Rob so perhaps Henry going back to FMRS would be a good thing for her.

He'd helped her, albeit just for a week and now she was ready to return to the rescue centre, to Rob, to get another dog, one who didn't talk, who wouldn't act like a counsellor whenever she felt like sharing. No, this was definitely going to work out for the best. So why was he so unhappy?

They had a longer walk that evening, with the lead shorter than normal, as if Sally didn't want him to go any further away than absolutely necessary. They were both quiet, Sally hardly saying a word, Henry reluctant to wag his tail or bark for fear of upsetting her.

"We can't spend the evening moping," Sally said as she let them back into the house. "We're not going to have a party but we should be happy."

Henry looked up at her as she took off his lead.

"And you can stop looking at me like that."

Henry stared at the floor, ears down.

"Sorry, Har… oh damn it, Henry. I keep forgetting. It's just your big eyes, they look so sad. If I didn't know any better… You are happy going home, aren't you?"

Henry looked back up at her at wagged his tail nonchalantly.

"What am I supposed to deduce from that?"

He wagged his tail a little faster.

"That's better. Now, let's get some supper. As it's the last…

As a treat, I'm going to make yours first while mine's cooking. That makes sense anyway. Hang the rules."

Henry wagged his tail more enthusiastically as he watched her tip out his food.

Sally looked at the bowl.

Henry barked.

"Wait a minute. Don't be so impatient."

Henry barked again, making Sally laugh.

"Tomorrow's going to be horrible. Maybe I can come and visit you sometimes?"

Henry wanted to say, "Yes, it'll be awful. No, don't come and visit, you won't want to see me in a cage. Go back to the rescue centre and get another dog. Do it as soon as I've gone," – like getting back on a horse when it's bucked you off… although Henry could never understand that logic. There was also a saying about ripping off a plaster but that looked painful too, so he just wagged his tail. He stopped when Sally continued talking.

"No, probably not a good idea. We'll just move on. Be happy." Her smile didn't convince Henry one bit but he'd heard that time was a healer, although he'd never seen anyone helped with a clock or watch – Sally still seemed sad about her family despite having several clocks around the house and a red watch with tiny black dogs all over it on her left wrist – but he knew humans were complicated creatures, far more than dogs.

He'd eaten his dinner long before the cooker pinged. When Sally took out the dish, Henry approached it, sniffing.

Sally pulled it back. "Careful, it's hot."

Henry pulled back too.

"Beef lasagne. Too much for one but I always make plenty, force of habit. So I have some and freeze the rest, which I can't do with this because it's meat and you're not supposed to refreeze meat so I'll put it in the fridge and have it three nights in a row. I don't mind. It's comfort food and right now, I need serious comforting."

Henry nudged her leg and Sally smiled. She was determined not to get maudlin. This was their last night together and she didn't want him to feel sad, and remember her like that, if he did remember things.

She didn't know much about dogs, they'd never had them growing up, her parents were cat lovers, but she was sure they had good memories. She'd seen some dogs cower at swearing, Henry hadn't but then she'd never sworn and couldn't remember there being any on the television programmes they'd watched together.

Sally put the dish onto the heatproof work surface and cut the lasagne into three: two large portions and a smaller portion. "I know, it's silly; two adult servings and a child's. I have the first two pieces the first two nights, then the third on night three. As you know, I have sandwiches for lunch because we're usually so busy, so I like a hot evening meal. I just have to pad it out with something else on night three, either that or find I'm a bit bored with it by then so I'm happier to have a smaller bit… although I'd never get bored with lasagne."

Henry wanted to tell her that he felt the same but couldn't ever remember having any of it. He knew what it was but no one had ever made him any. He hoped that it would be different tonight – a little, cooled down in his bowl. It smelled so lovely.

Sally spooned one of the larger portions onto a plate, alongside some salad, a couple of slices of lightly buttered granary bread and a solitary fork. Covering the dish with cellophane, she left it on the side to cool. She put the plate, and a large glass of white wine, on a tray and Henry followed her into the lounge.

Putting the tray down on the glass-topped coffee table, she switched on the television and skimmed through some of the programmes. Henry had little time to take in each programme before Sally clicked onto another. She finally settled on one about building an ecological house deep in a wood, then started eating her lasagne.

"Andy and I were going to do this," Sally told Henry, pointing at the screen. "We were going to build a house in the middle of nowhere. Took us months to find the right spot. Not here, but not far away. Then Joanna came along, by surprise, although we had been trying, and we put it on hold. Then Joanna got sick and we started running out of money. After she died, we were going to build the house again – we'd done all the research – but we couldn't get planning permission. We hadn't bought the plot, which was just as well, but we made enquiries.

"There was no road leading to it, and of course we couldn't afford to make one, and the council wouldn't, so there was no hope even if they'd given us permission, which in our heart of hearts, we knew they wouldn't, which is why we didn't buy it. Don't know why the owner was even selling it really. They must have thought someone would be mad enough to keep it as woods, because it was pretty… and it really was pretty. And quiet. That's what I love about it here; it's so quiet. Then Andy spotted the DIY shop for sale, and by that stage we knew so much about doing up houses we thought it was something we could handle."

Henry wanted to smile at the thought of Andy the 'andyman but kept his amusement to himself.

Sally ate another forkful of lasagne, and washed it down with a swig of wine.

"Then one day, I was home, cooking dinner… shepherd's pie."

Henry tried to picture a pie full of shepherds and wondered how Sally had fitted one in let alone two or more. He wanted to frown but decided against it in case she misunderstood.

"I've not made it since. I was home cooking dinner. Had made it, dished it up. Andy had rung saying he was leaving so I knew he wouldn't be long. But it got later and later. The dinner was gone and going cold. I tried his mobile but there was no reply. I knew he wouldn't answer it on the way home, couldn't, he rode a motorbike, but I kept leaving messages, thought he'd got it on silent and was distracted, but then someone else answered it: a woman. I was about to have a go at her, ask her why she was with my husband but she was hysterical. I knew something was terribly wrong. I knew that really before she answered. He'd never go off with someone else. There's always the possibility, but..."

She caught her breath, took another forkful of lasagne, and another mouthful of wine.

"She was the driver. She'd pulled out, not looking properly, and hit him. He'd been doing less than the speed limit, he always did, but it doesn't take much, does it. I know I drive quickly but I'm always super careful at junctions. Kerry says it drives her nuts, not that she's a passenger very often but sometimes she just doesn't think."

Sally muted the television but kept watching it, despite talking to Henry. "It went to trial. She was prosecuted. Death by careless driving. Banned for seven years. I was really angry but I didn't want her to go to jail. She had... has a son. It's going to be hard enough for her to do everything she needs to do with no licence. They're quite wealthy, they own one of the factories on the industrial estate, so she can afford taxis, probably even a chauffeur, but even so. They live in the middle of nowhere too, in one of the villages the other side of the estate, so you need your car."

Sally looked down at Henry who was giving her his undivided attention. "I'm sorry, Henry. I don't know why I'm telling you all this." She laughed. "But you're a very good listener."

She chased the last piece of lasagne round the plate then stabbed it and put it up to her mouth, with her left hand underneath the fork in case the lasagne disintegrated. She then started on the salad. "I know, Henry. It doesn't make sense. I should take turns: lasagne, salad, lasagne, but I always eat the best stuff first. I only have the salad because it makes me feel like I'm being healthy."

Henry thought she looked quite healthy anyway. She'd never sounded out of breath when she went up the stairs, sometimes jogging up, she'd lift pots of paint and move other goods around as nimbly as Kerry did. Mick had got out of breath getting off the sofa.

After taking the tray out to the kitchen and refilling the wine glass, Sally settled back on the sofa. Henry was about to rest his chin on her knee when Sally got up again. She looked down at Henry and said, "Let's treat ourselves, shall we."

Henry would have nodded if it wouldn't have given away that he'd understood, so he just wagged his tail.

He followed her out to the kitchen and watched her dispense some chocolate-looking ice cream into a small clear bowl. Henry licked his lips. "Sorry, mate, this isn't good for you. I'd let you lick the bowl but don't want you getting into bad habits. Can't let your mistress blame me for leading you astray, can we?"

Henry tried to watch the television while Sally ate the ice cream but he'd look over at her occasionally and she'd spot him each time and laugh. Why couldn't he stay? Why couldn't Dr Moss say he was wrong? Bring different photographs with him and apologise. He'd know he'd done the right thing and... it wasn't the right thing, Henry knew.

He belonged to FMRS and he had to return to them. It wasn't that bad. But it wasn't Sally's. It wasn't chocolate ice cream and lasagne. It could be. *I am your prized possession, am I not? Yes.* They'd be so pleased to have him back that he could have whatever he wanted. He'd get a bigger cage, not that the other one had been small...

Neither of them slept well that night. Every time Sally moved, she woke Henry, not that he'd really been asleep, just eyes closed, pretending to count sheep. He couldn't understand why that would send people to sleep; sheep had to be one of the most boring creatures on earth.

That and koala (because they sleep twenty-three hours a day, although Henry had to admit that had its appeal). People thought tortoises were boring but they fascinated Henry and he'd always thought he'd love to meet one because they were so old and wise. They'd know everything about everything and be able to teach him far more than television ever could.

Henry felt like a zombie the following morning, not a good look to be going back to FMRS with, but after a hearty breakfast (including warm bacon – Henry couldn't believe his luck!) he felt much better… still desperately sad at leaving Sally, but at least back to something he knew, stability… until he was stolen again.

Don't be so pessimistic, Henry. They'll have tightened their security and put a guard on the door at all times. I'm worth a fortune. They wouldn't be so stupid to let him get away again… would they?

Chapter Twenty-One – Reunited

Every time the shop's doorbell went, Henry's heart hammered. Sally's did likewise but he wasn't to know that. She still smiled at all the customers, laughed at Kerry's jokes. Henry began to think Sally was happy that he was going, until he heard the sadness in her voice when Dr Moss returned.

"Hello, Sally."

"Hello, Dr Moss."

"I have the photographs and receipt from the rescue centre – the original centre, not PetCare, although he had a different name then. Henry did."

Sally looked at the paperwork. "Tim?" She pushed the staffroom door open and looked at Henry. "I can see why you changed his name. He's not a Tim at all."

Dr Moss opened the pack of photographs.

"I didn't need to see them," Sally said.

"But..."

"I asked for them to be sure but I knew. I saw the way you looked at him. I think maybe he felt disloyal to both of us, that's why he's been subdued since you came in."

"I'm sorry."

"No, I'm sorry. I should have trusted you, although the rescue centre – the one I went to – would have wanted some proof, I guess."

"Of course. What did they say?"

"They're fine... as long as I'm sure, they said. He's not stayed with them so they're not as strict as they would, could have been."

"That's good of them."

"I'll make a donation."

"I will too," Dr Moss blurted out. "I mean, we will. I know Gwynne–"

"Gwynne. Is that his mum?"

At the mention of her name, Henry barked.

"That's all the proof I need," Sally said, pushing the packet of photos back across the counter.

"Thank you." Dr Moss watched Sally go to the back room, unclip Henry from his lead then pick up the homemade bed and a bag of his toys. One squeaked as she lifted the bag.

"Can I help?" Dr Moss asked, moving round the side of the counter.

"Thanks, but it's okay."

Dr Moss nodded. "What will you do now?"

"What do you mean?"

"Will you get another dog? It's none of my business, of course."

Henry thought Sally looked guilty so he wagged his tail to reassure her. "Probably, yes," she said. "But not straight away." Henry barked agreement.

"Then keep the stuff."

Henry's heart sank and the thought of not being able to say goodbye to the alligator but he knew he had to be charitable and let his replacement have it.

Sally looked back at the doctor. "Are you sure?"

"Of course. You bought it all. It's been so good of you. You've clearly been so kind to him."

"We have had fun. Is he...?"

"Go on."

"Is he happy with Gwynne?"

Dr Moss looked at Henry. "I think so. I hope so. Seemed to be. I know she's been in pieces since he went missing."

Henry imagined Gwynne in pieces, her shattering like glass as she dropped to the lab floor.

"About his toys..." Dr Moss hesitated.

Sally looked at the bag then back at Dr Moss.

"I know I said to keep them but..." he hesitated, "and there's a whole load of new toys at the l... office, so feel free to say 'no', but would it be okay if he kept one of those?"

There is? Henry looked up at Sally and barked. *The alligator, please give me the alligator.*

"Sure."

"Which one would you like then, boy?" She put her hand into the bag and pulled out the bear. Henry wanted to shake his head but dipped it instead, but then realised that had resembled a nod.

"Not that one, then. So the... alligator?"

She swapped the bear for the alligator, and Henry barked and wagged his tail. "The alligator it is," Sally said, and handed it to Dr Moss who said nothing but smiled. "You'll need to do something about the chip in his leg. It didn't work at the rescue centre, and they tried several times."

"I will, thank you."

As Sally brought Henry through, Dr Moss pulled out a collar and lead from his overcoat pocket, swapped it for the collar Sally had bought and gave it back to her. "Thank you for everything. You don't know how much this means."

Sally smiled. "Yes, I do. If the same thing happened to me, I'd want him back. He's... he's very special. Take care of him."

Dr Moss nodded, smiled, then led Henry out the shop.

Henry watched Dr Moss strap him into his car. He looked down at the harness. "This is new."

Dr Moss blew out a long puff of air and grinned. "Oh, thank God for that."

"What?"

"You can still talk."

"Oh... yes." Henry copied Dr Moss's puff of air and grin. "Yay."

Dr Moss laughed and shut the passenger door. He then walked to the driver's door and got in. Watching Henry from the rear view mirror, the doctor looked serious. "I thought maybe..."

"What?"

"You haven't been talking to anyone, have you?" he asked, turning round to face the back.

"Of course not."

Dr Moss nodded, turned back to the front, and started the engine. "Good."

"And I'm telling you, it was torture! I couldn't even talk in my sleep. At least I don't think I did. No one said anything."

"Tell me what happened," Dr Moss said, pulling away from

the kerb.

"When?"

"Henry."

"Oh, the dognapping. Yeah, that was weird. Bit tired now though. Been an eventful morning. Can I just have forty winks?" Henry winked in rapid succession to prove the point, then laughed. "Oh, man. I've been wanting to do that since like forever."

"Henry."

"Yes?"

"What's happened to your English?"

Henry looked around him. "What do you mean? Where's it gone? Was I speaking Chinese or something?"

"No, it's just…"

"Just?"

"You've gone all common."

"Oooh…"

"I'm sorry. I shouldn't be telling you off."

"No, you shouldn't."

Dr Moss sighed. "We were so worried about you."

Henry's ears pricked up, eyes widened. "You were?"

"Of course."

"You said Gwynne was in pieces. Does that mean she was unhappy."

"Terribly. In pieces means very, very upset."

"Did you?"

"What?"

"Go looking for me?"

"Every evening."

"Really?"

"Yes, really. Gwynne's over the moon that I've found you."

"Over the moon. English is such a funny language." As Henry closed his eyes, he pictured Gwynne riding a cow as it jumped over the moon. He couldn't remember what the nursery rhyme was called but Gwynne was happy, as was the cow.

Dr Moss carried on talking until Henry snored. The doctor

smiled, turned left, and drove the twenty minutes to FMRS.

As they pulled up, Gwynne rushed over to the car and pulled open the passenger door. She gave Henry, who'd been asleep until then, the biggest hug, making him cough. Gwynne backed away, looking hurt.

"It's okay, Gwynne," Henry said. "Go for your life." He wasn't sure if it was possible to 'go for' until your life literally ended, but if she wanted to try then he wasn't going to complain. He loved cuddles. The word itself was his favourite… in English. The Spanish equivalent, abrazo, always felt hard, abrasive. He also liked the German 'schmusen'. That too sounded nice, although French was his second favourite, 'caresse'. He loved to be caressed.

"Oh Henry, it's been horrible without you. Awful."

Henry blinked and looked up at her. She looked terrible. Her eyes were all red and she looked odd without make-up, not that she normally wore loads but she looked older, much more than a few days.

"It's not been all that great for me."

"God. Are you okay?" She looked him over, brushing back some of his fur as if for signs of torture.

"Oh, no, not that bad. The first place was… just boring really." *This is my moment*, Henry thought. "Stuck in a cage hour after hour."

Gwynne looked at Dr Moss.

"There are going to be changes," Dr Moss said as Gwynne released Henry from the car.

Henry jumped down then looked back at the harness. "So I see."

"It's for your own safety. Gwynne has one in her car too."

Henry wrinkled his nose. "Huh? You got a dog, Gwynne?"

Gwynne laughed. "No, Dr Moss and I are going to alternate taking you home at night, stay over at the weekends."

"Really?"

"Yes," Dr Moss said, locking the car after Gwynne had closed the back door. "Really."

"Like a proper dog?"

"Yes, Henry." Gwynne patted him. "Like a proper dog. Like a pet."

Henry grinned again, showing all his teeth. There was a bit of bacon stuck between two of them but no one noticed, Gwynne and Dr Moss were too busy talking about how great it was to have him back. Henry didn't notice because he was too busy cocking his leg against one of Mr Wilson's prized roses.

Chapter Twenty-Two – Back Home

The lab looked the same, yet there was something different about it. Henry scanned the room, trying to work out what had changed. No cage, just the bed in its place – the bed with all the dogs running around. Strangely, Henry realised he'd missed them too.

"Erm…" He looked up at Gwynne.

"I know. The cage has gone. We have to trust you. We want to trust you."

"But what about burglars?"

Gwynne laughed. "We're not going to let that happen again."

"You're not?"

"No. As Dr Moss said…"

Henry looked back at the door. "Where is the doctor?"

"In his office, phoning Sir Alfred, Sir Walter, and anyone else who will listen."

"Anyone?"

"No, but the other members of the Board. You're still top secret, you know."

Henry rolled his head, blowing out air as he heard his neck click. "Bet they're pleased."

"Yes. I guess they are."

"You guess?"

"They've been breathing down Dr Moss's neck…"

Henry imagined someone breathing down his neck. He could do with that, especially if it was someone like Olivia. "Are they coming back?"

"Who?"

"The Board."

"I suppose so, at some stage. When there's some news to report, other than you being back, of course. That's big news." Gwynne held her palms apart, like a man relaying a story of a fish he'd caught.

"Uh huh."

"Dr Moss tells me you didn't speak to anyone the whole time you were away. He's very impressed."

"I had to keep everything in my brain and it's so full, I think it might burst." Henry was pretty sure that wasn't going to happen as long as he kept talking… but he didn't feel like doing that quite yet. There would be plenty of opportunities, he was sure, to talk later. "It's okay then if I just have the bed? The cage isn't coming back?"

Gwynne nodded. "Is that okay?"

"Sure." Henry didn't mean to sound so nonchalant but it had been an eventful few days. He'd said as much to the doctor when they'd got in his car. He'd slept badly the night before, and while he wanted to spend time with Gwynne, chatter with her until his brain emptied, including the list of things he wanted her to look up, he wanted to sleep more.

Things to look up. Firstly, there was Vic's English: the saying "you are" or its contraction "you're" forwards but not backwards, in a question. Secondly, how Polaroid cameras worked. Thirdly… he couldn't remember thirdly. He knew it wasn't the tool… the bolt cutters, so what? He shook his head to see if it would free up some of the thoughts going round his brain but it only made them crash into one another and give him the beginning of a headache.

He padded over to the bed, whispered a "hello" to his fellow canines, not waiting for, or of course expecting, a reply, then turned in a couple of circles until he knew the position and angle he wanted to sleep at, and plonked himself down.

Gwynne smiled as Henry rested his chin on his paws. She could sit and stare at him all day. The past few days had been awful, just as she'd told Henry… worse. It had been like losing a member of her family. Not like losing a child, she was sure, but there'd been a gaping hole, exacerbated by Dan's absence, lessened by his return, but there nonetheless.

She could easily understand how Sir Alfred had reacted to Henry's disappearance, although she knew it was more to do with money than any paternal feelings, but she couldn't understand why he'd been so unemotional, uncaring, about his imminent return.

She only had Dr Moss's report of the conversation but she was glad she'd not been the one making the call. She knew the doctor had been as stressed as her during those few days, more so as it was his reputation on the line, not just his job.

Henry had been asleep for less than half an hour when Dr Moss burst into the room.

"It's all good, Gwynne. Sir Alfred's happy, Sir Walter's happy. The Board is happy… that it's really him, and of course that he can still speak. Annoyed at the loss of the few days. 'Every minute costs us money, Moss'," Dr Moss mimicked. "But it's okay, everything's going to be okay."

Gwynne pointed to Henry. Dr Moss turned in his direction, in time to see him roll onto his side. "Oh, sweet. He's such a sweet dog."

"We still don't know what happened, Dr Moss. Do you think he'll tell us?"

"Of course. Why, don't you?"

"He might be traumatised."

Dr Moss laughed gently. "Henry? Traumatised? I don't think that's ever going to happen. He's such an easy-going dog. It's clearly done him no harm. The worst thing for him was having to keep shtum for so long. Bet you've not been able to shut him up."

Gwynne smiled. "He's hardly said anything, actually. I think it's all catching up with him. He won't stop when he wakes, that's for sure."

"Talking about me again?" Henry asked, opening one eye then the other.

"Thought you were asleep," Gwynne said, picking up his water bowl, emptying it into one side of the double steel sink and refilling it.

"Just having a few winks," Henry said, then winked.

Gwynne laughed but Dr Moss looked up to the ceiling.

"Yes, he's back," Dr Moss laughed and left the lab.

"I am!" Henry exclaimed, standing up. "And I'm hungry. What's on the menu?"

"Not sure." Gwynne picked up a printout showing the restaurant's selection for the week. "Choice of fish and chips or lasagne."

Henry's ears went flat at the mention of lasagne.

"You okay?"

Henry nodded.

"Henry?"

"Last night. Last supper."

"Eh?"

"Sally, the lady who found me, took me home and was there when Dr Moss saw me again. She cooked lasagne last night."

"Oh. Maybe not then. Fish and chips?"

Henry frowned. "What?"

"Would you like fish and chips?"

Henry looked past Gwynne then around the room. "Where's Gwynne, you imposter. What have you done with her?"

Gwynne laughed. "Nothing. I'm still here."

"I can have fish and chips?"

"Sure. A little. Fish without the batter, and one or two chips. Can't go too mad."

"Why?"

"Why what?"

"Why have you changed from giving me dried, boring food, with the exception of a couple of proper meat lunches and a very late steak-unlikely-to-ever-be-alligator breakfast?"

Gwynne shook her head. "A lot's happened in the past few days. We've…"

Henry pointed his nose to the floor but looked up at her with his eyes big and brown. "You've…"

"Okay. Don't get too big-headed, but we've come to appreciate you more."

"Thanks."

"We'll still make you earn your keep though."

"Earn my keep? What does that mean?"

"Pay board and lodging. Rent and food. Not with money, obviously, but in kind. Work for it."

"Oh, boy. Here it comes. Soften me up with all the new food, uncaged bed and tell me I have to work harder."

"Not harder. Promise. Although the Board wants to see results. I don't want to get all serious on you."

"No, it's okay. I know they've spent a lot of money on me, that you've all done so much to get me to be able to do this and I appreciate it, I do. I'll work hard."

"Thank you, Henry. I appreciate it too. We all do. It must have been tough for you, scary. Wasn't it frightening when they kid… dognapped you?"

"Not really."

"Really?"

"I was sort of asleep so I went along with it because I thought it wasn't happening."

"Oh."

Henry was about to continue when Gwynne raised her hand, stopping him. "Do you mind if I record this?" She held up a small digital dictaphone.

"Sure."

"Sure you mind or…"

"No. Don't mind."

"Sir Alfred said we've got to record everything. He wanted a video but Dr Moss said that would be too invasive. They compromised that I'd use a dictaphone, this, for our chats, then Dr Moss would use a camera for official interviews."

"Interviews." Henry sighed. That didn't sound like fun at all.

"Only short ones. Ten, fifteen minutes. I'm sorry, Henry. You're probably wondering why you came back."

"Erm…"

"Dr Moss told me how nice that lady was."

"Sally."

"Yes. She owns a DIY shop, doesn't she."

That was question number three! "Tell me, Gwynne. What does DIY stand for?"

"DIY? Do It Yourself."

"Only asking."

"No. It stands for Do It Yourself."

"What do you mean 'Do It Yourself'?"

"It's when you make repairs to your house yourself instead of asking an expert."

"Oh."

"Why?"

"Just wondered."

"Can we talk about your time away now?"

"Sure."

Gwynne got through two mugs of coffee and Henry a bowl of water in the three hours he took to retell the story. Three hours of minute detail. Enough for the dictaphone's battery light to come on.

"Thank you, Henry. You really didn't need to go into so much detail just for this." She held up the dictaphone. "You know Dr Moss is going to ask you to go through it all again."

Gwynne had also got through seventeen tissues as she laughed at the hilarious way Henry told the story and from the poignant moments.

While Gwynne was interviewing Henry, Dr Moss was typing up a report and emailing it to the Board. He knew Gwynne was going to be using the dictaphone but this was to be from his point of view, on the few days that Henry was missing up to finding him and getting him back in situ.

Gwynne, Henry and Dr Moss were exhausted.

"Why are they doing this, Gwynne?" Henry asked tucking into a well-earned plate of something meat related.

"What do you mean?"

"It must be costing them a fortune to do all this. Why?"

"I don't know. Research obviously, but I don't know exactly. You'd have to ask Dr Moss." Gwynne did know but also knew it wasn't her place to say, not the real reason why Sir Walter was spending millions on Henry and what it meant for people like his late wife and other Multiple Sclerosis suffers, to have a dog that could not only perform the tricks that guide dogs do but hold decent conversations, be a carer for them when humans weren't around.

Gwynne was finishing downloading the recording when Dr

Moss walked into the lab.

"Hi, Henry. How's it going?"

"Good, thank you. Bit of a sore throat from lots of talking but eased it with a bite to eat. How are you?"

Dr Moss laughed. "It's so good to have you back. And I'm well, thank you."

"Henry has a sore throat," Gwynne explained, "because he's dictated three hours' worth of his account of the last week."

"Wow."

"Wow indeed," Gwynne said, copying the files to their departmental shared drive. "It's on the G drive so you can access it. Henry dictate v.1."

"Lovely, thank you. We'll be asking you for more tomorrow. Did Gwynne explain?"

Henry nodded. "Video camera?"

"Is that okay?" Dr Moss asked.

"Sure."

"Great. We have a surprise for you."

Henry looked at Gwynne. "Really?"

Gwynne looked at Dr Moss, frowning, sort of knowing what the surprise was but needing clarification.

"You're going home with Gwynne tonight."

Henry wagged his tail, thumping it against one of the cupboard doors. "Really?"

"You are, Henry."

"And the surprise for both of you," Dr Moss continued, "is that you can go home now."

Gwynne looked at the clock. Four-thirty. A good hour earlier than she normally left, two when they were particularly busy. "Really?"

Dr Moss nodded. "Sure. You've both earned it."

Gwynne locked her computer screen, took her bag from the bottom desk drawer, sent Dan a quick text to let him know they were on their way, then retrieved the lead from the hook by the door.

Henry didn't need telling twice. He was there, sitting by her feet, panting and raring to go.

“Then tomorrow night,” Dr Moss said as he walked back to his office, the opposite way from the car park, “you get to come home with me.”

Chapter Twenty-Three – Meet The Osbournes

Gwynne clicked the harness onto Henry as he sat willingly on the back seat. "Ready?"

"Yep. Anything I should know about before we head off?"

"Like what?"

"Dan. You live with him, don't you?"

"I do." Gwynne got in and drove off.

"What's he like?"

"You know. We've talked about him before."

"No, I mean really like, not how he looks but as a person. What does he like, not like?"

"You mean, does he like dogs?"

"Yes, okay. Does he like dogs?"

"He'll love you."

"Because I'm cute and funny or because he likes dogs anyway? You didn't really answer my question."

"Sorry, trying to concentrate on the road," she said, almost overshooting a junction. "Yes, he likes dogs, although he had cats when he was younger so it's what he's used to. He's not allergic and he's a grown-up child so he'll play with you and your toys until you're both exhausted."

"Toys?" Henry didn't remember them putting any toys in the car and Dr Moss had the alligator he'd retrieved from Sally.

Gwynne laughed. "It's like Christmas at home. I bought some, Dan bought some. You'll be spoilt for choice."

"Sounds great. Just one other thing."

"Yes, Henry?"

"Does Dan know I can speak?"

Gwynne didn't reply.

"Gwynne?"

"Erm…"

"Let me guess. You weren't supposed to tell him but you accidently on purpose let slip."

"Please don't tell Dr Moss. I'll be sacked, or worse."

That made Henry ponder on what could be worse than losing a job? Could they kill her? He thought it highly unlikely but didn't press the matter. He'd only just got her back so didn't want to do anything to jeopardise that.

Gwynne pulled up outside her small detached house with 1930s bay windows. Unlike the houses either side of Gwynne's, hers still had the original red brick walls exposed. The house on its right was painted lemon, the one on the left pastel pink. It reminded Henry of the Battenberg cake Carmen used to like so much. She'd thought it was a traditional English cake because they served it at the Ritz – a fact courtesy of a television programme rather than actual experience.

The smell of cooking hit them as soon as they walked in the door. Like Sally's house, it was cosy and felt like home. Henry didn't feel the need so much to be good company with Gwynne. They knew each other already. He'd promised himself, Gwynne and Dr Moss, that he would behave, not be too cheeky, just amusing and speak when spoken to, which he assumed because it would certainly be a novelty for Dan, would be most of the evening.

Henry followed Gwynne into the kitchen and raised his head as he sniffed at the smells wafting around the room. It smelled a little like lasagne but it wasn't quite right.

Dan pointed to the oven. "I know it's early but I thought it would be a nice homecoming."

"It is, thank you, darling." Gwynne smiled and blew Dan a kiss.

"Pasta bake. Used up some bacon before it went off."

Henry wondered where the bacon would have gone off to if Dan hadn't used it but didn't ask.

Gwynne got on her tiptoes and kissed Dan on the lips. Henry wanted to giggle but thought best not to, not at least until he and Dan had got to know each other.

Dan looked at Henry. "So this is the boy wonder. He… llo Hen… ry," he said slowly and loudly, as if talking to a foreigner.

Henry looked at Gwynne.

"I didn't tell him enough, as you can see." Then she turned back to Dan. "Just speak normally. He's not retarded."

"I don't think that's PC anymore, Gwynne," Henry said. "I think you should say disabled or mentally challenged."

"Sorry, Henry. See, Dan?"

Dan was staring at Henry with his lower jaw dropped open. "He..."

Gwynne had to nudge Dan to move a couple of times as she laid the kitchen table.

Henry nodded. "Yes, Dan. I talk."

"He..." Dan repeated.

Gwynne dished up the dinner as Dan stared at Henry. "Treat him as you would another human being... or better. Say something to him."

"Do you watch the footie?"

Henry looked at Dan's feet, making Dan laugh. "You mean football?" Henry said looking back up again.

"Yeah. Do you follow it?"

"Not unless I have to. Who do you support?"

"West Ham."

Gwynne sighed. "Yes, I'm a football widow."

"Oh, Gwynne. I'm so sorry to hear that." Henry's face crinkled. "I didn't realise you'd been married before."

Gwynne laughed.

Henry looked up at Dan. "Her husband died and it's funny?"

Dan smiled sympathetically. "It's okay, Henry. Gwynne wasn't married. Her husband, that she didn't have, didn't die."

Henry frowned, trying to work that out.

"A football widow means someone, usually a woman, whose partner – husband or boyfriend – spends too much time watching football or at matches so she never sees him."

Gwynne put her and Dan's dinners on two mats on the table. He'd poured some red wine and they sat down. "There's a little left for you, Henry, but you have to wait for it to cool."

"It's okay," he said. "I should have mine afterwards anyway."

Gwynne frowned. "Where did you get that from? Not that I'm complaining."

"Sally."

Dan looked at Gwynne. "Who's Sally?"

"The lady with the DIY shop where Henry ended up after escaping."

"Oh yes. You've had a fun few days."

Gwynne and Dan tucked into their meals, interspersed with chats between themselves and some including Henry. Dan put the empty plates on the draining board while Gwynne served out some trifle. "Only out of a packet, in case you were wondering, Henry."

"I wasn't really but thanks for telling me. It looks very pretty. All those multi-coloured bead things on the top."

"Hundreds and thousands," Dan explained.

Henry thought it lazy, not counting the little specks of colour. Were there hundreds or thousands? He'd want to know which.

"Red jelly at the bottom, then custard... Have you ever had custard, Henry?"

Henry shook his head.

"No, I don't suppose you would have done. It's not really dog food, but then nor is pasta bake," he said, looking into the dish. He stuck in his finger, pulled it out then licked it.

"Nice," Henry said. "And you want me to eat that?"

Dan laughed. "You did tell me he has a sense of humour but I didn't know you were serious."

Henry wondered how someone could be serious about a sense of humour but knew that the English language seemed to have so many of its own rules that were inexplicable so didn't add that to the list of things for Gwynne to explain or look up.

Dan let Henry lick out the trifle bowl so he'd finally have some custard. There had only been a scraping, but a dog's sense of taste is more finely tuned than humans so it didn't take much for Henry to get enough to critique it. "It's very creamy. Nice."

"Isn't it," Dan said. "It's one of Gwynne's favourites."

"And the hundreds and thousands are crunchy."

"They're my favourites. Little coloured crunchy balls." Dan laughed and looked at Henry. He didn't know what was so funny but smiled to feel included.

Dan was washing up when the doorbell went.

Henry barked instinctively.

"It's okay, Henry," Gwynne said. "Dan'll get rid of them." She turned to Dan. "We're not expecting anyone, are we?"

"Erm…"

"Dan?"

"I might have mentioned to my sister that you were bringing him home."

"Dan! You know we have to keep him to ourselves. We're not supposed to have anyone else here when he's here. What were you thinking?"

"Sorry, darling. I wasn't."

Gwynne scowled. "No, you don't."

"I can't tell her to go away, she'll suspect something's up."

"I'll just not talk," Henry butted in. "I'll be an ordinary Jack Russell who can bark, shake paw, lie and roll over. But don't get me to do any begging. Don't talk to me and I won't have to reply. I've done it for almost two weeks, another evening won't be hard."

"Thanks, mate," Dan said and winked.

Gwynne closed her eyes and shook her head. "Just don't let her stay long, okay? Say you're really tired and you have to get up early. She's not the sharpest to pick up on hints but do your best, hey?"

Dan nodded and went to the front door as the bell rang again.

"Claire's always been the impatient type," Gwynne explained to Henry. "Used to getting her own way so there's no good being too subtle with her. She's always the last to leave at parties, helps clearing up, providing there's wine to be had."

Before Dan and Claire appeared, a small white West Highland Terrier rushed into the kitchen and went straight up to Henry. It sniffed Henry's backside which didn't impress him at all, especially as he was sitting down.

"Fifi!" Claire called, then came into the kitchen. Henry thought she looked like someone off the television: a model, ready to walk the catwalk, hair pumped up on end, almost as if she'd seen a ghost. Her lips were bright pink and her lipstick had smudged so it looked as if she was smoking a two-dimensional cigarette, a bright pink one.

She was dressed entirely in pink, a matching jogging suit, although Henry suspected her feet had never pounded a pavement, other than perhaps for the January sales. She had pink boots almost up to her knees. They looked like leather and Henry wanted to go up and sniff them but felt that she'd think that rude.

Although no worse than her dog sniffing my bum, he thought. Everything she wore was coordinated to the shade, even her nail varnish matched her attire and mouth.

Henry wanted to have a go at Fifi, who was still sniffing his backside, the diamantes on her pink collar sparkling in all their fake glory. She was clearly as negligent at subtlety as her owner.

The penny finally dropped, with Claire anyway. "Fifi, that's not nice. Say hello nicely."

Henry, just for a second, expected Fifi to actually say 'hello' but she just whined, not even a nice whine but a little wimpish screech. It reminded Henry of Victor 'Dullard' Mullard.

"Can't stay long," Claire said, but then looked at the wine. "Ooh, Zinfandel. May I?"

Dan looked at Gwynne who nodded. Dan took the smallest wine glass from the cupboard and filled it.

"Thanks, Danny," she said, ignoring Dan but looking at Henry.

"So who's this then?"

"Claire, this is Henry. He's the office dog and usually lives with the owners but they're out for the evening so Gwynne said we'd have him and take him back in the morning."

Henry looked up at Gwynne. *Really?*

Gwynne nodded at Claire.

"But she has an early start," Dan continued, "so we won't be late–"

"Oh, me too. Taking Fifi to a breeder up in Yorkshire first thing."

"Interesting," Gwynne said, clearly uninterested.

"What's the story there?" Dan asked, then looked as if he regretted it.

Claire sat down, holding her glass out for a refill. Gwynne, who was nearest, filled it halfway. Claire looked at it, then nudged it nearer to Gwynne who topped it almost to the brim. "Thanks, Gwynny."

Gwynne hated being called Gwynny. Why Claire had to add a 'y' to every name, she didn't know. She'd be calling Henry Henryy next and probably Fifi Fifiy. If Gwynne dared to call Claire Clairey she'd be excommunicated, although at the moment that wasn't a prospect that bothered Gwynne all that much.

Fifi had stopped sniffing Henry's backside for long enough to be sniffing up at the leftover pasta bake. "Oh poor darling," Claire said. "Mummy forgot to feed you. Any of that going spare?"

No, Gwynne thought. *Henry's been waiting for that.* She was about to say, "No, sorry, it's for Henry," when Dan poured it onto one of their plates and put it on the floor. Before Gwynne could scowl and Fifi could reach the plate, Dan picked up the Westie and sat her on his lap, across the table from Claire.

Henry stared at the plate, Gwynne, Dan, Fifi, Claire, then back at the plate again. Claire squeaked and obviously wanted to say something but she opened her mouth only to close it again.

"Fifi's a spoiled little brat, like you, Claire," Dan said. "Mum's let you do whatever you like all your life. Your boyfriends have been the same, pandering to your every whim. You're not going to get away with it here. And your precious dog certainly isn't. Help yourself, Henry, and Fifi here can watch."

Gwynne thought that a bit cruel but agreed it was about time Claire was put in her place, and while Gwynne had never thought she'd get away with it, who better to do it than Claire's brother.

"And that's the last glass of wine you're having," he continued. "If you've got to be in Yorkshire in the morning, you'll have an early start. Any more and it won't have cleared your system in time."

Gwynne didn't know if that was true but she loved Dan even more for saying it.

Henry was still staring at Dan.

Gwynne noticed him waiting. "It's okay, Henry. You have it."

So Henry did; quietly, politely and with no belch at the end, as he had been known to do, usually when no one was around.

Dan put Fifi back on the floor then removed the bowl when Henry had finished, adding it to the washing up pile. He wanted to ignore his sister, do the washing up and chat with Gwynne, then play games with Henry, but the eyesore in the room spoiled his plans for the evening. Limiting her wine would probably do the trick.

He decided to do the washing up anyway while Claire talked about this wonderful breeder that her equally wonderful boyfriend, Luke, had found. He'd suggested that Fifi would have wonderful puppies. "Don't you think it would just be wonderful?" Claire said to the room.

Gwynne and Dan looked at each other as Gwynne dried up the dishes and put them away.

Fifi was sulking under the kitchen table, ears pricking every time her name was mentioned, too often in Gwynne, Dan and Henry's opinion.

Gwynne could see Henry struggling to contain his frustration so took away Claire's empty wine glass and put it on the draining board. "Thanks for calling in, Claire. I know how busy you are–"

Claire opened her mouth, Gwynne assumed to protest, but she was on a roll. "As Dan said, we have an early start, although not as early as you by the sound of it."

"It is a long way. Luke is driving his Jag of course so Fifi and I can travel in style."

"Harnessed in, I hope."

"Er..."

"Fifi. You don't want her hurt in case of an accident."

Claire looked wounded. "Oh, there won't be an accident. Luke's a brilliant driver. Passed his advance test four times."

Passed a test four times? Gwynne wondered. *Do you mean taken four times? Who would need to take it again if you'd already passed it?* She got up and walked through to the hall, with Fifi following her.

Claire then appearing to realise she had no choice but to move, did so.

"You haven't driven tonight, have you?" Gwynne asked.

"Oh no, Gwynny. Of course not. Luke drove. He knows I like to have a glass or two of wine."

Or twelve, given the chance, Gwynne thought. "Shall Dan give him a ring to say you're ready? One of us would give you a lift but we've been drinking too."

"No need, darling. He's outside."

"Good timing."

Claire shook her head. "He dropped me off and waited. Probably snoozing, expecting me to be longer."

"He waited all this time?"

"Of course." Claire looked as if Gwynne had asked the most stupid question in the world.

"Why didn't he come in? We wouldn't have minded." *Would have diluted the conversation,* Gwynne thought.

"Oh no, he's fine. Has this thing about meeting family."

Dan shrugged, washed up Claire's wine glass, dried it and put it away, as Gwynne slammed the front door behind Claire and the beloved Fifi.

"Ah ha!" Dan slapped the kitchen table with the tea towel, making Henry jump. "Sorry, mate."

Gwynne came through and sighed. The boys looked at each other.

"All right?" Gwynne asked.

"Dan's had an epiphany," Henry explained.

"You have?" Gwynne asked, looking at Dan.

"Not really. Just relieved another royal visit has ended. I don't know Luke that well–"

"Not surprised if she keeps him tucked away."

"We did meet in a pub once, by accident. He was tucked away then too, in a corner, dark, and they were snogging. It wasn't pretty."

Gwynne screwed up her face.

"He's a good-looking lad. I think she's afraid to let him out of her sight."

"Except when visiting here."

"Because he sits in the car and falls asleep."

"Probably bores him to it," Henry added.

"You're very astute, Henry," Dan observed.

"Thank you, Dan. Now what was this epiphany?"

"Toys. Lots of toys. Did Gwynny tell you?"

Gwynne scowled at Claire's version of her name.

"She did mention something to that effect. Something about it being Christmas? Do I have to wait that long? Are they wrapped up so I get to tear the wrapping open?"

Gwynne laughed. "No, don't worry. You can have them now. Not wrapped, sorry about that. Come Christmas, we'll wrap something up for you."

Henry looked up at Gwynne. He had made the right decision, to come back. He'd expected a life shut away in the cage but here he had the best of both… no, all worlds, not that he know how many worlds there were – something else to ask Gwynne. Yes, Henry got to spend his time with Gwynne at work and here, in her home, with her can't-work-him-out-yet-but-think-he'll-be-cool boyfriend, even if that did occasionally come with psycho-in-pink sister, Claire.

In theory, Henry shouldn't like Fifi either but there was something about her that appealed to him. He'd never really given much thought to having a girlfriend but now that one had been presented to him, of sorts, he'd quite warmed to the idea. He'd have to be firm with her, and he was pretty sure that FMRS would never approve but if there were going to be others like him, a feisty little Scot could be just the ticket.

Henry followed Dan and Gwynne into the lounge, and to a large blue plastic box. It was almost as tall as him, around shoulder height, so Henry craned his neck to look into it. "Oh, my." It was filled with a multi-coloured array of toys, made of a variety of different materials. Henry squealed as he recognised the racoon.

"All right?" Gwynne asked, her face looking as if he'd been shot.

"You got me a racoon glove puppet."

Gwynne looked at Dan, who shrugged.

"I saw one at the rescue centre," Henry explained, "the second centre, with Sally. She'd bought me a lot of stuff already…" Henry looked at the box. "Though nowhere near as generous…"

"It's okay," Dan said.

"It's a pleasure," Gwynne added.

"I didn't like to ask for it. Of course, I couldn't ask, especially as she'd already picked out some other toys and that was plenty for the week. Not that I knew it was going to be a week."

"So," Dan knelt by the box. "before we get maudlin, what do you fancy playing with?"

Henry looked down at the box then up at him.

Dan frowned. "Oh, God."

"What, Dan?" Gwynne asked, looking worried.

"Do you want to play with these?"

Henry pouted. "Is that a trick question?"

"I thought maybe because you can talk that you'd have outgrown them."

"I'm nineteen months old."

"In human years," Gwynne pointed out.

"But still, a mere baby. I'm a dog, it's what we do."

"Now where have I heard that before?"

"I don't know." Henry's eyes widened. "Oh yes, the cat."

"Cat?" Dan asked.

"I had a cat toy and I got a bit hungry with one of its ears."

"Oops," Dan said, smiling at Gwynne.

"It wasn't funny," she said, frowning. She then smiled. "Actually it was hilarious. You should have seen him. He was so defensive."

"So, is it the racoon?" Dan asked.

Henry barked. "That would be great."

Dan struggled to get his large hand inside the glove puppet and could see Henry almost salivating as he waited. As Dan had had little practise with dogs, he wasn't really sure what to do but waved it around to see what Henry did. The dog acted like he was chasing a butterfly, nipping at the racoon's over-emphasised nose.

Once or twice he got it, making Dan go "ow", but he was quick enough to pull back so Henry lost the grip. They only stopped when it was clear that the racoon was losing the will to live, both Dan and Henry were happy to keep going, although Dan's hand ached more than he'd expected. "I need practise," Dan said, not realising he'd said it out loud.

"Looks like you're doing pretty well to me," Gwynne assured.

Henry panted and nodded. When he got his breath back, he agreed. "Can we go again? That was fun."

"Here, let me." Gwynne pulled the glove puppet off Dan's fingers and it fitted much better on her smaller hand. Henry was quicker to snap at the racoon's nose, pulling the glove puppet off her hand. "Hey!" Gwynne growled. "That's cheating, I wasn't ready."

Henry laughed. "You're a soft target."

"Right!" Dan stood, put the glove puppet back on his hand, and prepared for war.

Chapter Twenty-Four – Bringing Back Memories

In theory, the following day was no different to the previous one but somehow – after a night at Gwynne and Dan's – it felt different to Henry. Because he belonged.

In his previous life at the lab, he'd been a 'belonging', serving a purpose, but now he felt like a pet… no, not a pet, but he had more than a purpose, he had a mission, a reason to earn his keep. He wanted to please them more than ever, to push himself, to show not only them but himself what he could do.

Even the breakfast had improved; fresh meat rather than tinned. Still milk and the *i* newspaper – which had replaced *The Times* in his favour just before he'd been stolen, and Henry liked that. It gave him stability.

"What's the plan for today?" Henry asked, a remnant of meat threatening to ooze off his whiskers.

Gwynne was engrossed in something on her computer screen. "Huh?"

"So, what's the plan for today?" Henry repeated, the remnant of meat dropping onto the floor. He sniffed at it, licked it, and belched.

Gwynne turned to him sharply. "Oh, Henry!"

"Sorry. It came out before I could… It got your attention though."

"Why?"

Henry sighed, his shoulder slumping. "So… what's the plan for today?"

Gwynne turned back to the computer and Henry thought she was going to ignore him again but she appeared to read from the screen. "Dr Moss has emailed me a list of things he'd like to cover. He says if we could do them all today, that would be great, but he thinks it might be a bit much."

"Things?"

"Questions, tasks. Nothing too strenuous physically but this is only day two–"

"Day two? I've been here much–"

"Day two of Henry part two."

"Henry part two. Isn't that a Shakespeare play?"

"Henry the fourth and sixth, parts two. I think there was even a part three in one of them."

Carmen, despite being named after an opera – or at least that was the conclusion Henry had come to – hadn't been a fan of Shakespeare, or anything historical come to that. 'Nothing before the Beatles,' she'd said to the TV once.

Henry didn't know why the television had wanted to know about her preferences, especially as she controlled the remote – but it had been something else learned about his 'owner'. Henry then realised that he knew little about Gwynne. He knew where she worked, where she lived, and who she lived with, but not about her interests.

"What are you interested in?" Henry blurted out.

Gwynne turned to look at him. "Interested in?"

Henry nodded. "You know, what TV programmes do you like? Do you have any hobbies?"

"You know what TV programmes I like – you stayed with us last night."

"That's just one night. Besides, we watched what Dan wanted to watch: documentaries about people with no jobs, people with bad relationships, people who can't help but be criminals. I'm surprised Victor Mullard wasn't on there. Or Norman and Billy."

"Norman and Billy? Who are Norman and Billy, Henry?"

"Oh yes… The two men who dognapped me."

Gwynne wheeled her chair with her feet to move nearer to him. "You know who kidnapped you?"

"Yes. Norman and Billy. And Victoria. She's Billy's girlfriend… no," Henry corrected himself. "That's Rebecca, his wife. Victoria is Norman's daughter who's having a baby. Billy's baby. So yes, girlfriend. It's like something out of that programme we watched last night. Jeremy Kyle."

"You've got a brilliant memory, Henry."

"I have. It's pornographic."

Gwynne leaned forward. "I think you mean photographic?"

Henry blushed, although Gwynne wouldn't have been able to tell as his fur covered it. He grinned. "Er yes."

"It is? Your memory… photographic?"

"Of course."

"What do you mean 'of course'?"

It was Henry's turn to look puzzled. "I can talk."

"I know, Henry, but what's that got to do with your memory?"

"It follows suit, doesn't it?" That was a phrase that had baffled Henry since he'd first heard it. The only suits he knew of were the ones that people wore – not that anyone here seemed to wear them – they were all in lab coats – other than Sir Alfred, Sir Walter and Mr Notetaker – and suits from playing cards. He'd enjoyed watching Carmen play Solitaire… while listening to the Carpenters song of the same name. It had become a favourite of his, although he'd not heard it since, which was just as well because he'd probably burst into tear–

"Gwynne?"

"Yes, Henry."

"Do you have any playing cards?"

Gwynne screwed up her face then shook her head. "Erm… no, I don't think so."

Henry blew out a puff of air. "That's a shame. A CD player?"

Gwynne shook her head again. "What do you want a CD player for?"

"It doesn't really have to be a CD. It could be a tape player, although I know they're older. Mick had one in his car – Carmen told me – but I notice yours has a CD player. Oh yes. Oh…"

"What?"

"You can't take the CD player out and bring it in here, can you?"

"No, I can't. What's this all about? Why do you want a CD player? You want it to play music?"

"Of course."

"What sort of music?"

"I don't know. I don't know what sorts of music there are. Just the sort that plays out loud. The Carpenters."

Gwynne shrugged. "I don't have any Carpenters. My dad

loves them so he's probably got what you want but why…?"

"It's only one song. *Solitaire*. Do you know it?"

Gwynne shook her head again.

Her neck's getting lots of exercise today, Henry thought.

"I can download it," Gwynne suggested, pointing to her computer screen.

"'Download', what's that,?" Henry asked. Computers – although he'd seen enough of them on TV, were a fairly new concept to him. He'd known that Mick had one but it had been in a locked bedroom and not only had Henry been banned from there but so had Carmen. Mick had put the lock on it, said it contained the 'shit' and didn't want Henry coming to any harm, or anywhere near the 'shit', should he get out from the cage – which he never had in Mick's presence – and Carmen never took anything more than an aspirin for a headache, which Mick said she got too often. Henry wasn't surprised considering all the arguing they did. It had given him a headache too.

"It means that I can get it from the internet – you know what the internet is, don't you, Henry?"

Henry nodded. Of course he knew what the internet was. It was mentioned on TV often enough, and something Mick shouted at when locked in his room. "Stupid internet" being the only polite phrase Henry heard in amongst a barrage of offensive threats and very strange noises. Heavy breathing but worse – like a Dutch chicken being strangled. Henry only knew what a conscious Swedish chef sounded like and that was weird enough.

"Do you want me to?"

Henry – his eyelids drooping – lifted his head. "What?"

"Do you want me to download *Solitaire* – the song – onto my computer?"

Henry looked at the thin silver screen then back at Gwynne. "You can do that?"

Gwynne smiled. "Of course. It'll have to come out of one of my budgets… or better still, YouTube will have it."

"My Tube?"

"YouTube. It's a website that has loads – tens of thousands,

I'm sure – of videos: clips from films, songs, cute kittens, almost anything really."

"Cute kittens?"

"Oh yes. They're the most popular."

Henry scoffed. "Why would people take videos of cats when all they do is make the carpet wet… then probably eat it… or at the very least scratch it to bits."

"Because they're cute."

"You didn't think that when I chewed the ear off a–"

"Let's see, shall we? Carpenter's *Solitaire*."

Henry watched as Gwynne moved the screen round, typed something into a long thin bar then frowned as an advert for Saga holidays appeared on the screen. "Isn't that a bit insensitive?"

Gwynne looked at the advert. "I don't suppose it's been planned like that. I can skip it in three… two… one… There we go."

Henry closed his eyes as *Solitaire* started. Neither of them said anything during the four minutes and fifty-five seconds as Karen talked about the lonely man and his lost love. Henry had never been in love with another dog – and he knew dog-to-dog love was different to dog-to-human love – but having lost Carmen, then Sally, he knew how it might feel.

Gwynne reached over to a box of tissues and pulled out a couple. She wiped away the tears that had been trickling down both cheeks. Dropping the tissues into a wastepaper basket, she turned to Henry and gasped. "Henry. Are you crying?"

Henry sniffed. "No."

Gwynne walked nearer. Henry's face glistened. "You are. You're crying, and not just a tear or two. You're howling. Not actually howling but… I didn't know dogs could cry." Gwynne took a step back. "Dogs can't cry, can they, Henry?"

Henry shrugged. He'd not had a lot of experience with other dogs; just the ones at the rescue centre but they were kept apart most of the time, the cages were separated with sheets of wood in between, which Henry had thought most antisocial. At the dog park with Carmen, he'd not been there long enough to form any kind of bond with other dogs, especially the ones who had wanted nothing more than to sniff his backside.

Fifi was as good as it had got recently and he had thought she had potential but not if Claire came as part of the package. They said that dogs looked like their owners – or was it the other way round? – but fortunately Claire and Fifi were nothing alike, in looks or mannerisms.

"Henry?"

"Huh?"

"You really are crying, aren't you?"

Henry nudged his face with his paw then looked down at the lab floor. There was a pool – albeit a small one – of tears circling his front feet. "Yes!" he shouted and whooped in a trio of circles.

Gwynne laughed but then went serious. "Did you suspect you could cry?"

"Huh?"

"You look like you're surprised but something tells me you'd considered it."

"Of course."

"A human emotion."

"Er… yes."

"What else can you do?"

Henry stretched his neck. "That would be telling."

"Hen… ry."

"Gwy…nne."

"What else can you do?"

"That's for me to know and you to find out."

"Mmm. That's not fair. I thought you liked me."

Henry looked wounded. "I do like you. I like you a lot. A very lot. Not that that's good English but you know what I mean."

"Alright then. If I guess something, will you say whether you can do it or not?"

"Maybe. But maybe not."

"Oh, Henry! You can be so infuriating."

"Life would be too easy if everything was given to us on a plate." He looked up at the clock then back at Gwynne.

"Speaking of which, I had a really nice breakfast – not that they're not always nice, especially the ones that aren't quite alligator – do I get something different for lunch?"

"I don't know. I'd have to find out. It's too early. Another hour at least."

Henry's stomach growled.

"Already?"

Henry shrugged.

"Let's do some work, take your mind off it."

Henry sighed and lay down, head on paws, eyes still focused on Gwynne.

"Okay. Dr Moss has some questions for you…"

"As he always does."

"Mmm. But I'd like to ask a few of my own. Okay if I dictate… record them?"

"Sure."

"So we know you can talk. And it's clear you know some… French and German?"

"My Spanish is best."

Gwynne noted that on a fresh piece of paper. "Can you swim?"

"Of course. All dogs can swim. Try something harder."

"Fly?"

Henry laughed. "Of course not. I'm not a wizard. I'm no Harry Potter. Even he had a broomstick. I'm no witch either, by the way."

Gwynne smiled. "Harry Potter. Invisibility cloak. Can you turn invisible?"

Henry shook his head. "No wizard. No, no invisibility. Unless you have a cloak I can try."

Gwynne looked at a spare lab coat hanging up near the door.

"That wouldn't work. It would have to be an invisibility cloak and even I know Harry Potter's fiction. JK Rowling, pronounced row as in row a boat, not row as in argue. Bet that drives her nuts."

"There are things," Gwynne said, studying her screen, "you

can do that other dogs can't. You can talk, for instance. You're not supposed to be able to talk."

"I thought you wanted me to talk."

"Of course, Henry. You're the only dog in the world that can do that."

Henry doubted that. There would be other labs, other companies, far richer than FMRS, who had tried and succeeded, and not told anyone. Gwynne and Dr Moss weren't shouting it from the rooftops, were they. Henry pictured the two of them on top of a roof, wobbling as a gust of wind threatened to topple them. Henry shivered.

"You okay?" Gwynne asked, leaning forward in his direction.

"Fine, thank you." Henry then pictured another set-up like theirs, another Gwynne talking to another Henry, another two-way conversation. He wondered whether anyone had tried to steal Henry mark II.

"We don't know how to handle…" Gwynne continued, "…what else to expect. So we're going to be grilling you, asking you lots of questions, but you…"

As Gwynne prattled on, Henry imagined himself on a spit roast above an open fire. He'd seen enough westerns – Carmen had loved them, especially as they were often in Spanish – to know how things were grilled out in the open. He'd be too big to fit in a normal indoor oven. He didn't like the thought of that. Questions he could handle but not a long metal spike going into his bum and out through his mouth… or would they put it through his mouth and it come out through his bum? Henry dropped his tail between his legs.

"Sorry, Henry. We'll stagger the questions. Won't bombard you all at once. There's plenty of time. The police will be coming in at some stage. It's not such a priority, now that you're back… not that it ever was. You're just a dog, as far as they're concerned, and we're… FMRS isn't anywhere near the top of their list, even on a good day. The protestors are enough hassle for them without anything going on inside the buildings." She sighed. "Anyway, you're back. That's the main thing." Gwynne got up and walked over to Henry, crouching down, then twisting her head so she and Henry were face to face.

"I want to catch the people who dognapped you, even if the police don't. What do you think, Henry? Want to play detective?"

Henry's tail sprung up and wagged furiously. He'd loved watching old Poirots, Marples, and Castles – Henry thought it would be great fun to be a writer following the police, even better than just being a Joe Public solving crimes – he'd love to have a chance of being either. He'd never held a pen or used a computer so perhaps he'd be a Poirot (he was the wrong gender to be a Marple) but Castle never seemed to do much writing anyway. "Does anyone else know about me?"

"What do you mean?"

"They kid… dognapped me. Me. No other dog. Me. The talking dog."

"There aren't any other dogs here, talking or otherwise. Lots of rats… It's just you of the dog variety here."

"Someone had to know I was here. There was no sign… sorry, were no signs of forced entry, were there. I heard you say that."

"There weren't, no. So you think it's an inside job."

"What does that mean?"

"That someone who works here had something to do with it."

"Dr Moss."

Gwynne shook her head. "No, Henry. Not Dr Moss. He was as worried as I was."

"You were worried?"

"Of course."

"For me?"

"Of course. It's the not knowing that's the worst. When there was no ransom demand, we–"

Henry pricked up his ears. "You thought they'd want money for me? I did think…"

"Sure. It was the next logical step."

"They didn't look very rich."

"Do you remember where they lived?"

Henry bowed his head and squinted. "Not from here. If you

could take me to the DIY shop, I could work it backwards, look around, and see what I recognise. There was lots of turning right so if I turned left a lot."

"We'd have to think very carefully first… probably tell Dr Moss. I don't suppose the police would be too interested unless we had proof."

"The bad guys… and not guys…"

"Gals… girls…"

"Yes, the bad guys and gals, girls, didn't look very rich, although Billy had enough money to smoke and drive a van."

"He had a van? Of course he did. Do you remember anything about it?"

"Erm…"

"You did say you had a photographic memory."

"I did, didn't I. It's usually when I need to remember something."

"It would be very useful if you could remember something about the van."

"It was white."

Gwynne jotted the colour on her notepad. "The most popular but anything else?"

"The number plate was B1 LLY."

"Really?"

Henry laughed. "Course not. Billy couldn't afford a number plate like that."

"Did you see it though? Enough of it to remember?"

"I did see it drive off but I was hiding under a bush. I came out when I knew it was far enough away…" Henry squeezed his eyes shut. "Think, Henry, think."

Gwynne waited and smiled as Henry wiggled his bottom.

"D…"

Gwynne wrote down the 'D'.

"M…"

Gwynne wrote down the 'M'.

"Like Danger Mouse has on his t-shirt." Henry said, eyes still clamped shut but mouth smiling.

"Very good, Henry. Now it should have two numbers after

that. Any idea?"

"07... or was it 09?"

"2007? 2009?"

"009 definitely. Billy's no James Bond. So yes, 09."

"And the three letters after that? Or the model number?"

"D... A... D... I remember because I thought how ironic it was that he was going to be a dad but that Rebecca didn't know that Victoria was going to have his baby. Billy's baby. I said that already, didn't I?"

"You did, Henry, but good to have it again. So DM09 DAD?"

"Yes. I think so. Pretty sure. No, really sure."

"Well done, Henry, although I don't suppose the police will do anything with that information – we certainly can't – but it's a great start. Maybe if, as you suggested, we go to the DIY shop and work our way to the house... it was a house?"

Henry nodded.

"We might spot the van outside."

Henry shook his head.

"No?" Gwynne asked.

"He kept the van in a garage."

"Oh... so at least we're looking for a house with a garage."

"I think there were a lot the same."

"Do you know how old the house was? No of course you won't."

Henry dipped his head at the suggestion that there was something he didn't know. He could learn anything. Nothing – he was sure – was beyond his comprehension. It was just a case of it going in his brain's archives then recalling it when he needed to. "Could you show me a picture?"

"Sure," Gwynne said and returned to her computer. She tapped a few keys and an array of houses appeared on the screen. She turned the monitor to face Henry and pointed at the first picture.

Henry was too far away so squinted.

"I can't bring the computer nearer to you as it's all plugged in but you could come here."

Henry shuffled around on his bed and decided since he

wasn't overly comfortable anyway, he would cross the room to look at the pictures. There would be tedious details with any investigation, he surmised, and as long as they were investigating together, it wasn't too painful. He took a sip of water – he didn't know how long the age-guessing would take – and plodded over to Gwynne's desk.

Henry looked up at the first picture and shook his head. He did the same for the next few until he went, "Hmmmm. Something like that!" He sniggered and hummed C+C Music Factory's *Things That Make You Go Hmmmm* as he padded back to his bed.

Chapter Twenty-Five – Grilling Henry

Gwynne clicked on the dictaphone. "Henry, how far back do you remember?"

Henry closed his eyes. "Let me think."

Gwynne looked at the clock. Five minutes. "Henry?"

Henry shot his eyes open. "Sorry. Nodded off there for a minute."

"Five, but it's okay. It's been a trying time."

Henry opened his mouth a fraction then shut it again. "Trying? I don't remember trying anything."

"How far back do you remember?"

Henry closed his eyes. "Let me think."

"Henry!"

Henry grinned a white-toothed smile. "Only joshing. How far back do you want to go?"

"How far back *can* you go?"

"All the way."

Gwynne frowned. "What do you mean 'all the way'?"

"All the way. I remember being born and–"

"You do?"

"Of course. You don't?"

"No. No one does."

"I do."

"Okay, no human does."

"I'm a dog, not human."

"I know, Henry. A very special dog."

Henry grinned. He liked that. He liked being special. He knew there was more than one type of special, that one type wasn't very nice, the type of word that Mick had used all the time.

Henry looked around the lab, and thought about Gwynne and Dan's house. If Dr Moss's was anywhere as nice as theirs, Henry would be in for a treat. Gwynne and Dan had a large double bedroom for themselves, and two spare bedrooms: one almost as big, one small one, for a baby maybe.

"Are you and Dan going to have a baby?" Henry looked up at Gwynne with his big brown eyes. He wasn't sure what he wanted the answer to be.

Gwynne had just taken a sip of water and spluttered it over her desk. She pulled out a tissue from a box in one of the drawers and dabbed the desk dry. "What made you ask that, Henry?"

Henry shrugged. "Nothing made me."

Gwynne smiled. "Maybe in the future, but not right now. We're not even married. I want to be married before I have children."

"Are you going to get married?"

It was Gwynne's turn to shrug. "We've been together a couple of years so it's the next step. We've not lived together all that long so we're getting to know each other properly. It's going well so… I'm sure I'd say 'yes' if Dan asked me to marry him."

Henry watched Gwynne look at her left hand. He didn't know why – he'd never lived with anyone who was married – Carmen and Mick hadn't been – and wedding programmes weren't the sorts of shows that Carmen had watched. She did say that her parents had gone through a terrible divorce and it had put her off getting married, so Carmen turned over the channel when anything on the topic of marriage came on the TV. Probably just as well, it spared her from a life with Mick. Actually, the drugs raid has done that.

"So you really remember being born?" Gwynne asked, taking another sip of water.

Henry nodded. "I'm like that woman on that American TV show Unforgettable. Oh what was her name?" Henry grinned again. "Messin' with ya," he said impersonating Poppy Montgomery, the actress playing New York detective Carrie Wells. "I forget nada."

Gwynne laughed. "You really forget nothing?"

"No. Give me a date and I'll tell you what I was doing on that day, what anyone else around me was doing on that day."

Gwynne shook her head. "That's not possible. You could tell me anything."

Henry scowled. “Have I ever told you a lie?”

“Maybe. How would I know?”

“Mmm. I never have and–”

“The cat.”

“Pardon me?”

“The cat toy. You said you hadn’t pulled off its ear when I knew you had. You knew you had. You lied about that.”

Henry pondered. “Yes… but I told you the truth after the lie.”

“Not the same, Henry. Not the same.”

Henry whimpered.

“But if that’s as bad as it gets…” Gwynn leaned forward and rubbed his cheek then laughed as he purred like a cat. “Then I can live with it. With you. Now, let’s get back to it. Tell me about your birth.”

Henry screwed up his face. “It wasn’t very pleasant, I can tell you.”

“Yes, you can.” Gwynne smiled and waited for Henry to continue.

“I was covered in goo. Then my mum licked it off. Yuk. I didn’t want to go near that tongue again but being so young, I had no choice. And the others didn’t seem to mind.”

“Others. Of course. How many siblings did you have?”

“Siblings?”

“Brothers, sisters. Like Dan and Claire. They’re brother and sister. Siblings.”

“Oh.” Henry imagined the filing cabinet in his brain opening, filing the word ‘siblings’, and closing again. He liked storing new words and had plenty of room. Now that he was telling Gwynne all about his former life, it felt like it was freeing up lots of space. He liked sharing things with her, with anyone else. He’d kept so much to himself for so long. He wondered if the quicker he spoke, the freer his brain would feel… a bit like him bounding around a field on a breezy day. He smiled at the thought of that.

“What?”

“Nothing. You asked about siblings. I had four brothers and two sisters but they didn’t stay for long. None of us did. Actually I had three sisters but one died. Mum got really sad but she was busy with the rest of us. The woman we were living with took Sis away and we never saw her again. She wasn't sad at all, the woman.

She growled as she picked up Sis so I growled at her but she didn't hear me... she was too busy shouting at her daughter. I wanted her to die... the woman's daughter, so the woman would know what it was like but then I felt bad because the girl was lovely so I changed my mind.

We were lucky really because the daughter spent more time with us than the woman so... Then Carmen came and chose me. By then, my sisters and one brother had gone. It was really tough because..." Henry stopped and stared at Gwynne.

Gwynne sniffed and used the damp tissue to wipe her face. She smiled, a little unconvincingly in Henry's opinion, then screwed the tissue into a ball and chucked it at the bin next to her desk. The tissue made a dull thud against the bin's metal bottom. Henry's tail went down again as he imagined metal connecting with *his* bottom.

Gwynne frowned as the dictaphone beeped. She looked at the display. "Memory's full. I'd have requisitioned one with a bigger memory if I'd known," she said then smiled at Henry.

"Can you requisition me a bigger memory?" Henry asked, then took a slurp of water while Gwynne plugged the dictaphone into her computer.

She tapped a few buttons and stared at the screen while she downloaded the latest files. She clicked on 'confirm' when asked whether she wanted to 'delete original files from device' then safely removed hardware and turned back to Henry. "You are funny." She laughed as he looked up at her, water dripping from his sticking-out tongue.

He grinned, returned to his water bowl to take another drink. All that talking had made him as thirsty as... what was as thirsty as a thirsty thing? He plodded back over. "Gwynne?"

"Yes, Henry."

"You know these sayings, similes, 'as cold as ice' and so on."

"Clichés but yes, similes."

"What's as thirsty as?"

Gwynne pouted then frowned again. She turned back to the computer and typed 'as thirsty as' into Google's search bar. "As thirsty as..."

Henry leaned forward.

"As thirsty as..."

Henry leaned forward again then pulled back as his body threatened to tip.

"As thirsty as a jokes? Oh, no, 'as thirsty as' jokes. No, don't want those..."

Henry wouldn't have minded but let her continued.

"As thirsty as a simile. Eh? Oh, yeah. Okay. As thirsty as you are a soundgarden?"

"Eh?"

Without looking in Henry's direction, Gwynne said. "Yeah, I know. Doesn't make sense to me either. Here we go. Bartleby.com. Frank J Wilstach. Dictionary of Similes. 1916. Thirsty as a fish. Anonymous. Don't really get that one as they're surrounded by water. Thirsty as a sponge. Anonymous. That's better. Thirsty as a dry road. Not sure about that one, Mr Cyril Harcourt... or Thirsty as Tantalus. Sydney Munden. What's Tantalus?"

Henry sat and watched Gwynne dig deeper into the brains of early twentieth century scholars. "Here we go. 'Tantalus was a Greek mythological figure, most famous for his eternal punishment in Tartarus. He was made to stand in a pool of water beneath a fruit tree with low branches, with the fruit ever eluding his grasp, and the water always receding before he could take a drink.' That's mean.

"'He was the father of Pelops, Niobe and Broteas, and was a son of Zeus and the nymph Plouto. Thus, like other heroes in Greek mythology such as Theseus and the Dioskouroi, Tantalus had both a hidden divine parent and a mortal one.' Thank you, Wikipedia. Doesn't say what he'd done."

Gwynne mumbled the rest of the Wikipedia entry until she got to the part she was after. "'Misbehaved and stolen ambrosia and nectar…' Ambrosia. Don't suppose it's the custard pudding we know and love… 'to bring it back to his people, and revealed the secrets of the gods.' Oh yes, that's not good. 'Demeter, distraught by the loss of her daughter, Persephone, absentmindedly ate part of the boy's shoulder...' Eh? How do you do that? Never mind."

Gwynne continued mumbling until she got to the 'See Also' and 'Notes', then swung her chair round to face Henry. "Gruesome lot, those gods, Greeks, and so on. Better behaved now. Dan and I went to Greece."

That reminded Henry of Vic 'Dullard' Mullard but didn't say anything.

"Anyway… Feeling better? Okay to continue?"

Henry looked at the clock. "Mind if I don't? It's gone five and I'm a bit peckish."

Gwynne looked up at the clock too. "Gosh. Didn't realise it was that time. Dr Moss will be in shortly to take you home. I don't suppose he'll want to be too late on your first stay with him and Irene."

"What's she like?"

"Irene?"

Henry nodded.

"I've only met her a couple of times but she's lovely. A pussy c… er, lovely. Quiet and unassuming. Yes, very nice."

"Uh huh. Bit like the doctor then."

"Down to earth, as the saying goes."

"From where?"

"Sorry?"

"Down to the earth from where? From another planet? From the sky?"

Gwynne laughed. "You're right; English is such a strange language. Down to earth means they are grounded, ordinary. No, not ordinary. I'm not explaining myself very well, am I."

Henry was tempted to say "No" but didn't think that would be very polite.

"He's…" Gwynne hesitated but looked relieved when the lab door opened and Dr Moss stuck his head round it.

"Too early?" he asked the room, not looking at Henry or Gwynne but somewhere in between.

Henry waited for Gwynne to reply but she wasn't forthcoming. "Fine by me. Beyond peckish now. Way past chicken-hungry. Not quite dinosaur-hungry but…" He stopped when he could see that Dr Moss was looking at Gwynne and then Henry realised he'd not spoken loudly enough for anyone to hear.

"Oh yes, absolutely. I've downloaded our conversation this afternoon and there's a lot to go through. I won't get it all done tonight but I'll start on it before I leave."

Dr Moss smiled at her then grinned at Henry. "Okay, buddy?"

Henry liked that. He'd never been anyone's buddy before but knew it was a good thing. He'd thought it was just men who were buddies with other men, and women with other women, although it sounded like a male word and thought there would probably be another word for women with women.

"Lesbians," Mick had said, but Henry was pretty sure it wasn't the word he was looking for. He, Henry, was male. Dr Moss was male so why not be buddies? Did they both have to be human? If Dr Moss said they were then they were. He'd been alive much longer than Henry, although Henry didn't know how much longer but Henry knew Dr Moss was older than Gwynne and she wanted to have children someday so Dr Moss probably would too. "Do you have children, Dr Moss?"

Dr Moss didn't reply so Henry thought his question couldn't have been loud enough. He wondered whether they'd added a volume drug and they'd turned him down low but then realised when he went to take another slurp of water, that he'd had his alligator toy in his mouth the whole time… for the past few minutes anyway.

He couldn't remember picking it up – and normally Henry had a brilliant memory – but unless he was paying attention, some things wouldn't sink in. He pictured him with thicker fur and various objects bobbing about, trying to penetrate his skin. He didn't like that thought at all so spat out the alligator – then apologised to it.

His stomach rumbling loudly drew Dr Moss's and Gwynne's attention to him.

Dr Moss laughed. "That's a yes then, Henry. Okay. Let me finish up and I'll be with you in a few minutes."

Henry grunted. He couldn't see why the doctor had asked whether he was ready if the man wasn't himself? Henry knew it was human logic but it certainly wasn't dog logic and that, to him, was… well, much more logical. He'd be ready when he was ready and that was that.

Chapter Twenty-Six – The Mosses

"Are you okay in the back there?" Dr Moss asked as they set off.

"Fine, yes, thank you. The harness seems to have loosened itself a little though. Either that or I've shrunk since I was in Gwynne's car."

"Jolly good. No, it's not hers. We've both got one."

"Oh yes, you did say… or did Gwynne say." Henry was beginning to worry that he was forgetting things… or not remember things he knew he knew… if there was a difference.

"Comfortable though, yes?"

"Yes, thank you." Henry knew the doctor was posh but hadn't expected a 'jolly'. He wanted to laugh but the urge to sneeze was more powerful. He waited for a few seconds until the feeling went away. "Dr Moss?"

"Yes, Henry."

"Anything I should know about before we get to yours?"

"Like what?"

"Irene."

"Yes?"

"What's she like?"

"She's small, smaller than Gwynne. Grey hair. Six months older than me but you'd never tell."

Henry was sure he wouldn't tell anyone… not that he was sure what it was he wasn't supposed to tell. "Does she like dogs?"

"She'll love you."

Henry wasn't convinced that had answered the question so repeated the one he'd asked Gwynne. "Because I'm cute and funny or because she likes dogs anyway?"

"Yes, she loves dogs. She grew up with dogs. Bigger than you… Border Collies, I think, but dogs are dogs."

Henry knew that wasn't true but didn't like to correct him. "Do you have any toys?"

"Oh, no. Sorry, mate. I forgot to bring any with us. We have no children so nothing remotely toy-like. I could pop in the shops on the way home."

"No problem. One other thing."

"Yes, Henry?"

"Does Irene know I can speak?"

Dr Moss didn't reply.

"Dr Moss?"

"Erm..."

"Let me guess. You weren't supposed to tell her but you accidently on purpose let slip."

"Please don't tell Gwynne. I'll be sacked if anyone finds out... or worse."

Henry imagined Dr Moss in a sack, jumping along as if in a race, laughed then apologised.

"I know, weak-willed. But Irene would have found out eventually. A trip home like this, especially on a regular basis... if you're cool with that."

"I'm cool." Actually, he *was* feeling rather chilled. The coat that nature had bestowed on him wasn't doing a very good job of keeping him warm, or at least not until the doctor put on the car's heating.

"Oh good. I do hope you like her... and vice versa. She's not renowned for being... you'll see. Don't take her too seriously, although that's not difficult as she takes herself far more seriously than anyone else I know. You'll warm to her once you get to know her. Perhaps I should tell you that we couldn't have children so she... how should I put it? She clammed up a bit. So don't be surprised if she's not very talkative."

"I'll make up for that then. It's okay to talk, is it? I don't have to wait until I'm spoken to?"

"No, that's fine. You and I can chat, and I'm sure she'll chip in when she wants to. Maybe it'll bring her out of her shell."

Henry imagined a little grey-haired woman wearing a tortoise shell on her back. He hoped it was a small one.

"Something has to. No, that's not fair. She's lovely – everyone loves her – she can just be... a little hard work sometimes. Anyway, I don't want to give you a bad impression before you get to form your own. Impression, I mean, not a bad impression. Okay, Temp, shut up now."

Henry frowned, unsure why the doctor had named himself after someone who works at different places because he'd been there every day they'd known each other, not every day, every weekday, sometimes popping in at the weekends as well.

Ten minutes later, they were swinging into his driveway. The house was not dissimilar to Gwynne's: old, 1930s she'd told him, with bay windows but this one had four; two either side of the front door, which was red instead of Gwynne's blue one.

Henry spotted a figure at one of the windows, a petite woman with a neat haircut and matching jumper and cardigan. Henry expected there to be pearls but he knew that was being very stereotypical. Someone who looked like Agatha Christie had to be into reading.

He'd loved it when Carmen had read books to him. He knew the start of dozens of them. The trouble with Carmen was that she'd get easily bored and if she didn't like a book, she'd quite happily put it back on the shelf and pick another one.

She'd toyed with the idea of buying a Kindle but (a) she didn't have the money and (b) she preferred to 'handle' a book. There'd been a few that she'd narrated in their entireties to Henry, her favourite The Bible. Carmen being Spanish, there'd been little chance of avoiding it, and while he'd found most of it interesting, he didn't believe much of it, and he couldn't keep up with the names. It was at times like that he wished he could draw so he could create a family tree, and wondered why whoever had drawn the illustration on the front cover hadn't included a tree inside.

Dr Moss let them into a spacious and airy hall. Irene came out from the right-hand side room so confirmed it had been her who had been peeking from behind the net curtain. She was tiny. Not tiny like 'Drink me' Alice in Wonderland tiny but a lot smaller than her husband. Little and large.

"Here he is, Irene."

Irene smiled but made no move towards Henry, no outward

sign of affection. "He's lovely, Temp, just lovely."

There it was again. So Dr Moss was named after a short-term worker? That made no sense at all. Henry looked from Dr Moss to Mrs Moss. Henry wanted to speak, tell her to say something but words failed him. *That makes a change*, he thought. He couldn't see her getting down on the ground, and playing rough and tumble with a racoon hand puppet, not that they had one, or anything like it. Henry had visions of a sedate tea party with bone china cups and saucers.

Irene smiled again and led the way into the lounge, the room on the left of the main door, opposite the office that the woman had been hiding in. Henry could hear a machine whirring. It sounded like a printer or even possibly a fax machine. Sally had had one of those in the staffroom, which had doubled up as an office, kitchenette and wardrobe. Trebled up.

Henry couldn't stop yawning as he followed Dr Moss into the kitchen. He watched as the doctor filled a lipped plate with some dried dog food. Henry widened his eyes in the hope that he might inspire something a little more interesting. "Sorry," Dr Moss whispered. "House rules."

Henry wondered why a house would have rules but then it was an English house and that made sense, although that in itself didn't, he decided seconds later. Sally had mentioned rules but that was humans vs canines, not a person vs a house. A house was always bound to win because it was bigger. A human would therefore want to win against a canine because the human was bigger.

So a canine would have rules over… what? There were plenty of smaller things on the planet than a dog, a cat for instance, but that example was blown out the water (that he would like to have seen) because cats were a rule unto themselves, in law or otherwise, and there was no controlling them. Dan had told Henry that, and Dan was the expert on cats because he'd lived with them for so many years and had faded scars on his hands to prove it.

Henry munched away at the food, and was pleasantly surprised that it didn't taste as bad as he'd expected. It was funny how not having something for a few days would make you miss it, like Gwynne and Dr Moss, although he had hoped that this would be a one-off and that the next time he visited the Mosses, for however long, he'd be treated to something a little more exciting.

"I'll go and..." Dr Moss mumbled as Irene walked in the room. She tilted her chin in recognition, although they'd known each other for years, Henry knew that.

Irene picked up Henry's plate, looked at it, and tutted. "I don't know why he gives you that stuff," she said, tipping the remainder into a small bucket marked 'compost'. Henry wondered where on the internet, the dot com, it would be posted to but didn't like to ask.

"Here..." She picked a tin of stewed steak and emptied the contents onto a matching plate, scraping out the remnants with a fork. She then lowered the fork neatly into the tin and put the tin on the draining board, which was devoid of any other washing up.

Henry scanned the spotless room. It looked like she washed up every time a single item was dirty. The counter almost sparkled, a container had regimented rows of utensils. Henry imagined that if he were able to open the cutlery drawer that the knives would all be facing the same way – to the left or right – the spoons and forks in their separated compartments, facing upwards like babies in a hospital room waiting to be claimed.

Henry sat and waited as Irene placed the plate on the immaculate tiled floor. He looked up at her, back at the plate, then up at her again. It was only after she'd said the word, "OK" that Henry began to eat.

"Thank you," he said, expecting her to scream or shout for Dr Moss who had returned to the lounge – Henry knew that from the dull sound of the TV – but she did neither.

She was still standing there when he finished eating.

Henry wanted to say something else, start a conversation with her but knew he shouldn't speak with anyone he hadn't been given permission to speak to, despite what Dr Moss had said earlier.

Irene smiled and picked up Henry's bowl. "It's okay, sweetie. I know all about you."

Firstly, 'Sweetie'. He kind of liked it but felt it ever so slightly patronising. He sighed. No, sweetie was fine. It was more than fine. Sweetie it was. He grinned, making Irene laugh. Secondly, "I know all about you."

A gangster had said that in a movie and Henry knew what had followed but didn't think Irene was capable of all the awful things the gangster had done, and none of the cupboards were big enough to contain a machine gun. No, Irene was a 'good guy'. What was the female version of 'guy'? Oh yes, gal.

Irene leaned towards him. Henry leaned back until he bumped against a chair. "I know you can talk," she said and drew away.

Henry puffed out a breath of air… a long meaty breath, then smiled, hoping none of the sinews of steak had trapped themselves between his teeth. Irene didn't say anything, so he was either sinew-free or she was too polite to point it out. Despite the lack of pearls from the twinset, he suspected the latter.

"Dr Moss told me all about you. How you'd been kid… dognapped and escaped. You're very brave."

Henry liked the way she smiled. It was genuine, caring, as if Henry were the child she'd never had, not just an animal who'd come to stay for the night. He wanted to ask where he'd be staying but thought she'd think he didn't want to chat and would rather go to bed, which was partly true because it had been a long day, despite it not yet being six o'clock. "Thank you."

"So," Irene said, sitting at the kitchen table, "tell me everything about you."

Henry sighed, but made sure it didn't show on the outside. "Everything?"

Irene nodded.

"Which bit of everything?"

"Oh, I don't know. Tell me about your day today, yesterday.

Was it good to be back?"

Henry smiled. "Yes, it was… is, good to be back. It's better than before, not that before was bad but it's like… it's…"

Irene lowered her head. "It's?"

"It's like I'm a pet now rather than an object."

"You like it? You like being a pet?"

"Oh yes. It's really nice, especially getting the steak. That was really nice, thank you."

Irene laughed. "You're welcome. That was meant for Dr Moss's supper tomorrow night but don't tell him."

After everything that had happened to Henry, he was pretty sure that he had become an expert at keeping secrets, so nodded. "Won't he notice if there's nothing for him to eat?"

Irene laughed again and Henry wondered if she was laughing at him rather than with him, like when Keith Harris had tried to convince Orville that the audience wasn't being rude. "Don't worry, dear. There's always food in."

Henry looked around the stark kitchen and wondered where it was kept but most of the kitchen units had solid doors so without x-ray vision, Henry had to assume that it was all behind them. He made a mental note to ask Dr Moss whether that could be something they could inject him with but then remembered that they hadn't planned for him to talk so had to keep his paws crossed that it would be a side-effect when they wanted him to do something else like juggle or quack.

"How are you getting on?"

Henry looked up and saw Dr Moss had changed his clothes. Instead of the formal trousers and shirt he wore underneath his lab coats, he was wearing blue jeans and a dark green sweatshirt. It had a little logo of a man on a horse with some kind of stick and Henry wanted to ask what it stood for but Irene was already speaking.

"Henry was just saying how much he's enjoying being back."

"Yes?"

Henry nodded when Dr Moss looked in his direction. Henry was surprised that the doctor was surprised as they'd already had that conversation but then he knew that humans were quite forgetful so Henry doggie-shrugged by which time Dr Moss had turned back to face his wife.

While they were talking about dinner – normally a topic he'd be interested in – it meant that they weren't talking about him. *It's not always about you*, a voice inside his head told him. He shook his head as if trying to get rid of a fly or bee.

"Are you okay, Henry?" Irene asked.

Henry said nothing but pretended to scratch his ear.

"Maybe he has fleas," Dr Moss said to his wife. "I don't think we've ever done all that. You know worming, fleaing, and getting rid of any other pests. We don't even have him registered with a vet, although of course we have many employees far more qualified than your average vet who could see to him."

Henry wasn't sure if he wanted anyone 'seeing to him' and he was certain he didn't contain any pests, fleas or otherwise. Just the thought of that made his ear itch.

"I'm sure it's not fleas, darling," Irene said then turned on the oven, and waited for the gas to ignite. "Cottage pie, is that okay?"

Henry wanted to giggle at the thought of a pie full of cottages but didn't know how Irene would take it, and being a guest in her house he thought it might have felt rude. He then wondered if Sally's shepherds lived in the cottages in the pies and made a mental note to speak to Gwynne about it. Dr Moss probably could have helped but Google and Wikipedia seemed to be her best friends, next to Dan… and Henry of course, now that he was more than a lab rat… dog. Another thought came to him and he closed the pie drawer to make way for the new one.

"Is your first name Doctor, Dr Moss?"

Dr Moss stopped sorting out some recycling and looked at Henry, ignoring a lemonade bottle that was threatening to dribble onto his hand. "Sorry?"

"Is your first name Doctor, like Doctor Who?"

Dr Moss shook his head but didn't elaborate.

Henry wanted to ask the question again, this time swapping Doctor for Temp, but didn't want to annoy anyone so changed the subject. "We've been lucky with the weather today." Wasn't that what humans did, talk about the weather?

The Mosses laughed but again didn't answer the question. Dr Moss took the recycling outside while Irene put a dish into the oven.

Henry frowned but then decided it didn't matter. He looked around the room. He liked the kitchen. It was where all the parties ended up – the good ones anyway – and it was warm because of the cooking so he was happy to stay there until he knew where he was supposed to be.

The evening turned out much as he'd expected. He'd sat underneath the kitchen table while the Mosses ate their pie then Dr Moss and Henry went into the lounge while Irene cleared away. Henry wanted to stay. He couldn't have helped her clear away but he could have kept her company, talked to her, while she worked.

Henry thought that Dr Moss should have helped as Irene had done the cooking but then Dr Moss worked during the day so maybe Irene worked at night instead.

Henry wasn't sure what she'd be doing in the daytime but he supposed he'd find out. He usually found out something he wanted the answer to, although he knew this time that he'd have to ask Irene rather than get Gwynne to consult her digital friends.

The evening was, Henry imagined, a fairly typical affair. Irene and 'Doctor' sat on the sofa, talking mostly about the current situation in Bolivia, which had dominated the news the previous night. Geography had never been Henry's strength, and when the programme had shown a world map, Henry had spotted Mexico not that far away and he'd whimpered just as Irene had stretched her legs.

"Oh, sorry, boy! Did I kick you?"

Henry wanted to say "No" but didn't. He wasn't sure why.

Irene reached down to Henry and made a fuss of him before going to the kitchen and bringing back a treat.

After wolfing it down, as if never being fed, he'd whimpered again but Irene had not fallen for it that time, laughing and looking at the TV.

Henry's mind going back to the map, he remembered that Carmen hadn't lived in Mexico for years so was safe, albeit probably in an English jail somewhere, but she still had family there. So Henry crossed his paws and hoped they'd be okay.

Despite all that, he slept wonderfully. Irene had made a dog bed for him. It was rather feminine with red roses on it but she'd filled it with material that felt like pillows, so when he'd finished padding round in circles, working out which angle he wanted to sleep at, he'd slumped down, lowered his head onto his paws and nodded off as soon as his eyes were closed.

He'd not even dreamed of anything, or at least nothing he could remember. He'd not worried about any South American countries, not worried about what he was going to have for breakfast – he knew it wasn't likely to be stewed steak again, that would have been too much to take.

It had turned out to be tuna and a strange kind of pasta and vegetable mix which looked far too healthy but had tasted nice, if not rather dry. It had been accompanied by a promise to buy "proper dog food" by the next time he was to visit, and after a very polite and heartily meant "thank you", he'd smiled at the thought of being a regular fixture at the Moss household.

Chapter Twenty-Seven – The Investigations Begin

"Not too tight?" Dr Moss asked before closing the passenger door.

"No, I'm good, thanks."

"And you slept okay?"

"Like a log," Henry said, then frowned. "Do logs sleep? I didn't think they had brains."

Dr Moss laughed. "I don't think they do. I'm not sure where that phrase came from. Sorry, Henry."

"That's okay," Henry replied, then opened the drawer of Gwynne-to-lookups and stored that in it too.

Henry stared out the window as the doctor drove his black BMW estate to FMRS.

Henry would pin his attention to a particular tree and follow it until his neck clicked and he had to let go and pin something else. Buildings were bigger and in built-up areas so moved slower… or rather their car moved slower… Henry wasn't stupid.

He'd been doing the tennis spectator thing for most of the journey when he heard his name being shouted. "Huh?"

"You okay in the back there?"

"Oh yeah. Just pretending I'm at a really slow tennis match."

"As you do. Looking forward to seeing Gwynne again?"

Henry frowned. He'd only seen her the previous day, barely… Henry counted… sixteen hours? "Half-past five to half-past five… twelve. Half-past five to…" Henry peered between the front two seats. "Half-past eight. Three hours. Fifteen."

"Fifteen?"

"Practising my… er, twenty-four-hour clock."

"Oh, right. So, you okay about going back to the lab?"

Ah, that was what it was about. It wasn't seeing Gwynne again, it was where they were going. "Yes, I'm okay about going back to the lab. You're being very kind to me… not that you weren't before but, you know."

"Yes, Henry. I know."

Henry continued looking forward as they pulled up to the security gates. Henry hadn't noticed before but wondered why the estate had no company name emblazoned at the front and added that to the Gwynne-to-look-up drawer.

It was getting quite full so he hoped she'd have some Henry time that could be about him asking questions rather than the other way round. Once he had an answer or solution to something, he never needed to ask again so he didn't think she'd mind.

Gwynne was already in the lab when they got there although she seemed too busy at her computer to pay much attention.

Henry walked over to her desk and coughed. Gwynne looked up – at human level – then down at dog level. "Oh, morning! How are you?"

Before Henry could answer, she carried on speaking. "Did you sleep okay? Isn't Irene nice. What did you have for supper? Did you have a good breakfast? I should have given Dr Moss some of your dog food, sorry. It went straight out of my head. But you had a good time."

Endeavouring to keep track of the order of the questions, he answered, "Good, thank you. Yes, fabulous. She's lovely… made me a bed of pillows. Stewed steak. Er… tuna and some pasta concoction…" Henry beamed at the use of such an impressive word… not realising that he still had some of the concoction stuck between his teeth.

Gwynne peered at him, frowning, then smiled and nodded.

"No problem, and yes, lovely time." Henry sat, flexed his shoulders and puffed out a stream of air, dislodging the bit of broccoli from his teeth.

"Right… nearly nine. We should get cracking. Anything I can get you before we start?"

Henry's shoulders slumped a little. He wondered if Google and Wikipedia fell into the category of 'anything' but decided that he might have to earn some credits before she would take time out of proper work to look things up for him.

"Your water's fresh this morning. Is that okay? Are you

okay? Anything you need?"

Henry shook his head and plodded over to the bed. He couldn't quite work out why he wasn't more enthusiastic but being grilled, as it turned out, was quite tiring, and although he'd slept really well the previous night, he didn't feel fully charged.

He smiled as he thought of his body as a battery with a plus at one end – the head, he thought – and the minus at the other… yes, the poop end was definitely the negative. He'd seen the battery level indicator on Gwynne's mobile phone and imagined the green shading covering most of his body, being topped up when he was plugged into some milk and…

"I'd like the *i* for later, if that's okay." He wasn't sure when he'd read it as he'd rather spend the time asking Gwynne to do the research for him but he was worried about Bolivia and thought he could take some sneaky peaks while Gwynne was busy.

"Done. I picked one up on the way in. I've had a word with Iain in the post room and Lauren on reception and between them they'll put it with our post so it won't be as early in future but mid-morning at the latest. So you could be a proper employee and have a lunch break like the rest of us." At that, Gwynne laughed.

Henry wasn't sure which bit of that was funny but smiled anyway. "Thank you." *A proper employee*. "A proper employee? Does that mean I get paid?" Henry grinned.

Gwynne laughed again but a different type of laugh, a more genuine one this time, Henry thought.

"I don't think so but in kind, maybe."

Henry frowned. Kind of what? Then he remembered something Mick had said when he'd bought something for Carmen and her repaying him 'in kind'. She'd not looked too happy about that. Henry gulped. This time, he didn't open the Gwynne-to-lookup drawer as he decided he wasn't in a hurry to find out.

He coughed, straightened up. "Okay, to business. What would you like to know?"

Gwynne smiled, grabbed her clipboard, and walked her

chair over towards Henry. He giggled as the soles of her feet padded against the cold grey floor. Henry's bed was quite near a radiator so despite most of the room being the same colour as the floor, he didn't feel particularly cold.

"Okay," Gwynne said, looking down her list. "Ooh, hold on."

Henry sighed but then giggled again as her feet padded backwards.

She returned with the dictaphone, laid it on top of the clipboard, and shook her head as she stared at the first question.

"Something wrong?" Henry asked.

"No. Not really."

"Not really?"

"The first question was about your memory."

"Which we answered yesterday."

"You did."

"Then we talked about you getting married–"

"You're getting married?" a voice screeched from the doorway.

Gwynne and Henry turned round.

"Congratulations!" Dr Moss beamed as he strode towards them.

"Oh… er, no, Dr Moss. It was… er, hypothetical."

The doctor stopped striding, hesitated, turned one hundred and eighty degrees so his back faced them, then turned another one-eighty. He frowned. "I'm er… sorry?"

Gwynne laughed. "It's okay, Dr Moss. Really. Henry and I were recapping on yesterday's session."

The doctor looked over at Henry who was in the middle of drinking from his bowl of still-cool water. His face stayed put but he moved his eyes upwards and tried to say "yes" but it came out as "yeth", water dribbling out of his mouth. *Nice look, Henry.*

"Okay, well, I'll leave you to it."

"You weren't coming in for a reason?" Gwynne asked, eyebrows raised.

"Oh, yes. Sir Walter phoned… or rather his P.A. He's going to call in sometime this week. Didn't say when. A spot check, I suppose, but nothing to get worried about. Everything's fine. He's delighted… okay, happy, that Henry's back…" Dr Moss looked over at Henry who had stopped drinking, although his mouth was still open. "Sir Walter doesn't really do delight, Henry. He's more of a… he's a businessman. Everything is business, serious. Pleased is about as enthusiastic as Sir Walter gets. Even 'happy' was probably an overstatement."

Henry shrugged. "But you're happy… pleased… delighted?" he tested.

"Of course, Henry," Gwynne said, leaning forward on her chair and stroking him under his chin.

He giggled as it tickled.

Gwynne looked down at her hand, got up, and walked over to the sink where there were a couple of tea towels sitting on the draining board. She wiped her hands on one then hung them both back on a couple of hooks.

She returned to the chair but rather than sitting back down, she stood and faced her boss. "Sorry. That's fine. No problem. We have a lot to talk through so we'll probably just be doing that. We have breaks of course; walking, eating, erm…"

"Reading the *i*, researching…" Henry offered.

Gwynne frowned. "Yes, reading, researching. Thank you, Henry."

Dr Moss nodded a little too enthusiastically then left the room.

Gwynne picked up the clipboard from the chair and sat back down. "Right… where were we?"

"You not getting married, not having children."

"About you."

Henry frowned and shook his head. "Me getting married and having children?" He shuddered.

Gwynne laughed. "No, we were talking about what you remember – everything, it would seem."

"Yes, my memory, you getting married or not, then we moved onto Greek mythology, Tantalus and his eternal punishment in Tartarus."

Gwynne smiled and shook her head. "Wow."

"Is that not right?"

"It is, spot on, which will come in really handy as we go through more what-happened-to-you-over-the-past-few-days reminiscence."

Henry sighed and slumped onto his bed again.

"I'm sorry, Henry, but it's got to be done. The Board will want to know, but…"

"But?"

Gwynne looked around the room then leaned forward. "We can do some investigating," she whispered.

Henry sat up. "We can?"

"Absolutely. We'll be the next… Rosemary and Thyme."

"Who?"

"They're amateur sleuths… detectives. Like Rizzoli and Isles but not paid and they didn't wear suits."

Isles made Henry think of a tropical holiday. "Ooh I like that. Which one's me?"

Gwynne frowned. "I don't know. I've never watched it. Okay, I'll be the older one."

"That does make sense. I'm assuming neither is a dog."

"Correct."

"Rosemary is the woman and Time is the man because he's got a super-power watch?"

Gwynne laughed. "No. No super-power watch, and no, both women. And it's Thyme like the herb, nothing to do with time or watches. In case you were wondering."

"Oh, okay. I'm definitely going with the younger one then." Henry relaxed. "Off you go. Fire away."

Gwynne cleared her throat and looked at the clipboard. "Tell me more about the place you were taken to."

Henry took another slurp of water then gave Gwynne as much detail as possible.

"So you remember the route you took to the DIY shop."

Henry nodded.

"Dr Moss will know the way to that as he brought you back. But we could do your way to the shop from the house in reverse," Gwynne suggested.

"Huh?"

"We were talking about this before. If you tell me the route you took and I write it down, draw a map, we could work it backwards. You know, you said left instead of right, or was it right instead of left? Anyway…"

"That makes sense."

"Shall we do that?"

"For the Board or for Rosemary and Thyme?"

Gwynn laughed. "Both. They'd want the culprits… criminals caught too."

"Too. You do?"

"Of course. They might try it again."

"Oh, I don't think so."

"You don't?"

Henry shook his head. "I got the impression I was somewhat of a… an inconvenience."

"Oh. That's…. good?"

"So I don't think they'll be in a hurry to risk it again."

"Do you think they had any connection to the guy who was here first, the one on his own, the…"

"Stupid one."

"Yes. Victor Dullard Mullard." Henry and Gwynne wore matching grins.

"No. No relation, although I thought there was initially."

Gwynne leaned forward. "Really? Why?"

"Because they were both called Vic."

"Oh, good. So we have something to go on. Another man called Vic."

"No, she was a woman. Quite young, your age."

Gwynne beamed. "Thank you, Henry."

He nodded.

Henry told Gwynne everything he could remember – which was literally everything, filling several pages of notes – and she built a picture of his route. She didn't know the area well but was confident they'd be able to retrace it. It would be easier to do it in the daylight so suggested they wait until the weekend.

"Why? Don't you want to go now?"

Gwynne laughed and looked at the clock. "I have to work until five which will be too late as we really need to do the run when we can see what we're doing, where we're going."

"Run? We're running there? I thought we'd take a car."

Gwynne leaned over and gave him a hug. "You're so funny. Yes, we're taking the car, my car, the red one."

"The Focus, yes," Henry said, squinting as if focusing on a particular spot on Gwynne's face.

"But we need daylight."

Henry nodded. "I don't suppose they're going anywhere. I'm just a dog after all."

"And we need to do this right. They can't suspect anything. We have to snoop, make sure they're not there when we… when we…"

Henry raised his eyebrows.

"We're going to have to break in. I've never broken in anywhere before."

"Not necessarily."

"What do you mean?"

"Billy's got a white van."

Gwynne looked down at her notes. "Yes, white van."

"And Billy usually leaves the garage door open."

"Oh, yes, you mentioned that too. But would he be stupid enough to–"

Henry nodded. "Not as stupid as Mr Mullard, but yes. I got the impression Billy wasn't the brains behind the operation."

"That was…" Gwynne looked at the notes. "Norm… Norman?"

Henry nodded again.

"But you said you didn't think he lived there, that it was just Billy and Rebecca."

Henry nodded a third time. "So they'll be there at the weekend, won't they?"

Gwynne sighed. "Yes, they probably will. I suppose there's no time like the present."

Henry raised his eyebrows at the word 'present'.

Seeing the expression on his face, Gwynne said, "Sorry, Henry, I don't mean it like that. I'll get you some treats in a minute." Henry wagged his tail. "No, I meant now… well, not now now but after work."

Henry knew he should be getting excited; their first mission, first case to solve – an easy one he felt – but a little shiver ran down his spine, making him shudder.

"Sorry, mate. Cold? Would you like the heating turned up? Actually I don't know if it's even on. Should be. I can go and–"

Henry shook his head, still angled so it brushed his shoulder, making Gwynne laugh.

"So you're okay about this?" she asked.

"Sure."

"You sure you're…"

Henry smiled. "I am. Looking forward to it, just nervous."

"Nervous? Why?"

"In case something goes wrong."

Gwynne held the clipboard to her chest. "What could possibly go wrong?"

Henry had heard that before. He took a deep breath and sighed.

Chapter Twenty-Eight – Finding The Proof

Gwynne gave Henry a hug as she strapped him onto the front passenger seat of her car. "Are you sure you want to do this?"

"Thank you. That was nice. Of course. We'll be like Rosemary and Thyme, like you said."

"Thelma and Louise."

That had been one of Carmen's favourite movies and he remembered every minute of it. "I hope not."

"Why?"

"The ending."

"Ah yes."

"I'd like to be Brad Pitt though. Pitt, what a silly name. William Pitt of Chatham, the Elder. Son, William Pitt the Younger. Born 1759. Died 18-oh…" Henry looked up to his left. "6. 1806. Conservative party. Educated at Cambridge, Pembroke, I think. "

"History was my worst subject at school, especially the years."

"Oh, I like history."

"I can tell. That's because you remember everything."

"There was a programme on him. He became the youngest Prime Minister at twenty-four. I thought twenty-four was quite old but–"

Gwynne coughed.

"But it's not."

Gwynne smiled. Henry continued. "And he was PM again for the last two or three years of his life."

"Two or three? You don't know?"

"They just said 1804 to 1806 but…"

Gwynne started the car. "It's okay. So you're comfortable? I'm not supposed to put you on the front seat because if we had an accident you'd hit the dashboard and not the seat in front which would be bad enough but…"

"But it often isn't… an accident. They aren't, are they."

"Not usually, no. Only when Mother Nature has something to do with it, you know, if the weather's really bad."

Henry conjured an image of a tree dressed in a pinny and hairnet like Hilda Ogden from Coronation Street, one of Carmen's favourites, despite not understanding much of what was said because of the accents, but didn't change the subject. "And drivers are speeding."

"Speeding or not concentrating, yes."

"But you don't speed, do you, Gwynne. And you concentrate, don't you, Gwynne."

"Yes, Henry. I stick to the speed limits."

"Limit not a target."

"True. I've never thought of it like that. Where did you hear that from?"

"Probably Sesame Street." The other 'Street'.

"Oh."

Henry knew it wasn't, that it was a speeding campaign advert but he liked to think of the American children's TV programme so that had come out of his mouth first.

Gwynne put the car in gear and set off in the direction Henry had given her for Sally's shop. He hoped they'd visit but it would probably be shut and Sally would be home with a new dog, Henry's replacement, because her house – and the shop – would have been too quiet without one.

He was going to sigh until he remembered where Sally would have gone to get Henry number two; the rescue centre. The rescue centre that Rob worked at. So Sally would have her family, not another child but perhaps a female dog so a daughter number two, of sorts.

"Am I a child?" Henry asked Gwynne without thinking.

The car wobbled a little as she turned to look at him then looked back at the road. "You're a dog. You know that."

"I know but some people say that they treat their animals like children."

"They do, it's true. Dan's sister, Claire, with Fifi."

Now Henry did sigh at the thought of the spoilt but very cute West Highland Terrier.

"You okay?"

"Huh?" Henry looked over at Gwynne who was

concentrating on driving but he knew she'd asked the question. There was only her and him there.

"We're nearly there," Gwynne replied.

Henry had forgotten to look where they were going but stretched his head and peered out the windscreen. He recognised the road leading to the DIY shop. He didn't know why but his stomach hurt.

It had been a long time since he'd had lunch and the treats Gwynne had given him hadn't been very filling but it wasn't a hungry ache. He already knew he missed Sally but couldn't explain why he felt the way he did. Maybe it was excitement at being on his first ever investigation but he thought it more likely to be nerves. What if Billy or Norman caught them snooping. The image of Snoopy reappeared in his head.

"What sort of dog is Snoopy?"

"Snoopy?"

"The cartoon character."

"Oh, I thought you knew a dog called Snoopy."

Henry frowned. He did know a dog called Snoopy, the cartoon character. Were they not talking about the same dog? He didn't reply.

"He's a beagle."

"A beagle? Like the brown and white beagles?"

"Yep."

"But he's black and white."

"It's a black and white cartoon."

"Not when it's in colour. He's still black and white in colour."

Gwynne shrugged. "We're here."

Henry waited for her to switch off the engine but she didn't. That confirmed they weren't going to even try the shop door, check whether Sally was working late.

"Okay?"

"Uh huh."

Gwynne looked at the notes and map she'd made. "So we turn right at the end of the road.

Henry nodded. He took one last look at the shop then mimicked a sat nav until they reached the road Henry knew as the one Billy and Rebecca lived in.

With Henry peering out of the side window, Gwynne drove slowly until he said to stop.

"Good thing these houses all have something different about them," Gwynne said.

"It's the bushes. I remember the bushes." Henry shivered as he recalled those damp few seconds.

"Henry?"

"I'm fine." He wriggled his nose. "It's the one over there. Number… forty-two. The answer to life, the universe, and everything."

"Hitchhiker's Guide." Gwynne laughed. "You do watch a lot of TV."

Without answering, he looked at the garage. It was shut. "We're going to have to wait."

Gwynne nodded, although Henry couldn't see it because he was still staring out the window. "Just as well I brought some snacks."

Henry whipped his head round and grinned. "You did?"

Gwynne nodded again.

Henry looked down at a packet of treats. "Bacon sizzlers. My favourite."

Gwynne grinned. "I know." She opened the packet and pulled out a long curly strip and placed it in front of Henry. He looked down at it, then at Gwynne.

"It's okay. I'm not going to make you wait."

He grabbed the treat, broke it in half with his teeth, one half bouncing off the seat and onto the floor, the other half skilfully balanced in his mouth. He snapped his mouth, thinking of the alligator trying to get Danger Mouse, then chomped on the treat until it was gone.

He stared over the edge of the seat and the other half of the sizzler. He felt like Indiana Jones staring over the edge of a cliff, although Henry couldn't remember which film that scene was from. He couldn't remember. There was something else he couldn't remember. He sat up straight. "I can't remember."

"Can't remember? Can't remember what?"

"Which Indiana Jones film has him at the edge of a cliff."

Gwynne frowned. "Nope, got me there."

Henry shook his head, as if shedding the dampness from his ears. He watched as Gwynne leaned over and picked up the second half of the treat, placing it gently back in front of him. Not waiting for an "okay", Henry equally gently took it in his mouth and munched it, licking his lips when he was done. He looked up at Gwynne and smiled a 'thank you'.

"Another?"

"No, thanks. Maybe one an hour, depending on how long we have to wait."

"Good plan," Gwynne said as she reclosed the packet, rolled down the top, and stuffed it into her door's side pocket.

Henry looked at the car's LCD clock which was still visible despite Gwynne having switched off the engine. "Won't that drain your battery?"

Gwynne followed Henry's line of sight. "The clock?"

Henry nodded.

"I wouldn't have thought so. It'll just be a trickle and designed so…"

At the word 'trickle', Henry shivered again.

"Are you cold?"

"No. Just right."

"Nervous?"

Henry hadn't thought about that for a while but now he'd been made to, he did feel a little nervous. Either that or his stomach flipping was telling him he was hungry, or grateful for the treat – he couldn't decide which.

"Excited?"

Henry grinned. That was it! His stomach was doing what it was because he was excited.

Henry and Gwynne spent the next hour and ten minutes chatting about life, with Gwynne filling in any gaps in Henry's knowledge. One thing Gwynne could never remember was the order of Henry the Eighth's wives. Henry, the canine version, started by telling Gwynne that 'eighth' was the only word in the

English language that ended 'hth'. She nodded as if she already knew but was too polite to say so.

"I know it's divorced, beheaded, died, divorced, beheaded, survived," she said, "but I can never remember which was which."

Henry nodded sagely. "CAJAKK. The Catherines are at either end; that's Catherine with a C starts (married 1509, divorced 1533... twenty-four years, which turned round is forty-two – the answer to life, the universe, and everything). Katherine with a K was last. They married in 1543 and Henry died four years later.

"Another four. Second was Anne Boleyn (1533 to 1536) then Jane Seymour – a great actress by the way... have you seen her film *Somewhere in Time* with Christopher Reeve (my favourite Superman... no one can replace him in my opinion)... just lovely. Anyway, yes. Jane was the same year, but died the next year. 1537.

"The other Anne, Anne Cleves – they're both Annes with an 'e' by the way, was January 1540, divorced in the July. I think after a three-year gap he must have raced into marrying her. He married Kathryn with a y later in the year then had her executed in 1542, marrying Katherine with an e the next year. No wonder he died; he must have been exhausted!"

Henry had rattled off that information so quickly that he knew how Henry must have felt, although Henry, the canine version, had never been married. The picture of Fifi appeared in his brain.

"You're drooling."

"Huh?"

Gwynne pointed to his mouth.

Henry wiped his chin. "Oh yes, must have been that treat." He looked at the clock. 6.50. "Another one in ten minutes?"

Gwynne laughed and was about to reply when a man in his thirties opened the garage door.

Henry recognised Billy and growled softly so as not to alert him.

"Silly question but is that one of them, the younger one,

Billy?" Gwynne asked as she put on some gloves.

Henry stopped growling. "Yep."

They watched as Billy reversed his white van out of the garage. As before, he didn't stop to close the door.

Ducking down in their seats, Gwynne and Henry twisted their heads as the van went past.

When Gwynne, with the clearer view, confirmed that Billy had gone, she got out then went round and opened Henry's door, releasing him from his harness. "Come on then. It's now or never."

Henry wondered whether that was true but knew they couldn't hang around. They didn't know how long Billy would be so had no time to waste.

Gently closing Henry's door, Gwynne led him to the garage.

As sure as they could be that no neighbours were nearby or watching, Gwynne and Henry went to the internal door that connected the garage with the rest of the house. Gwynne gave a low 'whoop' when it opened with no resistance.

Before she could hold him back, Henry went in first, sniffing and looking around. There was no radio or television on so it was a good indication that they were alone.

Henry went to the utility room where he'd been kept and was surprised to find that the cage was still there, along with two bowls: one containing water that looked as if it had been there since Henry had escaped, the other half-filled with less than appetising crusty food.

"Got it."

Henry looked up to see Gwynne holding aloft, in her gloved hands, his collar.

"Great, but that doesn't prove anything. The police will just say you planted it."

Gwynne deflated. "You're right but it's a start. You know we have to find more proof."

"Plans and so on."

"Exactly."

"So let's split up. You cover the high ground, I'll cover the low ground." Henry meant she'd look at work surfaces and shelves, he'd cover anything he could see from a normal standing position.

He first tried the lounge as he'd heard Billy and Norman discussing everything in there. Other than a couple of empty beer cans which Henry thought would have their DNA on them, there was nothing of interest; no plans, no notes, no pictures.

He could hear Gwynne in the kitchen, opening and closing drawers and cupboards. He hoped there'd be another 'whoop' but she was humming a tune he didn't recognise. Time was running out – they'd both know that – so Henry returned to the utility room.

There was a set of open steps at the end of a long strip of work surface so he carefully clambered as high as he dare and looked along the black melamine. There was some paperwork at the end but he couldn't see what it was. "Gwynne!"

At his calling, she came over quickly. "Found something?"

"Not sure." He pointed his nose to the other end of the room.

"Ooh." Gwynne lunged at the paperwork and squealed as she turned the pages. "Eureka."

"Some people attribute that word to Albert Einstein but it was Archimedes. It's not a German word is it? Then another mathematician, Carl Friedrich Gauss, echoed Archimedes when in 1796 he wrote in his diary, "EYPHKA! num equals delta plus delta plus delta", referring to his discovery that any positive integer could be expressed as the sum–"

"Sorry, Henry, but we don't have time for your photographic-memory references just this minute. You can tell me all about it when we get back."

Henry shrugged. He couldn't help but get excited that they may have found something. Actually, what had they found?

"It's not everything, I suppose, but it's certainly enough for the police to take us seriously. It proves they – Billy and Norman – had access to the labs. Unfortunately it doesn't seem to say who let them in but it's plans of a kind, instructions to and from the back gate, passcodes etc."

"Excellent. Then we can grab these and go?"

"I just want another quick–" Gwynne was interrupted by the

sound of Billy's van returning into the garage.

"Shit!" Henry exclaimed.

"Henry!"

"Don't blame me. It was the first thing I could think of. Quick, shut the door!"

Gwynne lunged for the utility room door and closed it without making a sound.

Henry joined Gwynne at the door and could almost hear her heart thumping but then realised it was his own. "What do we do if he comes in here?" Henry whispered.

Gwynne shrugged.

They both recoiled as they heard the garage's internal door open. They waited for it to shut but only heard two sets of footsteps – they assumed Billy and a companion – walk past the utility room and into the kitchen. Gwynne and Henry waited for a few seconds and were relieved when the kitchen door shut and they heard raised voices.

"That's Billy and Rebecca," Henry whispered.

Gwynne leant down to Henry's level. "Rebecca the girlfriend or wife?"

"The wife. The girlfriend is Vic. Victoria. Norman's daughter."

"Oh yes, of course, the love triangle."

Henry imagined a musical triangle covered in roses and chocolates, and wanted to laugh but said instead, "I think this is our time. Now or never, as you said."

Gwynne nodded, grabbed the paperwork, and cautiously opened the door.

The kitchen door was still closed, and Billy and Rebecca were still arguing – Billy more than Rebecca – so Gwynne and Henry dashed into the garage, leaving the utility room door open but neither of them cared.

After carefully closing the garage's internal door and switching on the light, Gwynne whispered a "No!" The metal garage door ahead of them was shut. Had they expected it to not be? Gwynne looked either side for a way of opening it and breathed a sigh of relief as she spotted a switch.

All they needed was for it to rise as high as Henry's back so he could get through and she could crawl underneath. The noise though would surely alert Billy and Rebecca. Gwynne hesitated a finger over the switch and leaned sideways, lifting her head as if better positioned to listen to events happening in the kitchen. She gave a low squeal at the crashing of something that sounded like a plate.

"Now!" Henry said, and Gwynne pressed the top of the button, raising the grey panelled metal a few inches. She stopped and listened for any interruption but the other pair were still going for it, Billy mostly but it sounded as if Rebecca was no longer the downtrodden wife that Henry had met previously. He smiled then nudged Gwynne's left leg to continue.

Once the door was as high as Gwynne dared it to go, Henry slipped underneath, as did she with some degree of difficulty, scraping one of her hands on the concrete floor.

"Shouldn't we put the light off and put it down again?" Henry asked as they ran to the car.

"The door? Why?"

"So they don't notice if they come out."

"It would only take time we don't have."

"Fair enough."

Gwynne let Henry into the passenger's side, glancing back to the house before shutting the door, then glancing again before getting in the driver's side and turning the ignition.

Her red Ford Focus was normally perfectly reliable but it refused to start. "No!" Gwynne hollered then said it again as a whisper. She turned the key again and the car burst into life, albeit jerking then cutting out as Gwynne realised she'd forgotten to press the clutch. She turned the key again, gave a quiet "yay" as the car started and stayed running.

"Calm, Gwynne, stay calm," Henry soothed, making Gwynne smile.

She reversed a few yards, delighted that all the houses had garages or driveways, then turned the car round as if leaving a neighbour's house then drove to the end of the road, looking in the rear view mirror every few seconds.

Both concentrating on the road for a couple of miles, Henry suddenly blurted, “That was awesome!”

It wasn’t how Gwynne felt particularly but it made her laugh.

“I could get used to this.” Henry then burst into song.

It wasn’t one Gwynne recognised as he hummed it rather than sang any words but it sounded nice and upbeat.

“Danger Mouse,” Henry said as if reading Gwynne’s mind.

“Oh,” was all Gwynne could think of saying. She’d seen clips over the years but it had been a bit before her time.

“So,” Henry continued. “What’s for dinner?”

“You hungry?”

Henry looked out the side window in the direction of Billy’s house, which was long gone. “Wouldn’t you be?”

“I was thinking of pizza and–”

“Not really a pizza fan, if I’m honest.”

Gwynne laughed again. “I wasn’t thinking of it for you. Dan’s not had it for ages.”

Henry sniggered.

“Henry!”

“Sorry.”

“Dan and I have not had pizza for ages.”

“Is it thin crust or deep pan?”

“I don’t know. I’d have to see what we’ve got in the freezer.”

“So you may not have pizza?”

“There’ll be at least one in there. We never run out.”

Gwynne couldn’t believe that after everything they’d gone through they were having a discussion about something as mundane as what type of pizza they were, or in Henry’s case wasn’t, having, but then again just having a conversation with a dog wasn’t exactly ordinary.

As they pulled up to Gwynne and Dan’s house, the security light came on, making Henry bark.

“You okay?”

“I’m good.”

"Good."

Carrying the paperwork, Gwynne let them into the house, which was already warm.

"Thank goodness for central heating," Henry said.

"Is there anything you don't know about?" Gwynne asked, putting the paperwork on the hall table, her keys into a shallow wooden dish, hanging up her jacket on the middle of five hooks, and kicking off her shoes.

Henry sighed. "There's loads I don't know."

Gwynne smiled. "I'm sure there is. You're only young."

"I'll be two soon."

Gwynne's eyes lit up. "Oh yes. We must have a party or something."

Although Henry had never been given a party himself – he'd been locked in one of the upstairs bedrooms during Mick's celebrations with the warning not to make any noise – Henry liked the idea of a party but asked, "Or something?"

"I don't know. A party then."

"Can we? I like surprise parties."

Gwynne pursed her lips. "Surprise parties are only for people who don't know they're being given a party."

Henry blew a raspberry. "Who doesn't know they're getting a party when it's their birthday. It's the same day every year."

"Some people just go out for dinner. A party is different."

Henry knew that much so nodded. "So the 'or something' is going out for dinner? I can have a party or go out for dinner?" He imagined the two of them – or three with Dan – sitting in a restaurant with a bib tucked into Henry's collar as he tucked into well-done alligator. The image of Danger Mouse teetering over the water came back into his brain and he sniggered, missing Gwynne's reply. "Sorry?"

"Let's see."

Henry followed Gwynne into the kitchen where she set the kettle boiling then sat down at the table. Henry stayed in the middle of the floor for easy eye contact. "So, what's the plan, Batman?"

"Plan?"

Henry looked out to the hall table. "The paperwork. We take it to the police?"

Gwynne nodded. "Dr Moss first though, I think."

Henry dipped his head.

"What?"

Henry shook his head.

"Henry?"

Henry shook his head again.

"Come on…"

Henry raised his head. "It's just occurred to me…"

"What has?"

"What if Dr Moss is in on it?"

"In on what?"

Henry blew a raspberry. "My kid… dognapping." All this raspberry blowing was making him hungry. His stomach agreed.

Gwynne scoffed then looked serious. She shook her head. "No. Impossible."

"Nothing's impossible. I'm a talking dog. Did you think that was possible? That you and Dr Moss could make it happen?"

"No."

Henry was about to continue when Gwynne added, "He wouldn't do that. Why would he? He can take you home whenever he likes."

"He does now. Maybe it's just an act."

Gwynne shook her head. "I've not worked with him all that long but no, he wouldn't. He loves you."

Henry could feel tears threatening to reach his eyeballs. "He does?"

"Of course." Gwynne leaned nearer to Henry. "As do I. Who wouldn't, you're adorable."

"Billy, Norman, Vic… that's Victoria, although we didn't actually have anything to do with each other. Rebecca was lovely – she was the one who'd feed and water me." Henry imagined him ankle-deep in a plant pot, being watered, then shook off the thought. "The other Vic, Mr Mullard, he seemed to like me too. We had a 'right laugh' as Mick used to say."

"Mick?"

"I told you about Carmen, didn't I?"

Gwynne nodded. "A little. She's the reason you know so much."

"She is, although it was the television really. We used to watch it together." Henry squeezed his eyes shut as threatened tears returned.

Gwynne lovingly stroked him under his chin. "I'm sorry. Now, what would you like to eat?"

Henry opened his eyes and smiled. "Ooh… Mmm… Er…"

"Not that there's really a lot of choice."

"Aw."

Henry watched Gwynne go to a human-eye-level cupboard and open the door. "Beef and vegetables, chicken and pasta, tuna salmon mix."

Henry looked down at his stomach as each option was read out. Waiting for his stomach to gurgle when it heard one it fancied, Gwynne had added 'Game hotpot, or lamb stew' without a sound from Henry's body. He looked up. "Sorry, can you go through that list again please?" She did but still no noise. "Maybe I'm not hungry."

"You've not eaten since lunch."

"Adrenaline maybe?"

Gwynne smiled. "Maybe. Out of those options, is there one your taste buds would like rather than your stomach?"

The picture of his feet in a plant pot was replaced by one of him sticking out his tongue to reveal a dozen young red roses. There was a theme running here. "Would you mind going through–"

Gwynne reeled off the list for a third time, and Henry thought of Danger Mouse and the alligator. "The fish one please. I fancy fish."

"Tuna and salmon coming up. And would sir like a drink?"

"Sir would love a bowl of chilled water, if that's not too much trouble."

"No trouble at all." Gwynne smiled and went to prepare his

meal.

As Henry watched, all thoughts of Carmen were filed back into the 'history' cabinet to make way for yet another folder in 'Henry & Gwynne'. The next day they would take the evidence to the police and the threat to Henry would be over.

Chapter Twenty-Nine – Turning Over The Evidence

Gwynne and Henry eyed Dr Moss nervously as he read each page.

"Mmm…" Dr Moss scratched his chin.

"Mmm?" Henry asked.

"Interesting."

Gwynne and Henry looked at each other but said nothing, waiting for their boss to continue.

"I think you have a solid case. There are names, notes, what they plan to do. Nothing afterwards of course but you got your collar back. Don't suppose you took any pictures while you were there?"

Gwynne sighed and thought of the mobile in her handbag which at the time of the search, she'd left in her car's boot. She shook her head.

"No, that's okay. It's just that you need it to tie to them. The names are good but no surnames. Billy, Norman… they're the main two, are they?"

This time, Dr Moss looked at Henry who nodded.

"We have Henry's testimony." As soon as Gwynne had said it she knew how futile that option was, and felt stupid for saying it.

"We do."

Gwynne and Henry looked at each other but said nothing, waiting for their boss to continue.

"Did anyone see you go in or come out?"

"No," Gwynne and Henry said in unison.

"At least I… we don't think so," Gwynne added.

"Then why does Henry have to be Henry?"

"I could be Henry," Dr Moss offered. "What I mean is that if you and I go to the police… all three of us – it was Henry who was stolen after all. I could say I was a witness."

Gwynne smiled. "That's kind of you but I could just say Henry led the way. No one needs to know that he talks. I could say we walked there."

Henry and Dr Moss laughed, looked at each other then back

at Gwynne.

"OK then. We went by car but he barked once for left, twice for right."

"And three times for straight on?" Henry offered.

"No," Gwynne agreed. "That wouldn't work."

"Then what's the answer?" Dr Moss asked.

"A map?" Henry offered then shook his head. No dog could understand a map, not even Penfold. Henry frowned. It occurred to him that he'd never found out what kind of dog Penfold was. Was he a dog? If he was... or was it 'if he were'? Anyway, If Penfold was a dog he'd have eaten Danger Mouse, certainly would have had he been a cat. Neither a cat nor dog would have come to the rescue of a mouse. Plus they would have been much bigger. "What was Penfold?" Henry asked.

"Excuse me?" Dr Moss scratched his chin again and Henry noticed how red it looked.

"Danger Mouse," Gwynne explained. "I think he wants to know what type of creature Penfold was."

"A hamster," Dr Moss replied without hesitation.

"How do you know?" Gwynne laughed and Henry grinned. It did make sense. Two types of mice. He was glad that they didn't experiment on mice. Gwynne had assured him they only had rats, and rats were nasty – other than Ratatouille. He was funny, caring and... Henry hesitated to use the word but 'sweet'.

"One of my favourites as a child."

One thought went through Henry's brain as Dr Moss had said that; that Dr Moss was younger than he looked; perhaps late forties rather than fifty-something. Henry equated his dog months to human years and but then realised that Dr Moss had to be older than ten.

Henry shrugged. Humans were weird. What did one dog year equating to seven human years mean anyway? Henry knew one of the dogs at the park had been eighteen which in human terms would have been one hundred and twenty-six, and he didn't think a human had lived that long. He looked up to the ceiling, trying to dredge up that particular nugget of knowledge but struggled. He looked at Dr Moss. “How old was the oldest person?”

“Pardon me?”

Henry repeated his question.

Dr Moss turned to his computer screen and typed in a few words. “According to Wikipedia, the oldest verified person on record was a French woman Jeanne Calment (1875–1997), who lived to the age of 122 years, 164 days.”

Henry blew yet another raspberry while Gwynne said, “Wow.”

“Ooh.”

“Ooh?” Gwynne’s mouth remained in an ‘ooh’ position.

“Could we have raspberries tonight?”

“Dr Moss was going to have you tonight but…” Gwynn turned to Dr Moss.

“I don’t see why not. We can get some on the way home.”

“That would be lovely, thank you.” Henry beamed but then looked serious. “Can’t we take what we’ve got to the police?”

“I don’t see why not.” Dr Moss repeated then scratched his chin for a third time.

“But you said…”

“I know, Henry, but it’s not just dognapping… not that that’s not serious of course…”

Henry nodded confidently.

“But it’s breaking and entering into here. These premises.”

“Technically they didn’t break in,” Gwynne pointed out.

“True,” Henry agreed.

“We must have them on CCTV.”

Dr Moss shook his head. “Inside job. Got to be. Nothing recorded on the way in or on the way out. Trevor said it was a blip. I blame him, always had my suspicions about that Trevor. Something not quite right.”

Henry smiled and turned to Gwynne. “You know you were going to bring in a camcorder…”

Gwynne’s face dropped. She shook her head. “Sorry, Henry. Went straight out my head. I have a video option on my phone but…"

"So what do we do now?" Henry asked.

Gwynne stood so Henry did likewise. "We go anyway. Tell the police what happened and that they left some paperwork here."

Henry shook his head. "They'd ask why we hadn't handed it in earlier when we reported the break-in. The non-break-in."

"No," Gwynne said. "We need to stick as near to the truth as possible."

"Where did Billy and Norman live?" Dr Moss asked.

"Billy and Rebecca, husband wife," Henry corrected.

Dr Moss nodded.

Gwynne went pale. "I didn't make a note of the address. We'll have to go back."

"No need," Henry said.

"Why?" Dr Moss asked.

"Google Earth, Google maps. We could trace it on your computer. We know it's number forty-two."

The doctor and Gwynne smiled. "You're too clever by half." Gwynne chuckled.

Henry frowned. That didn't make sense. How could only being half clever be too clever? He shook his head. Humans were even weirder than he'd thought.

The three of them huddled around the office's computer screen and after various confusing moves, finally got the route printed out and the address written down.

"So now we go to the police?" Henry suggested.

"We try," Gwynne replied.

"Would you like me to come with you?" Dr Moss offered.

Gwynne removed the maps from the colour printer. "Thanks but we'll see how we get on. Is it okay to go now? We could wait until after work."

"No, no. Go. It's fine. We're up to date with all our reports, the Sirs are happy, Henry's doing well…" Dr Moss looked over at Henry.

"Oh yes, very well, thank you," Henry confirmed.

"Then go. Let me know how you get on. Give them my mobile number if they need to speak to me. Tell them we'll cooperate fully."

Gwynne nodded at Dr Moss then to Henry. "Ready?"

"As I'll ever be."

Gwynne winked. "Come on then, partner."

Henry glowed. He'd never been anyone's partner before. He wondered which one of them was Holmes and which was Watson, but then remembered Gwynne mentioned Rosemary and Time, no Thyme like the herb. Henry couldn't remember Gwynne explaining which was which but Henry had settled for the younger one.

Chapter Thirty – Persuading The Police

Even looking at the police station across the road made Henry nervous. He wasn't sure why as he'd never done anything illegal… as far as he knew. He wasn't an expert in law but he'd never been told off for anything other than chewing a toy cat's ear and being cheeky.

He knew the latter wasn't illegal as almost every child he'd come across had been far worse than him, and even had the cat been real, he didn't suppose he'd be locked up for that. He smiled as he thought of the cage that no longer confined him.

Gwynne had tuned the radio to Classic FM when they'd left the research centre, and the theme tune to *Chariots of Fire* had come on. Henry would have recognised it even if the presenter hadn't have told them in advance. It had been one of Carmen's favourite movies. "Very English," she had said in her very un-English Mexican accent. Henry had been surprised when it had been introduced as the theme tune by Vangelis and not a fancy title by an older composer. Henry liked Erik Satie and Beethoven.

Switching off the engine, Gwynne got out of the driver's side then went to help Henry. He'd been strapped into the back this time. "Safer," Gwynne had said, "and more legal."

Henry had wondered whether being more legal meant slightly illegal but given where they were going, gave Gwynne the benefit of the doubt.

With the theme tune still in his head, Henry pranced like a show horse up the steps, pretending to be one of the *Chariots of Fire* runners in slow motion, as he followed Gwynne on a long lead. Of course Henry was sensible enough to have gone in without a lead but he knew he had to be on one in public, especially outside a police station.

Gwynne took a deep breath as she opened the front door then held it long enough to gently usher Henry inside. The door, not the breath.

The sight that greeted them was familiar to Henry as he'd

watched many British true crime documentaries. There was a desk sergeant to greet them behind a tall curved reception desk, with other uniformed staff milling around.

Sitting on a short row of grey chairs was a small array of a people: a couple of old ladies, a man who looked around the same age as Dr Moss, and two people dressed head-to-toe in what looked like plain black dresses, each with a postbox-sized opening to see out of, and a small group of teenage boys towards the end of the corridor. Fortunately no one other than Gwynne had a dog with them so at least Henry didn't have that to contend with.

As Gwynn asked to report a crime, Henry wondered whether the visitors were doing the same or awaiting conviction. None looked to be handcuffed so he assumed they were innocent, although the more Henry looked at the teenagers, the more he wondered.

He looked back at the two dressed in black. From their eyes, he couldn't tell whether they were male or female but from what he'd seen on television, he assumed they were female. He would be able to tell from looking lower than their eyes but knew that would be rude so turned back to Gwynne.

He saw her nod, smile, and head over to the seats. There were two empty ones: one the other side of the old ladies, and one to the right of the people dressed in black. He didn't know why but only being able to see their eyes made him nervous. One had very pretty eyes, and although their chair was nearer, Henry willed Gwynne to take the other one. He knew that would be too obvious though and Gwynne wasn't the sort of person to be that picky.

As he suspected, she chose the nearest chair and sat with a slight huff.

She looked down at him and raised his eyebrows as if to check he was okay. He knew better than to speak or nod so wagged his tail and licked his lips.

As if that were a cue, Gwynne opened her bag and pulled out a packet of treats. "Thought I'd forgotten, didn't you?"

Henry wagged his tail harder. He wanted to bark but knew it

wasn't the time or place.

They'd literally only just sat down when a plain-clothed detective came out of a back room and greeted Gwynne, holding out a hand. "Hello, Miss Davies. I'm DI Richard York, do follow me."

Henry hid a laugh as he thought of the colours of the rainbow: Richard Of York Gave Battle In Vain – red, orange, yellow, green, blue, indigo, and violet – although this Richard looked tough enough to win any battle. Feeling Gwynne pull at his lead, Henry followed the pair into the background scenes of the police station.

Again, the office looked like any other open-plan that Henry had seen in the documentaries. There was an air of busyness despite almost everyone being engrossed in something at their desks. Henry assumed it would be paperwork; he knew the police always had too much of it, which was why you no longer saw the 'bobby on the beat', as the old crime dramas had called the constables.

DI York led Gwynne and Henry to an individual office at the end of the room and invited Gwynne to sit. Henry did likewise, a few inches from her feet.

"He's very obedient," DI York said, looking at Henry.

Gwynne laughed. "When he feels like it."

Henry, of course, didn't respond.

"Can I get you something to drink?" the DI asked, looking at Gwynne. "Cup of tea? Coffee?"

"Just some water would be fine, thank you."

"The same for this young man?" The DI turned his attention to Henry.

Young man. Henry liked this Richard of York.

The detective inspector popped his head out of the doorway to pass the request to a young male colleague, then returned and shut the door.

"Now then," he said, sitting opposite Gwynne. "I understand you're here to report a quite serious crime."

Gwynne sighed and Henry took that as frustration that she

would have to go through everything she'd told the desk sergeant.

"My colleague has written down the basic details but if you don't mind starting from the beginning, so I have everything from you rather than a piece of paper. I have also pulled out the report that was made when the two burglaries occurred. You've been very unlucky but then I suppose somewhere like that is a bit of a target."

Gwynne nodded and told him the whole events, minus the talking-dog bit. She stuck to the truth as much as she could, making the going-back-to-the-house bit plausible.

"Ah yes, our old friend Mr Mullard. You really don't think he was connected this time?"

Gwynne shook her head. "No, the Vic, I think is coincidental. Victoria rather than Victor."

"Right. And how do you know this from just these plans?" DI York tested.

"We overheard Billy and his wife Rebecca talking," Gwynne lied. "Arguing, actually. I got the impression he'd been unfaithful to Rebecca with Vic, Victoria, so they told us quite a lot without meaning to."

"Because they didn't know you were there."

"Exactly."

"In the utility room."

"Yes," Gwynne squeaked but then looked up and smiled at the colleague as he placed a glass on the desk in front of Gwynne and the bowl on the floor by Henry, who wanted to say "thank you" but resisted the urge.

"But you didn't break in," York continued, acknowledging the colleague's kindness with a slight nod.

"Absolutely not," Gwynne protested. "Billy had left the garage door open when he'd gone out. Unfortunately he, they, returned while we were still there so we had to hide."

"For someone who's good at getting in secure buildings, he's not very good at locking his."

"No, he's not."

"Mmm."

"Is there a problem?"

"Only the matter of trespass."

"Oh."

"Okay so you didn't break in, didn't do any damage, didn't steal anything – as such – but you still weren't there with permission."

Gwynne sighed again.

DI York winked. "But we don't have to mention that."

Gwynne took a sip of water then smiled cautiously. "We don't?"

"No. You see we've been keeping an eye on the Maitlands and the Quinnells for quite some time. We're very close to pinning a lot on them and this is just one of a string of burglaries that have been attributed to them. We're very grateful that you've come to us, especially given that you suspect an inside job. Trevor..." York looked down at the paperwork. "Thompson."

"Something like that. I'm not sure. Other than doctors or Sirs, we just call each other by our first names."

"Sirs?"

"The two main investors: Sir Walter Forsyth and Sir Albert Crawley."

"Forsyth is the boss, yes?"

Gwynne nodded. "He started the centre after his wife was diagnosed with MS. That's what we do there, research into a cure for Multiple Sclerosis."

"Very good, very worthwhile."

Henry felt that a little sarcastic but let it go.

"And Crawley. Where do I know that name?"

"Downton Abbey?"

"Ah yes, my wife is a fan." He went to swivel a wedding ring that no longer sat on his finger. "Ex-wife."

Gwynne nodded again, more sympathetically this time.

"I believe we interviewed this Thompson man after the incident with Mullard. I'll check Thompson's story but we don't think they're connected." York pushed back his chair and stood.

Gwynne remained seated until York put out his hand indicating the door.

"We'll ring you if we need you. Thank you very much again, Mrs Davies."

"Oh. I thought… No problem."

Henry wondered whether she would correct York's use of Mrs rather than Miss but it didn't look like she was going to. Henry followed them both out of the office, back down the corridor past the desks which were producing more of a hive of activity.

Before they parted at the reception desk, DI York took a piece of card out of a pocket and handed it to Gwynne. "There's my direct number if you think of anything else. What you've given us is invaluable and of course there will be a full investigation so that anyone involved will be brought to justice."

"Will I need to testify?"

"I can't say at this stage but I will keep you informed of our progress, although it'll be reported in the papers so you'll probably see it there first."

"Thank you, detective."

He nodded, and after tapping a four-digit code onto a keypad Henry hadn't noticed on the way in, DI York returned back into the realms of the main office, leaving the door to shut behind him.

Gwynne looked down at Henry. "You okay?"

Conscious of people still milling around him, he just wagged his tail.

Gwynne smiled and led him back to the car.

Chapter Thirty-One – What Next?

The drive back to FMRS was held in silence other than the classical tunes on the radio, interspersed by brief introductions and chat from the presenter.

Henry wanted to say something but couldn't think of anything. He hummed along to a rather depressing and heavy Richard Wagner track – the presenter had said the title but Henry hadn't caught it and wasn't keeping up as he didn't know it.

He grimaced as Gwynne wrenched the handbrake.

"Sorry, chap."

Henry smiled. Although he liked his name, he also liked being given nicknames, and 'chap' sounded grown up.

Gwynne let him out and took him back towards the labs, past the gardens – roses suitably 'watered', reception, and the kitchens where there was a delicious waft of food.

Henry's stomach rumbled.

"Was that you?" Gwynne asked.

Henry – knowing they weren't in the safe confines of their laboratory – dipped his head in acknowledgement.

"Okay. I'll drop you off then get something for you. Any requests?"

Henry remained silent.

"Sorry. We'll have this conversation when we get there." Gwynne gave a fleeting smile to another woman of a similar age who'd looked at Gwynne strangely when talking to a dog.

"If only she knew," Gwynne said to Henry when the woman was out of earshot.

Closing the laboratory door behind them, Gwynne let Henry off his lead and waited for him to settle onto his beanbag before discussing lunch. "You look tired."

"A little."

"Do you want to wait to have something to eat or have a bite now?"

The alligator scene from Danger Mouse flooded back into

Henry's brain. He gave a weary smile. "Could…" He lowered his chin onto the beanbag. "I…" He puffed out a little breath of air. "please…" He twitched his nose. "have…" He closed his eyes. "some…"

"Ahh." Gwynne gently laughed as Henry alternated between a snore and another sound similar to a raspberry.

She looked up from her desk as the door opened.

"How did it go?" Dr Moss asked, straightening his glasses. "You weren't very long."

Gwynne shook her head. "Apparently it wasn't big news. Good news but not big news."

"Oh?"

"We saw a very nice detective but he said they'd been monitoring the Maitlands – that's Billy and Rebecca – and the Quinnells – Norman and his daughter Victoria – for a while. Of course he was pleased we'd gone there and the evidence we gave them is useful despite us not getting it lawfully."

"Not lawfully? Why not lawfully? You didn't break in."

"No, but we were trespassing. We weren't invited."

"They wouldn't invite you in."

"Exactly but we shouldn't have been there, free access or not."

"But they can do something with what you gave them, the police? They can build a case?"

"Another string to it, I think."

Dr Moss looked over at the sleeping Henry. "And he's okay, is he?"

Gwynne followed the doctor's line of sight. "Oh yes, just a little tired."

The pair laughed as Henry snorted, rolled over onto his back, kicking one foot, and whimpered.

"They'll keep me informed," Gwynne continued. "I'm not sure if I'll need to testify but I get the impression this is low-key, especially given that all they took was a dog, and no harm came to him."

It was clear from Henry's well-being that this was true. If anything, it had been the best thing to have happened to him – and Gwynne – as solving his dognapping was just the start of a series of adventures for the modern-day Rosemary and 'Time'.

Note from the Authors

Thank you for purchasing 'Oh, Henry',
the first novel in the Henry Houdini series.

We loved writing it and hope you enjoyed reading it. We will be bringing you more, including some short stories, in the series available in the next few months.

Thank you to all our beta readers –
especially Anita, Anthony, Lynn, David, Deborah, and Renu.

We welcome feedback (and am always grateful for honest reviews) and you can either find Morgen through her website, www.morgenbailey.com or via email: morgen@morgenbailey.com.

Rachel can be found lurking on Twitter at:
https://twitter.com/RachelCavAuthor.

Rachel's books

Fiction

The Serial Dater — 31 dates in 31 days

The Serial Dieter — 31 dishes in 31 days

Various Henry Houdini long short stories

Morgen's books

Fiction

After Jessica — money and a girl gone missing

Hitman Sam — a trainee hitman and love triangle

Oh, Henry — the first in the Henry Houdini series

One for the Road — a hit-and-not-run novel

Short Story Collections: Shorts & Flashes

Non-fiction

The 365-day Writer's Block Workbooks
1000+ exercises and 50+ tips per book

Editing Fiction ~ A Writer's Guide
Morgen's guide to writing a story then pulling it apart

About the Authors

Rachel Cavanagh was born a southerner and will always be at heart. She transplanted herself, indirectly because of her job at the time, to the East Midlands, UK, in the early 1990s and has dreams of 'retiring' to Sussex, further south than her original roots, where she'd love to write full time with a sea view.

Short stories have always been her first love. A regular at her local library as a child, she devoured novels (sometimes under the covers with a torch) but often returned to short stories. Inspirations include Roald Dahl and Kate Atkinson.

Rachel will always be grateful to her father, with whom she would love to have had more time, especially to hear about his working relationship with Mr Dahl. Rachel knew how proud her father was of her, and she will always be a daddy's girl.

You can find Rachel at https://twitter.com/RachelCavAuthor.

Morgen Bailey (Morgen with an E) is an author, speaker, mentor, tutor & lecturer of writing courses as well as a judge of writing competitions. She is an editor for publishers and indie authors and former columnist for Writers' Forum magazine 'Competitive Edge'.

The former chair of three writing groups, she has judged the Flash 500, H.E. Bates, BBC Radio 2, BeaconLit, and Althorp Literary Festival short story competitions as well as the RONE. She also runs her own monthly 100-word competition. Talks and workshops have included the W.I., U3A, Troubador's Self-Publishing Conference, Delapré Book Festival, and NAWG Fest with her 'Editing your Fiction' weekend residential course.

Morgen can be found almost everywhere including Twitter, Facebook, and Instagram. Her website is www.morgenbailey.com where you can sign up to her monthly newsletter.

Published by **August Publishing UK**

Printed in Poland
by Amazon Fulfillment
Poland Sp. z o.o., Wrocław

61748789R00150